IF YOU CROSS

Lock Down
Presents

If You Cross Me Once 3

Too Many Secrets

Written By
ANTHONY FIELDS

Copyright © 2023 Anthony Fields
If You Cross Me Once 3

All rights reserved. No part of this book may be reproduced in any form or by electronic or mechanical means, including information storage and retrieval systems without permission in writing from the publisher, except by a reviewer who may quote brief passages in review.

First Edition 2023

Printed in the United States of America

This is a work of fiction. Names, characters, places, and incidents either are products of the author's imagination or are used fictitiously. Any similarity to actual events or locales or persons, living or dead, is entirely coincidental.

Lock Down Publications
P.O. Box 944
Stockbridge, GA 30281
www.lockdownpublications.com

Like our page on Facebook: Lock Down Publications
www.facebook.com/lockdownpublications.ldp

Stay Connected with Us!

Text **LOCKDOWN** to 22828 to stay up-to-date with new releases, sneak peaks, contests and more…

Like our page on Facebook:
Lock Down Publications

Join Lock Down Publications/The New Era Reading Group

Visit our website:
www.lockdownpublications.com

Follow us on Instagram:
Lock Down Publications

Email Us: We want to hear from you!

Acknowledgements

The praise I give to the creator of the worlds is warranted first and foremost because this talent to write is a God given gift. I thank Allah for all the blessings in my life. Although I can't seem to stay in the streets, my presence is still felt by many. I was a good dude and left a lasting impression on all the people I touched in one way or another. I see that now manifested as I do this new bid. Out of the blue, people will send me money and pics, and I haven't talked to them in years. People will reach out and check on me, and that's a good look. Makes me feel like I mean something to the world. And sometimes a dude in the joint needs that, so thank you to my family, to my man Black Junior, Kevin Clayborne also known as Cat Eye KK, to Vincent 'Vee' Elliot, Ducksauce Lassiter, Lacy Hamilton, Antwan 'LA' Thomas, James Venable, Sammie Gaither, Antone White, Eric Hicks, Fat Bug, D.C. (Greg Wright), Redds, Nunu, LarryMoe, Rich Young. Kendall Hinton, Reggie 'Champ' Yelverton, Chico, Andre Rose and others. If I didn't mention you, it's because I forgot about you. Don't blame my heart, blame my head. Maybe you need to reach out to remind me of our bond.

This series, just like the others, wasn't intended to be a series. It was originally just supposed to be two books, If You Cross Me Once and You'll Cross Me Twice. But as always, the feedback and demand dictates all. The people wanted more, so here it is, the third installment of the Cross series. I hope that you enjoy it because I happen to be in a federal penitentiary that stays on lockdown, so writing these series keeps me sane. They keep me busy, and they keep me out there. The most positive responses, I get from dudes in jail (majority of them from D.C.), is that I 'take them out there' in my books. I always smile at that, because that's always my intention. If you have read the first two books, answer this question for me, don't you hate Greg Gamble? I do, and I created him ... lol. I have a lot more stories in store for you guys and gals. Trust me.

What's next? Angel 5: The final Chapter, the second installment of In the Blink of an Eye. It's entitled 'Blink Twice and You Missed it'. I believe that that book is one of my most slept on books. If you have this book, and you're reading this right now, please check out 'In the Blink of an Eye'. It's a little different from what I usually write, but the story is great. It's about a group of females who go hard for theirs in the city of dreams (Washington, D.C.). You won't be disappointed. Trust me. I gotta take this opportunity to thank everyone whose supported me from the very beginning of this literary journey. To all the dudes who read Angel as a manuscript and encourage me to continue writing it. To Wahida Clark, who was there at the outset while she was still in prison. She gave me a lot of great advice early in the process of becoming a published author.

To all the publishing houses that ignored my mail and rejected my manuscript, thank you. It inspired me to continue. To Teri Woods and Lucas Riggins. They gave me my start in the game. Things got shady as time went on, but I gotta acknowledge them. To Crystal Perkins-Stell, the Detroit homegirl who tried but never seemed to break through, thank you for Bossy and Ghostface Killaz. To Kiki Swinson, don't hate me for how I portrayed you in this series. I meant no real ill will. All you did was try to help me. Thank you. The many conversations we had back in 2007 and 2008 encouraged me and helped me in my bid. To my man, Jason 'J Rock' Poole, who introduced me to T. Styles and and The Cartel Publications, who signed me but dropped me due to conflict and ego, thank you. Again, I have to shout

out Wahida Clark, who in 2008 signed me to her label, Wahida Clark Presents. She gave me the platform to give the people the first four Ultimate Sacrifices. Thank you. Now with that said, can I please have all the money you owe me for books sold in 2013, 2012, 2014, and beyond? And please don't try to blackball me again with Amazon, when I'm only trying to eat off my own books. To Nene Capri, who guided me once I got home in 2016. To Keisha Scott and her mom who typed for me. Rest in peace to Lashonda Johnson and Kano (he did all my book covers for NDA streets Publishing). To all the book clubs, vendors, online booksellers, bookstores, and other platforms that distribute books, thank you. My books are now in libraries, stores, online everywhere books are sold and on book carts in state and federal prisons all over the country. Thank you to everyone. I'm humbled by it all. Thank you to Kwame Teague and his wife. Lastly, thank you to Cash and Lockdown Publications for allowing me to continue this journey. I can't get out of here without getting at the men.

Whether I shout out the same people or not it's warranted because often, we are the forgotten ones. The ones still behind the fence or wall. To all the incarcerated men. To D.C. Nick, Dirty, Greg Bryce, Angelo 'Nut' Daniels, Pretty B., Apple Head Rob, Brook Tolliver, Boy Wonder, Jamal 'Handsome' Johnson, Don Juan McCowley, Project Pat, KD, Joe Ebron, Redhead, Trey Manning, Cochise Shakur, Erron Robinson, Abdul 'Dulee' Fields, Larry Wilkerson, EL, Buck, Poo Poo, Reck, Tonio, Black Shit, Dave, Vee, Floyd-EL, Jojo Davis, Tony Rone, Mark 'Flavor' Ford, Boy, Marco, Ray Bob, Huff Tha Great, Andre 'Dree' Becton (Trenton Park), Andy Daniels, Big Wali, Tweez, Rick, E, 88, Fat Shawn and others. There're too many men to name in this one, but you all know how I feel about you. Especially those of you who can navigate the bull jive and recognize the real. To all the people smart enough to avoid me with the whispers and rumors, thank you. Always standing on the code of silence. I'm out! Death before dishonor always.

D.C. Stand Up!
Buckeyfields

Chapter 1

Greg Gamble
Central Detention facility
(D.C. Jail)

"David, David, David. I knew that you'd do something to fuck up your release from jail. You're an animal, a beast, a cold-blooded predator. One who just couldn't help himself. All you had to do was chill out, and eventually you would walk out of this place. The gun only carries a year. With time served you would have left sooner than later, but you couldn't chill. Why? Because all the men in this jail today understand is violence, right? And you definitely speak the language of the land. I talked to a couple witnesses already. That kid had the audacity to be jacking his dick on the tier. Disrespected you, right? And you made him pay for it just like you did Solomon Robinson. I couldn't get you on the Robinson murder, David, but I got you on this one. That kid you stabbed... Warren Stevenson. He was only twenty years old, and unfortunately, he will never see another birthday. He died an hour ago at UMC, and guess what else? I'm dropping the gun case just to prosecute you personally on the new case. With all the video footage available and all the witnesses in that unit that are lined up to tell on you, I got you dead to rights on this one. Your friends can't kill all the witnesses on the case, David. Sorry! I know you're wondering why I'm here, David. The sitting United States Attorney for D.C. was standing outside of your cage conversing with you hours after you killed a man in cold blood. You're wondering why I'm here, aren't you?"

I waited to see if David Battle would speak, but he didn't so I continued. "I'm here to help you, believe it or not. I can make the new murder charge disappear…" I snapped my fingers. "Just like that. That twenty year old kid, Warren Stevenson, was here on murder charges of his own. He terrorized his Fort Totten neighborhood. No one is going to miss him. Only his family will be saddened by his death. This is called a quid pro quo situation, David. You help me, I help you."

"Help you how?" David Bathe asked suddenly.

"By confessing your sins, David. That's how. Confess to the Robinson murder and tell me who killed Yolanda Stavens, Thomas Caldwell, and Khitab Bashir, for starters. Tell me about your buddy, Quran Bashir, and what role he played in any of the murders. I listen to your phone calls, David. Tell me about Jihad Bashir and his role in all of this. Tell me about your lawyer, Zin Carter. I know all about her connection to Quran Bashir. What role does she play in this besides defending you in court? You're from the Sayles Place, Sheridan Road crew. So, I know that you know Zin Carter, Mike Carter . Tell me what you know about him and his connection to Sean Branch. I'm the only person that can help you now, David. I'm the wizard of Oz who can send you home to Southeast. All you have to do is talk to me, David. Confess your sins to me. Close your eyes and picture yourself in a confession booth inside a church somewhere, anywhere. Picture me as the priest you're confessing to behind that screen. Give me any of the people I just named, David, and I promise you that you'll get to go home. In the next 48 to 72 hours, you can be free. What's it gonna be, David?"

David Battle used both hands to cover his face momentarily, then he stood up. He walked up to the bars of the holding cage until we were only inches away from one another. "Picture myself in a church, huh?"

I nodded, but my eyes were now on the stained blood that covered the bright orange D.C. jail uniform top David had on. My eyes were riveted to the blood stains. "Picture yourself inside a confession booth with me on the other side of the screen listening to you." I lifted my eyes from the bloodstains and held David's gaze. "Confess and go home. Save yourself."

"Okay, I confess."

My heartbeat skipped inside my chest. Breaking David Battle and closing multiple cold case murders would get me elected mayor in the next election. "You confess to what, David? Talk to me. Wait … as a matter of fact, I need to record this." I pulled out my cell phone and used it to record whatever David was about to say.

"I confess that I might be gay because I really want to fuck you. Word on the street is that you're a fag, and ever since I heard it, I been wanting to fuck you in your ass. I got a closet fetish for old gay men. Seeing you right now makes my dick hard. I know that you're a vicious freak too. Probably eat a nigga's dick straight up, swallow his seed, then burp and say 'excuse me'. So, you got me, I confess to fantasizing … I can picture me fucking you in the confession booth in one of them Catholic robes on that them pervert ass Priests be wearing. Me, bending you over the seat and lifting the robe. Then fucking you real good …"

"Is that right, David? That's what you picture, huh?"

"Yeah, that's what I picture because I can't picture none of that other shit you just said. You got me fucked up, bitch boy nigga, if you think I would become a rat under any circumstances. I don't know no Quran Bashir, Jihad Bashir, Mike Carter or no fucking Sean Branch. Zin Carter is my lawyer, and that's all I know. So, fuck you, gay boy. Don't ever disrespect me again by trying to get me to be a rat. I'd rather die than do that. Fuck outta here, bitch before I pull out my dick and piss on your faggie ass."

With that said, David Battle turned his back to me and walked back to the metal bench. He pulled off the uniform top stained with blood, balled it up, and used it as a pillow before lying down.

Deep inside, I seethed. My blood boiled in my veins, but I never stopped smiling. "You're going to regret those words, David. I promise you that."

"Promise this dick in your mouth."

I left D.C. jail's infirmary and slowly walked through the jail. I put my phone away as I walked. On the ground floor adjacent to the command center, I navigated my way to a bevy of offices. All of the office doors were shut, except one. I knocked on the door before entering the office.

"How did it go?" Major Bruce Culbreath asked. "Did he talk?"

"No. Piece of shit cursed me out." I replied.

"Disrespected the shit out of me."

"Sorry to hear that, buddy."

"Don't be, it was worth a shot. Getting him to talk would have gotten me elected mayor. I appreciate you calling me like you did and getting me in here to talk to him. I offered David Battle his freedom, and he invited me to his dick. Some people just don't know when they are defeated, but he'll learn after I put him away for the rest of his life."

"Listen, I've seen your brand of vengeance firsthand. I almost feel sorry for the guy."

"Don't. He made his bed, so he's the one who'll have to lie in it."

"You're right about that. So, what now?"

"The usual. I'ma put Metropolitan all over this and when they finish, they will turn everything over to me. Then I'm gonna nail David Battle to the proverbial cross." I looked at my watch. "I gotta run, but thanks again for everything."

"Don't mention it, Greg. I will never forget what you did for my nephew last year. Whenever you need me, I'm here for you."

"Good to hear, Bruce. Good to hear."

Chapter 2

Zin

As I parked my car in the jail parking lot all I could hear was the voice of some anonymous inmate who had called my cell phone an hour ago. He'd said something about a stabbing in the unit and David Battle being locked up for it. I had been overseeing the interior decorator that was furnishing my suite in the building. I quickly did some research and then headed here to the jail. As I stepped out of my car, I spotted a familiar face. I stopped in my tracks and watched Greg Gamble exit the jail and walk to a dark colored new model Audi sedan. I watched as he ducked inside the Audi, then pulled out of a parking spot across the lot. I watched the retreating vehicle until it disappeared from sight.

"What the fuck was he doing here?" I asked myself, aloud. Baffled, I continued on towards the entrance of D.C. jail. At the visitor's counter, a female correctional officer that I had never seen before shook her head.

"No visitors allowed, ma'am. The jail is on lockdown," the CO said.

I pulled out my credentials and slid them across the counter. "That can't be true, Miss, because I just saw the United States Attorney exit the building. I have been informed that my client, David Battle, has been locked down for a stabbing. I demand to meet with my client immediately, or do I have to get the mayor on the phone?" I bluffed.

The female CO looked uncomfortable. Me mentioning the mayor vexed her. She turned my credentials over in her hand. "Uh … just wait a minute. Let me get on the phone with the Major and see what he says." After talking privately on the phone out of earshot, the female CO returned to the counter. "The Major says that you can see your client, ma'am. Please fill out the necessary paperwork, and then I will escort you to the first floor visiting room."

Twenty minutes later, I was seated inside the visiting room, waiting for David to be brought out. After what seemed like an eternity, he walked into the room with his ankles shackled and his hands cuffed to a belly chain that encircled his waist. He was escorted by a white shirted lieutenant.

Inside the small visiting room, David sat across the table from me. He looked as if he'd aged ten years in a few days.

"What the fuck happened, David?" I queried as soon as the room's door was shut.

David couldn't look me in the face. "I did some stupid shit."

"What stupid shit did you do? I got a call from one of your friends saying that someone had been stabbed and you'd been taken out of the unit in cuffs. What happened?"

"I lost my temper. I was on the phone, and I looked up … wild ass nigga had his dick out jacking off on the tier. We had two women CO's working the block and … man, fuck!!"

"It's too late for all that. Finish the story."

"When I saw the dude's dick, I lost my head. I felt disrespected. I went to my cell and got my knife. I stabbed the dude and killed him …"

"Killed him? No, you didn't kill him. He's in the hospital fucked up pretty bad, but you didn't kill him."

David looked at me like I was retarded. "He's dead, Zin."

"No, he's not fucking dead, David. I checked again before coming upstairs. The guy's name is Warren …"

"Stevenson. I know that. He died at the hospital."

"Are you in shock or something? Or have you finally lost your mind? Didn't I just tell you that I checked on his condition twice? Once before coming to this legal visiting room. Warren Stevenson is in critical, but stable condition at Howard University Hospital."

"Are you sure?" David asked, confused.

"Of course, I'm sure. Have you heard a word I just said? When I got the call about an inmate being stabbed here and you being involved, I made some calls. Found out who the injured man was and his condition. I made another call about thirty minutes ago before coming upstairs and checked on him again. Warren Stevenson is alive fighting for his life, but alive. Why would you think that he was dead?"

"That fucking faggie ass nigga …"

"What faggie ass nigga? Who are you referring to?"

"Greg Gamble."

"What about him?" I asked, confusion etched on my face.

"He came here to see me. That bitch nigga tried to trick me," David said.

"Wait … time out," I said, digesting what I'd just heard. "What did you just say? Say it again."

"After I was pulled off of the dude …"

"Warren Stevenson?"

"Yeah, him. I was roughed up by the CO's and dragged to the infirmary. After seeing a doctor, I was placed in a holding cage in the infirmary. I laid on the bench and fell asleep. I was awakened by someone calling my name. I thought it was the CO's, but it wasn't. I looked up and saw Greg Gamble standing at the bars outside the cage. He tried to get me to snitch."

"Snitch? Snitch on who?"

"On myself., Quran, and Jihad. He mentioned your father. He mentioned the dude, Sean Branch. And he even said something about you."

"Me?" I repeated, incredulously. "He wanted you to snitch on me? Snitch on me about what?"

David shrugged his shoulders. "Fuck if I know. He said something about you being connected to Quran. He believes you're doing some shady shit. He mentioned your father. Told me that I have to know him since he's from my neighborhood. He said something about Mike Carter being connected to Sean Branch or some shit. He told me to confess to the Robinson murder and tell him who killed the three witnesses. Told me if I told him something about the four of ya'll or any one of ya'll, I could be home in seventy-two hours tops."

I couldn't believe what I was hearing. I knew that Greg Gamble was upset about my string of victories against him, but to try and implicate me in crimes was a new low for him. The man was dead serious about making good on his threats to me. Greg Gamble wanted Quran, his brother, Jihad, and me in jail. He wanted to put Sean Branch back in prison and keep my father behind bars. The stakes were getting higher and higher right before my very eyes. What had started out as a game of wits between Greg Gamble, and I had now turned into a game of life and death.

"When I pulled up here, I saw Gamble leaving the jail. I wondered what he was doing here. Never in my wildest dreams did I think he'd be here talking to you and trying to get you to implicate me in some criminal acts. Trying to get you to LIE on Quran, Jihad and my father. He was never supposed to come here. He never should have questioned you. And he lied to you about Warren Stevenson being dead when he knew that he wasn't. His actions are unethical, over the line, and just plain wrong. Greg Gamble could go to jail for the stunt he just pulled with you."

"Well, let's tell somebody," David said.

"Who could we tell? He's the top prosecutor in the city. It took balls of steel to pull off what he did, and he's connected in high places. You don't get to come to DC jail and visit an inmate in the infirmary immediately after an assault unless you're well connected. Somebody here at the jail called

Gamble and told him about you and the assault. He was then allowed to come here and visit you while you sat inside a holding cage in the jail infirmary. If I did want to tell this story to someone … and I don't … there's no way to prove it ever happened. It would be basically your word against his. I'm betting that there's no record of him ever being here today …"

"There's cameras everywhere. All over this dirty ass joint …"

"Cameras can be manipulated. Footage can be deleted or destroyed. Somebody high up in the chain of command did him a favor, and I'm sure that someone covered his or her tracks. So, alerting someone is out. I have to figure out another creative way to deal with Greg Gamble. The more I think about it, I'm actually glad he pulled this stunt. He exposed his hand and let us know that all of the cards in the deck are marked. He let us know the degree of dirty pool he's willing to play. I see that you're wearing a white paper suit."

"They took my clothes before I came in here. My uniform had blood on it."

"That means that he means to have you charged for assault or attempted murder. Add that to the gun case, and you've just made my job hard as hell. I told ya to chill out …"

"And I told you that I saw that creep with his dick out and lost it. The voice in my head screamed, knife. I should've just beat his ass." David shook his head. "I can't believe this stupid ass shit."

"Well, believe it, because you did it. Let me go and talk to some folks. They got you locked down, right?"

David nodded.

"South One or Northeast One?"

"South One."

"That will hold you and keep you out of further trouble. Let me get on top of everything, and I'll be back to see you in a few days. Fall back, and remember, no talking to the tier about this case or any case. Muthafuckas are in here waiting to tell on your ass to go home Ya hear me?"

"I hear you, Ms. Carter. No talking about the case. I got it."

"Good," I said and gathered my things. "I'll see you in a few days."

***

The apartment that Quran called his 'trap spot' was immaculate. It didn't look like any trap spot that I had ever seen before. The walls were painted a pleasant shade of beige. The carpet was a caramel shade of brown. The leather loveseat, couch, and recliner were coffee brown. The coffee tables and living room table were brown wood. The table was glass, and the chairs around it were brown lacquer. A seventy-inch flat screen took up most of the wall on one side. All the other walls were bare. The apartment smelled of scented oils and weed. Jihad Bashir moved around the apartment with familiarity. His cell phone glued to his ear; he paid me no mind. I sat on the couch and furtively stole glances at Jihad. No matter how many times I saw Quran's younger brother, I couldn't get over how identical they looked. Their curly haircuts were similar. The wardrobes, , height and build were the same. Their eyes were an arresting shade of light gray. My reverie was broken moments later when the apartment door opened and Quran walked in.

He walked straight over to me, leaned down, and hugged and kissed me.

"Zin, what made you decide to come here? We could've met …"

"This was closer, Quran, and besides, I know that Jihad is often here. I need to talk to the both of you."

Jihad looked up from his phone conversation. "I heard my name. What did I do this time?"

Quran gave his brother a serious stare. "Get off the phone. Zin has something to tell us."

"A'ight. See you in thirty. Cool. One," Jihad said before disconnecting his call. He sat up on the couch where he had been lying down. "I'm listening. What's good, Zin?"

"You talked to David earlier today, right?" I asked Jihad.

Jihad nodded. "Yeah, he called and asked about Quran. He wanted to know why Quran wasn't answering his phone. I told him that everybody had new phones. I asked him about his situation. He said a little something about it before becoming distracted. Suddenly, he said, I'ma hit you back, Jay. I gotta go. Then he hung up. Why? What's up?"

"How much do ya'll trust David?" I asked Quran and Jihad.

"With my life," Quran said.

"Why do you ask that?" Jihad asked.

"Just curious. What I'm about to say to you both is somewhat public knowledge but some of it is what me and David talked about. That makes it attorney/client privilege. He hasn't given me permission to speak to ya'll about it, but I'ma do it anyway, since you both are involved …"

"Involved in what?" Quran asked.

"Yeah … involved in what?" Jihad seconded.

"I'm about to tell ya'll everything but it has to stay right here between us. That means no talking about it on cell phones, and no talking to David on jail calls. Nothing. Am I clear?"

Quran nodded.

Jihad said, "Clear as water in the Caribbean."

"Just left meeting with David at the jail. After he got off the phone with you, he stabbed a guy fifteen times. The guy had his penis out, jacking off to some female CO's. David went ballistic …"

"As he should have," Quran said.

"But that's not what concerns me. Somebody at D.C. jail made a call to the U.S. Attorney, Greg Gamble, alerting him to David's involvement in a serious assault. Greg Gamble went to D.C. jail and was allowed to go to the jail's infirmary where David was being held. Not the visiting room, but the infirmary. Greg Gamble talked to David without anyone else around. He lied to David and told him that the man he stabbed was dead. Told him that he was facing new murder charges, but he could help him if David talked."

"Talked about what?" Jihad asked.

"Look … let's not bullshit each other, okay." I stood up and said, "Ain't nobody in here but the three of us, right?"

Jihad nodded.

"And I ain't the fucking enemy here." I looked right into Quran's eyes. "I've proven that to you, correct?"

It was Quran's turn to nod .

"Okay, good. Greg Gamble wanted David to tell him who killed Yoland Stevens, Thomas Caldwell and Khitab … your brother. He wanted him to confess to killing Manny Robinson. He asked David about *me* and my connection to Quran. He asked about Quran and you, Jihad …"

"Me?" Jihad repeated.

"Yeah, you. He mentioned my father, and he mentioned Sean Branch." I paused to let my revelations sink in for the brothers.

"Man… this nigga…" Quran uttered. "I swear to God…"

"Greg Gamble offered David a get out of jail free card if he talked about any one of us."

"And what did Dave say?" Quran asked.

"I don't know what he said. All I know is what he told me he said. David Battle is your friend not mine. I'm just his lawyer. The both of you know him better than me. That's why I started all of this by asking ya'll how much do ya'll trust him. He said that he went off on Gamble. Disrespected him real bad. But I wasn't there. I'm just repeating what David told me. Somebody that knew he was my client called my phone and told me that there had been a stabbing, and David was snatched up because of it. I stopped what I was doing and went straight to the jail. When I parked in a parking spot, I saw Greg Gamble leaving the jail. The jail is on lockdown, but I was allowed in to see David. Everything that he told me, I'm telling the both of you. I'm not overly concerned about David talking because he doesn't know anything about me personally. I mean, other than the fact that I mess with Quran, I've done nothing wrong or committed any crimes. So, Gamble is just chasing ghosts by mentioning me. He's mad at me for repeatedly beating him in court. His reasons for mentioning my father, I believe, go a little deeper, and I have no clue about his motives. It's personal between him and my father, but my father won't say why. All I know is that Jon Zucker hasn't even filed the motion for my father to get back in court, yet Greg Gamble already knows that and all the details about the motion. I already know why Greg Gamble is beefing with Sean Branch, but what I don't know is why he's asking David about him. Like, is there a connection between David and Sean that I don't know about? And is there a connection between my father and David that I don't know about? Is there?"

Quran's eyes darted to his brother, and they shrugged their shoulders simultaneously. "Not that I know of," Quran said.

"I don't know Sean Branch or your father, Zin. I just know of him. I don't know who David is connected to," Jihad added.

They were both lying through their teeth. I could see right through their deception and denial.

"Well, I just wanted to put ya'll on point about Greg Gamble. This shit is getting more serious by the day. I already told you, Quran, that your name was mentioned in open court and now Gamble is using you … and Jihad as bargaining chips. Is there anybody else around you that can hurt you?"

"Anybody like who? You already know I'ma one man show," Quran answered. "Other than when I'm with Jihad."

"All I'm saying is, you don't have to convince me of shit. You don't have to tell me who's in your circles. But you have to be sure that whoever is around ya'll can be trusted because David is not the only person who's gonna be targeted by Gamble. That muthafucka is smart, and he's perceptive. He has an uncanny ability to know shit that he ain't supposed to know. So, if there's anybody that can be broken …"

"All my men solid," Jihad boasted. "Unbreakable."

"You sure about that, Jihad? What about you, Quran? Greg Gamble is a resourceful, manipulative piece of shit. He broke Thomas Coldwell, and he was David's first cousin. He broke your brother Khitab. Remember that."

"Leave my dead brother out of this," Jihad hissed.

"God bless the dead, but how can I when you and Quran thought that he would never break either?" I reached down and grabbed my purse. "I've done my good deed for the day. Ya'll got the heads up. The rest is on ya'll." I headed for the door.

"Jay, I'll be right back. I'ma walk Zin to her car," Quran announced.

Outside Quran said, "Thank you for everything, Zin. I appreciate it."

"I would do anything for you, Quran. But you already know that, right?"

"I do. And you know that's ditto for me, right?"

"I do know that. Do you remember what we talked about in reference to Greg Gamble?"

Quran nodded.

"That might end up being the only way to stop him, babe. Think about that."

"I will, and I promise you …"

"So, Quran … this is the bitch that you left me for?" a female stated emphatically.

As if on survival mode, Quran's head turned to face the voice. I moved him aside so that I could see the person who had just spoken. The woman was pretty. Her dreads were dyed burgundy, and her figure was nice, but the chick had me fucked up.

"Bitch! Who you calling a bitch, bitch!" I moved in the woman's direction, reaching down to remove my heels as I went. Quran's power full arms held me back.

"Tosheka … if you don't get the fuck on somewhere, I swear by Allah, I'ma …"

"You gon' what? You gon' what, Quran? What you gon' do? Kill me? Huh? You gon' kill me like you do all the people that get in your way or won't get out of your way? Well, kill me then, Quran! Because being without you ain't living!!" Tosheka shouted and started to cry. "Look what you have reduced me to! I can't have you, so I'm with your brother. Just to be near you … and this is all her fault!" the woman named Tosheka shouted as she pointed to me.

"I don't have time for this shit, Tosheka! We was just fucking. We were never exclusive. You know that. You chose to be with Jihad because that's what you wanted to do. Don't put that on me. This is my woman right here. I haven't touched you since we've been together. You know what it's hitting for. It's over between us. You got Jay. Let it go! I'm telling you some real shit, Tosheka. Let it go." Quran turned to face me. "Get in the car and go. I'ma call you and get up with you later." He leaned in and kissed me. "I love you. Go!" I could still hear the woman named Tosheka crying and shouting at Quran as I closed my car door and started the ignition. As I pulled onto Bowen Road, I looked in the rearview mirror one last time.

"I got a trick for your ass, Quran Bashir. Just you wait."

Chapter 3

Tosheka Jennings

"Look at this shit, Tosheka. Look at this scene you making out here. You know me. You know that I don't like muthafuckas in my business, and you doing exactly that. Putting everybody in my business. In your business. You out here screaming and shouting and shit. Crying and saying a rack of dumb shit. Talking about I kill all the people who get in my way or won't get out my way. People can hear you! Then what the fuck you think they gon' tell the police? Exactly what the fuck you just said. You lunching ! You slipping, and you being too dramatic for me. I ain't with that shit, Tosheka, and you know that. All this shit you just pulled in front of Zin was some bullshit. You on some bullshit. And why in the fuck are we even going through all of this?! You fuck with my brother now! I was in the spot when you told him how good his dick was, and how he fucked you better than me and all that shit. You said you fucked him to get back at me. To make me notice you. Well, that was the wrong way to get me to notice. All you had to do was fall back. I'ma dirty nigga by nature. I been with Zin for about six months, but I still would've come back to you because believe it or not, I fuck with you. But that shit you pulled with Jay ... that killed all that. I will never touch you again, and that's on my dead mother. So, like I said earlier, get over it, Tosheka, and let it go! We over with! You got Jay, and guess what? He feeling you. So, that's your move right there. You're his girl now. And don't ambush me no more, Tosheka. That shit is dangerous. You just popping up on a nigga. I got a rack of enemies and I'ma paranoid nigga. I might kill you the next time by accident. Do you understand what I'm saying to you?"

"I understand." I mumbled. "But, Quran …"

My words fell on deaf ears as Quran walked away from me. All I could do was lean on the facade of 1351 and cry like a baby.

***

"Tosheka, where the hell are you? We said thirty minutes."

"I was there, Jihad, but I left. Ran into Quran and his new bitch outside the building. We got into it, and I left."

"Got into it? Fuck that mean?" Jihad asked.

I looked at Jihad on the screen of my phone. I gave him the 'are you retarded' look that I was famous for. "Fuck does it sound like it means? We got into it …"

"Who got into it? You and Quran or you and Zin?"

"Both, kinda sorta. I called the bitch a bitch, and she acted like she wanted some smoke, but she was faking. She let Quran hold her back. He made her leave and then me and him got into it."

"Got into it, how? Did he hit you?"

"Hell no, he didn't hit me. You know that Quran don't beat up no bitches. He just cussed my ass out and then walked away from me. He hurt my feelings real bad. So, I left, Jihad. I had to leave. The shit he said …"

"What did he say?"

I had to keep my eyes on the road as I drove, but I wanted to look at Jihad's face so bad.

"Things … a lot of shit that made me think I'm dead ass wrong for fucking with you …"

"Did he say that? Did tough ass Quran tell you you were…"

"No, he didn't. He ain't no hater like that. He just kept saying that it's over between me and him and I need to let it go…"

"You do need to let it go. You're with me now."

"I'm with you, Jihad because…I can't let go. I love Quran with all my heart. He'll come around. I…I just…I just …"

"You just what, Tosheka? Gotta wait for him to wake up?"

"Exactly."

"If you believe that, you lunchin' like shit. Quran loves Zin, and you ain't her. I need you to tell me something though. A couple minutes ago, you said, I'm with you, Jihad because ..., but you never finished your sentence. Finish that sentence for me. You're with me because … what?"

I was stuck at a red light on Suitland Parkway and Naylor Road, so I could look at Jihad's face. I could see the hurt in his eyes. "You already know the answer to that question, Jihad. Don't make me say it."

"Naw, I want you to say it. Let me hear it. I need to hear it."

"I don't want to say it."

"Say it. I can handle it," Jihad pressed.

"I'm with you because … because I can't have him. I'm with you because you look just like him. Everything about you is just like him. I can be with you, Jihad, but it will always be Quran that I want. I'm sorry."

To my surprise, Jihad smiled and then started laughing. I was completely baffled.

"Fuck is so funny?"

"You. Looking all stressed because you had to tell me that. But guess what? I already knew that. I knew that going in … from jump street. And I'm cool with that. So, now that we got that out the way, can you come on back now, so I can see your sexy, bowlegged, pretty ass."

I couldn't help but smile. "You can see me, Jihad, but not there. You gotta come to my spot. I'ma text you the address when we hang up. I'ma be home in like fifteen minutes. Give me some time to shower, and you can pull up."

"Shower, huh? Won't you wait for me. We can shower together."

"Say no more, but do me a favor, please."

"What's that?"

"Stop and get some Patron. The watermelon kind and bring some of that gas you be smoking. I need that."

"Got you. I'm on my way. Text me the addy."

I disconnected the video call and texted Jihad my address. I was just about to put my phone in my purse when it vibrated. I thought the caller was Jihad, but it wasn't. It was my girl, Bionca Clark. Answering the call, I said, "Hey, Bee, what's up with you?"

"I'm good, girl. Just cooling. Haven't talked to you in a minute. How has life been for you?"

"Work is fine. The family is good. I can't complain. My only problem is these niggas out here. Can't live with them, can't live without them. Other than that, I'm good."

"Ain't that the truth. That grey eyed dude you be talking about all the time is driving your ass crazy, huh? What's his name again?!"

"Quran."

"Like the book the Muslims believe in, right?"

"Uh huh. You got it."

"That nigga got to be fine if he got grey eyes. I might need me somebody like that. You did say that your boo got some brothers, didn't you? I'm just saying …"

"One of them is dead and the other one is taken, too. Sorry."

"Damn, that's too bad, but I'll take a friend then. I heard that Quran be fucking with that fine ass old head nigga …"

"What fine ass old head?"

"The one that just got out of jail. The one …"

"Sean Branch?"

"Yeah, him. Get Quran to put me on."

"Gurl, Quran ain't gon' do that. He funny style as shit. Besides, what the fuck done got into your ass. I thought you like women? Now, all of a sudden you want some dick in your life."

Bionca laughed. "Never said that I didn't like dick and don't crave it from time to time. You know how that shit go. There's something about other bitches that I love, but I also love a fine ass man at times too. And for some reason, all the dudes I meet are lame as fuck. Dry as shit. Plus, they broke or got too many baby mothers, or they just plain clingy, too emotional or can't fuck for shit. You can say what you want, Sheka, ain't nobody eating a bitch pussy as good as another bitch. Add that to the fact that she's fine, sexy, and game tight, shit … I'm wet just thinking about it."

I pulled onto Iverson Street laughing at Bionca's crazy ass. "I feel you, Bee, but I'm good on a woman eating this cat. I'ma need some dick immediately after to feel muscles and nuts as the dick slam all up in this. When I'm bent over, the nuts slamming into my clit is what stimulates me the most. That shit be fire. If you can't see that, you missing out on a good game, bitch."

"Damn, Mr. Grey Eyes putting it in like that?"

Which one? "You better believe it. Got me acting crazy as shit out here in these streets."

"Got you hanging all in the hood and shit. Where Quran from again?"

"Sheridan Terrace. Him and his brother run shit around there."

"Now that you mention it, I think I heard about them already. Quran's brother's name is Bo, right?"

"No, girl. Bo is his brother's right-hand man. His brother's name is Jihad."

"And he got grey eyes, too, right?"

"Didn't I just tell you that both brothers are taken?"

"A'ight, then. Damn, bitch, if I didn't know better, I'd think you had 'em both the way your voice just changed when you said that. Sounded all possessive and shit. And I'm still tryna get Sean Branch. I'll put this pussy on his old ass …"

"Bionca, bye, girl, " I said and laughed. "I can holla at Quran and see …"

"Naw, naw… don't do that. I'm good. Just horny. Plus, you said Quran is funny style about shit like that. I'm good. I'll get him on my own. Do he be in Quran's hood with him and his brother?"

"Fuck no. Him and Quran are just tight. He don't hang out on Howard Road. At least, I've never seen him out there. They link up and do them. I know that Sean is from Langdon Park somewhere. If you really want him, you better go over there somewhere. Montana Avenue, Brentwood, Saratoga … somewhere over there."

"Fuck I look like to you, bitch? A stalker? I ain't going to all them places for no dick. No matter who it's attached to. I'm good."

After I finished laughing, I said, "Good luck reaching whatever goal you have in mind then, Bee. You sound confused to me. You horny, but don't know if you want a bitch to eat your pussy or a nigga to give you some dick. See, that's why I'm one way. Strictly dickly. I never have to choose. Sucks to be you."

"Sheka, fuck you," Bionca said in jest.

"Somebody is about to do that for me, so I gotta go. I'ma hit you back tomorrow and see how you handled your horny."

"A'ight, bitch. You be safe. Love you. Bye."

Tossing my phone in my purse, I got out of the car thinking about the night I was about to have. If I couldn't have Quran, his brother Jihad would have to do. Smiling to myself, I thought about a song by Luther Vandross. The lyrics to the hook were, "If you can't be with the one you love, then love the one you're with." And I was determined to do exactly that.

***

Once inside the apartment, I undressed down to my underwear and bra. I was straightening up when my cell phone vibrated. "Who the fuck ?" I said to myself, trying to recognize the phone number. I couldn't.

"Hello!" I snapped.

A female busted out laughing. "Bitch, chill out, sounding all vexed and shit. This ain't the IRS calling you. It's me, Tomasina."

" You too old to be playing on people's phone's Tom."

"Hooker, I'm on one of the landline phones at work. I just wanted to check on your ass. Haven't heard from you since …"

"Yesterday," I replied and laughed. "Bitch, we talked, yesterday. I was crying you a river about Quaran's ass … again!"

"Damn, you right. I gotta stop smoking weed. Shit killing my brain cells."

"They gon' piss your goofy ass and fire you if you keep it up."

"The D.C. Department of Corrections ain't firing nobody for weed. Shit, all my supervisors smoke sour diesel. We been doing smoke sessions. How dumb is you? What you about to get into?"

"It's nighttime, ain't it? I can't get into nothing but a good dream or a man's boxer briefs. And I ain't sleepy. You figure the rest out."

"Tosh, where you at, bitch?"

"In the house."

"Quran in there or somebody else?"

"Girl, I almost had to put these hands on his new bitch. Ran into them together leaving his spot on Howard Rd. Now, I ain't fucking with his ass. I got a new dick I'm sucking on."

"Bitch, you terrible," Tomasina said and laughed.

"You must not know 'bout me. You must not know 'bout me. I can have another nigga in a m inute. Matter fact, he'll be here in a minute, baby. So, don't you ever get to thinking you're irreplaceable," I sang.

"Yeah, okay, Beyonce. Make sure you call me tomorrow, whore."

"A'ight, boo. Love you."

"Love you too."

I tossed the cellphone and dance around my living room. The song, "Irreplaceable" by Beyonce played in my head. I imagined myself singing it to Quran.

"So go ahead and get gone. Call up and that chick and see if she's home. Oops, I bet you thought that I didn't know. What did you think I was putting you out for? Standing in the front yard telling me how I'm such a fool. Talking 'bout how I'll never find a man like you. You got me twisted. I can have another you in a minute. Matter of fact he'll be here in a minute. I can have another you by tomorrow. So don't you ever for a second get to thinking, you're irreplaceable."

I stopped dancing mid-step. "Hold up. Let me check something."

I reached into my panties, slid a finger inside my pussy, and moved it around little. I slid it out and placed my finger under my nose. I smelled my finger. There was no smell.

"Okay, I'm good."

Just as I started dancing again there was a knock on my door. I danced to the door and opened it. Jihad stood there looking just as good as Quran.

"Come on in, baby."

Chapter 4

Quran
Baby E. Jojo Morris. Kendra 'K.D.' Dyson.
I rode around the city with my next three targets in mind. I reread the text messages that Mike Carter had sent me. I looked at the picture of Baby E and KD together. Go figure. One rat was fronting weed to another rat. I shook my head and focused back on the road. I rode down 53rd Street and turned onto Dix Street. I looked around in hopes of spotting Baby E. For some strange reason I needed to kill him, or any one of the three targets. I needed to exorcise some demons inside me. I drove all through the Clay Terrace neighborhood but saw no signs of Baby E. As I gave up and headed Northeast to Sursum Cordas, I thought about several things at once. I thought about what Sean had said a few days ago about someone trying to kill him.

"So, I gotta find out who that broad and dude was that sparked at me. I gotta find this nigga, Doo Doo."

"You should have let me kill him that night on Third Street."

"I already know. I fucked up and now I was almost killed. Won't happen again. Ever. I'ma find Doo Doo and roast his ass. Then I'ma find that bitch and the nigga with her and do the same thing to them. Then I can resume settling all my old beefs."

I knew that Sean was a skilled killer, and he would make do on his own. He would also make good on his word to kill everybody that he had mentioned. I thought about Zin and everything she had told me and Jihad about Lil Dave and Greg Gamble. I couldn't believe what I had heard. Dave saw a dude jacking his dick on the tier and damn near killed him. Then somebody inside the jail alerted Greg Gamble to the assault. Who could that have been? How did that person know to call Gamble? How did Gamble get inside the jail to talk to Dave while in the infirmary? And why had Gamble mentioned me, Jihad, Mike Carter and Sean Branch? If Greg Gamble really offered to free Dave, did he really rebuff him and stand strong? If so, how long would he stay strong?

"How much do ya'll trust, David?" I could hear Zin's voice.

I shook my head suddenly to clear it of the doubt that creeped into me. I had known David Battle all of my life. I had killed for him on several occasions. I had stood beside him in every situation. He would never cross me. Then out of nowhere something that someone had said to me months ago came to mind. Something that Khitab had said while hanging from the pipe in that abandoned apartment. It came back to me with clarity.

"Bruh ... you gotta let me explain ..."

"Explain what, Tab? I read the paperwork where you explained everything to the cops. That's what got you in this situation. Explaining!"

"There's a lot of shit that you don't know, Que. Dave is jealous of you, and he's gonna cross ..."

"He's gonna cross me, and you were the only one who could see it? To protect me, you ratted on him to the cops? Is that what you're tryna say, Tab?"

"Yes ... No. Que, there's a lot more to it. You have to let me down and hear me out."

"Let you down, huh? Dave was gonna cross me? Did the cops tell you that?"

"I knew about it before I ever came across the cops. I tried ..."

"You knew that Dave was gonna cross me, and you kept that a secret?!"

"I told you, bruh ... there's a lot that you don't know."

"And how exactly was he gonna cross me, Tab? How was Dave gonna cross me?"

"Let me down, Que. don't leave me up here. I'm in pain, bruh. My whole face hurts, and I can't see a thing. I need ..."

"You need to make dua to Allah and pray that you are not tortured in the grave. Whatever it was that you knew or think you knew, you could've told me, Tab. You bartered Dave's freedom for your own. You crossed that man to make your gun charge go away. You are now a certified government witness. A whore for the government. A witness, a snitch, a rat. I can't forgive you for that, but Allah can. So, make your dues, Tab. Make 'em now."

"He was gonna cross you ..."

"So, you crossed him to keep him from crossing me?"

Without warning tears came to my eyes and fell down my cheeks. I could hear my brother's voice clearly in my head. Had he been right?

"Dave is jealous of you and he's gonna cross you."

Again, I shook my head to clear it of the doubt I now felt.

"How much do ya'll trust David?"
"With my life," I'd answered.

Dave would never cross me like that. He'd never become a rat. Would he? There was no way in the world that Dave would break weak.

"That muthafucka is smart and he's perceptive. He has an uncanny ability to know shit that he ain't supposed to know. Greg Gamble is a resourceful, manipulative piece of shit. He broke Thomas Caldwell, and he was David's first cousin. He broke your brother ..."

Before I knew it, I was coming out of the Third Street Tunnel. I made a right onto New York Avenue. Minutes later, I was in the Sursum Cordas neighborhood. I thought about the day I killed Franklin 'Diddy' Dorn on a street not far from where I was. I had killed the rat named Junie minutes later after he showed me who Diddy was. And here I was back in the area trying to kill two more rats who hung out here. Kendra Dyson and Jojo Morns. I wiped my watery eyes.

"Focus on finding the targets," I mouthed to myself repeatedly.

No matter how hard I tried not to think about Dave Battle and Greg Gamble, my thoughts went right back there. I zeroed in on Greg Gamble, the The United States Attorney for the District of Columbia. I thought about the run ins that Zin had with him and how worked up she had become after he had threatened her. I thought about the question she had asked me earlier.

"I'd do anything for you, Quran, but you already knew that, right?"

"I do, and you know that's ditto for me, right?"

"I do know that. Do you remember what we talked about In reference to Greg Gamble?"

I nodded.

"That might be the only way to stop him, babe. Think about that."

The question that Zin asked earlier brought back the memory of their conversation about Greg Gamble. It was inside my condo the first time we ever had anal sex. Zin asked me to fuck her ass and then afterwards, she said. "Now that you've had all of me, that's what I wanted you to have. And as you fucked me, I felt helpless. I felt vulnerable. I felt defenseless as you stood behind me and pounded my ass. And you know what? That's the same way I felt today outside of the courtroom when Greg Gamble threatened me. If I asked you to, would you kill Greg Gamble?"

> "Would I kill the United States Attorney?"
> "Yeah, would you do it if I asked you to?"
> "In a heartbeat, baby. In a heartbeat."

Zin asked if I would still kill Greg Gamble if she asked me to. I thought about the heat that would fall on everyone in the streets if I did in fact kill Greg Gamble. No judge, lawyer, prosecutor or elected official had ever been killed in D.C. Ronald Reagan was President of the United States in 1983 and had been shot by John Hinckley but survived. Even that hadn't happened in the city. Killing Greg Gamble was a big step to take. Killing regular people, rats of the humankind in the streets, was always explained away as everyday life in the dangerous streets of D.C. Killing a sitting United States Attorney was a whole different cup of coffee. One that would reverberate all throughout the country, not just in D.C.

"That might be the only way to stop him, babe. Think about it."

I parked the Cadillac Sedan on North Capitol Street by the Tyler House highrise building. I grabbed my head and ran both hands down my face. I exhaled deeply and wished that I had some weed to blow. I picked up my phone and dialed Zin's cellphone.

She answered on the second ring. "Hey, babe."

"Hey. Where are you?" I asked.

"At my Aunt Linda's. Why?"

"I need to see you. Touch you. Hold you …"

"Sex me?"

"Of course. You know I need that, too."

"Okay, but not here," Zin said.

"Go to my condo. I'll be there soon," I told her.

"Okay. I'm leaving out now."

"A'ight. See you soon. Bye."

I disconnected the call and pulled away from the curb on North Capital. I smiled to myself as I remembered when Zin was about to go at Tosheka. I saw her in my head as she was about to take off her heels hours ago. I wondered if Zin really knew how to fight. I knew that Tosheka could fight with the best of them. I imagined myself having to pull Tosheka off of Zin and laughed. I laughed now, but hours ago I was mad as shit that Tosheka had appeared out of nowhere and confronted me in front of Zin. Hopefully, she finally got the message that I was verbally and physically sending her. What we had was over. Done. My heart and mind belonged to Zinfandel Carter. And that was just the way it was. Thoughts of Zin led me back to the man she had helped free. Sean Branch.

"Greg Gamble wanted David to tell him who killed Yoland Stevens, Thomas Caldwell and Khitab … your brother … He asked about Quran and you, Jihad … he mentioned my father … and he mentioned Sean Branch … I already know why Greg Gamble is beefing with Sean Branch, but what I don't know is why he's asking David about him. Like, is there a connection between David and Sean that I don't know about? Is there a connection between my father and David that I don't know about?"

"There are a lot of things that you don't know, Zin. Things that you can never know."

I picked up my phone from my lap and sent a text message to Sean Branch.

Haven't heard from you. You good, big homie?
As I waited for a text from Sean. I could hear my brother Khitab's voice in my head again.

"There's a lot of shit you don't know, Que. Dave is jealous of you, and he's gonna cross you."

Chapter 5

Sean Branch
"Liv, what the hell is this that you got me watching?"
"It's called *Spartacus*. Supposed to a be true story."

I sat on the couch with Liv's head in my lap watching people on the T.V. screen use swords to rip right through other people. The main character, who I figured was Spartacus, was a beast with a sword and an animal in the bed with all the ladies. The scenes were set back in ancient times when men fought on the sand in coliseums until their death.

"You're lost because you didn't see last season's episodes. Spartacus was a slavehe under the foot of the Romans in the beginning. They used him as a gladiator to fight other men while the Romans waged bets on who would win. At some point Spartacus got tired of that shit and staged a rebellion."

My cell phone pinged to alert me of an incoming text. I grabbed the phone from the coffee table next to the couch and looked at it. The text was from Quran's new number.

Haven't heard from you. You good, big homie?
"I'ma call Quran right quick, baby. I'll be right back."
"Did Quran call you or text you?"
"Text me. Why?"
"Because when someone texts you, they are usually expecting a text back, not a call. But do you. You'll figure out how things work eventually."

I dialed Quran's number. He picked up after the third ring. "Youngin', what's up with you?" I asked and got up off the couch. I walked into the kitchen.

"Ain't shit, big homie. I need to get up with you soon."

"Business or pleasure?"

"Neither. Zi told me some shit that Greg Gamble said, and I wanna run it by you. Your name was mentioned."

"Is that right?" I asked not surprised that Greg Gamble had my name in his mouth yet again. "What are you doing right now?"

"I'm on my way to hookup with Zin. The day is over for me, but we can link up tomorrow whenever you're ready."

"A'ight, youngin'. That's a bet. I'ma holla first thing in the A.M. ."

"Cool. stay up, big homie. Assalamu alaikum"

"Walaikum assalaam. I'm out."

I walked back into the living room and saw a naked man jumping around on the screen. "Now, I see why you like this shit. Big, strong ass, naked muthafuckas filling the screen."

Liv laughed. "Boy, that's how they got down in the Roman days."

"My cock is magic!" The man on the screen bellowed to a room full of other people.

"Well, let it magically disappear from sight," a different man said to a round of laughter.

Shaking my head, I laughed and grabbed Liv's hand. "Come on upstairs with me. I got a few tricks I wanna show you."

"They better be better than that," Liv replied and pointed at the T.V. screen. "I told you that *Spartacus* is my favorite show."

"They gon' be way better than your favorite show. Trust me."

***

I sat the two trays of food on the hood of the four door Panamera. My shot up Porsche was at the dealership being repaired. The Panamera was a loaner vehicle. It was triple black with black tinted windows. I embraced Quran.

"Top of the morning, youngin." i told him before reaching around and grabbing the styrofoam tray on top. I passed Quran the food. "I hope you like regular shit, Que, because I ordered you scrambled eggs with cheese, turkey bacon, fried potatoes and wheat toast with buttered jam on the side."

Quran opened the tray and eyed the food. "It's perfect, big boy. Shukran."

"Afwan," I replied you're welcome in Arabic.

I grabbed my own tray and opened it. The food was fresh off the grill. My sunny side up eggs were done to perfection. I broke the yoke with my fork and tasted them. Standing, but leaning on the Porsche across from Quran, I shoveled turkey sausage links, fried potatoes and croissant into my mouth like a refugee. Once I had eaten enough to satisfy my hunger, I put the food down, opened my lemon and iced tea Nantucket. After taking a generous swig, I sat the bottled beverage down next to my breakfast. "Talk to me, youngin."

"First, I need your advice on something. You ever thought about killing somebody big?"

"Define big for me."

"Big as in a cop, lawyer, judge, prosecutor, councilperson."

"Is this about that punk, Gamble?"

Quran nodded. "This nigga ain't gon' quit until he's put you and me behind bars forever. I'm thinking about crushing his ass."

I thought long and hard about what Quran had said. "What happened this time?"

Quran opened the driver's side door of the GMC Sierra pickup truck he was driving. He put his food down on the seat. After wiping his hands and face with napkins, he said,

"I gotta man that's on body and a gun beef over the jail. I wiped down all the witnesses against him."

"You told me about that."

"A'ight. He beat the body, but they held him on a gun beef. All this geekin' ass nigga had to do was fall back, and he would have come home soon. This nigga saw a nigga jacking off on the tier."

"I hate that creep ass shit, youngin'."

"Apparently, he does, too because my man knifed the dude down on the tier in front of the whole block. Somebody at the jail had to be hip to my man Dave's situation because somebody called and told Greg Gamble. He knew about the body and all of his witnesses getting killed. . This nigga ... Gamble, went to D.C. jail and confronted my man in the infirmary."

"Get the fuck outta here."

"Wallahi. Somebody let Gamble confront Dave as he sat in a cage in the infirmary. Gamble lied to Dave and told him that the dude he blew up had died. Told Dave that he was going down and all that, but then threw the I can save you spill at him. Told him that he wanted info on his lawyer."

"Zin Carter?" I asked.

"Yeah, wifey. He told Dave to give up Zin, me, Mike Carter and you."

"Me?" I repeated. "Why would he mention me? I don't even know your man, Dave. he don't know me."

Quran shrugged. "Your guess is as good as mine, bruh. He knows, or thinks he knows something. Somebody been telling him something, but I don't know what that could be. The connections with Zin, I get. He knows that Zin is Mike Carter's daughter. He said some wild shit to her before that had her bent out of shape about a month ago. He beefing with her because she helped get you out, and he knows that she's helping her father with an appeal. She just helped Dave beat his body in court. My name came up in court."

"Your name came up how?"

"Dave's cousin, Tommy, was one of the witnesses against him. Before I wiped him down, he told the people that he feared for his life because Dave had a friend named QB that was dangerous and a vicious killer. Somebody in Gamble's office came up with Quran Bashir as QB."

"Do you think Gamble knows about your connection to Mike Carter?"

"I was what? Fifteen when Mike went in. I don't know how he could know about me killing for Mike then or now."

"Well, he knows about my connection to Mike. I been knew that. I'm wondering does he know about me and you being close. He can't know that we been killing together now, but he might know that you and I killed for Mike back in the day. That bitch nigga is like a blood hound dog sniffing shit out. He probably got so many muthafuckas on the payroll that he knows all kinds of shit. Now, rewind back to what you said, Gamble asked your man to tell him about us. You, me, Zin, and Mike Carter. Did he? Did he talk?"

"Zin said that he said he didn't talk."

"Do you believe him?"

"That's my man, slim …"

"That ain't what I fucking asked you, Que." I exploded.

"I believe him. Slim ain't no rat, big homie. He'd never eat government cheese …"

"Your man doesn't know me or anything about me … unless …"

Quran looked at me with bad intentions in his eyes. "Unless what? Unless I told him something about you? Is that what you were about to say?"

I nodded.

"If you were gonna say that, old head, it's obvious that you don't really know me like I thought you did. I never talk about anything that I did to anyone. So, I'd never discuss you with anyone. Dave knows that we're friends, but that's it. I killed my man, Dontay Samuels, for running his mouth too much. I learned that lesson almost twenty years ago. Dave is a solid nigga, slim. He won't talk."

"For your sake, I sure hope that you're right."

"I am right."

"Okay. if you say so, but like I said, your man don't know me. But to answer your original question, of course, I entertained the thought of bodying a big wig. A person that's usually off limits. But have I ever done it? Naw. Never really had to. Let me be clear on something, though, youngin'. Are you thinking about bodying Gamble?"

Quran grabbed his food and began to eat again. I waited patiently for him to talk. "He ain't gon' stop. You even said it yourself, he's a bloodhound. He's on our line, bruh. All of ours. Mine, yours, Mike's, Zin, and my lil' brother. I forgot to mention him. Gamble mentioned him, too. He ain't gonna ease up. He ain't going away. Can I afford … Can we afford to sit around and wait until he finds out something on one of us or outright frames us for some shit? That nigga plays dirty pool, bruh. He's motivated. Do we just sit back and …"

"I hear what you're saying, Que and to be honest with you, he was the muthafucka that I thought about killing before. Back when he was a regular prosecutor. You preaching to the choir about that nigga. He's definitely a vindictive, fag model ass nigga. He's probably tryna build some case on one of us or all of us as we speak. But killing him, youngin, is a big deal. It'll take a lot of planning and a lot of luck …"

"Muslims don't believe in luck, big homie," Quran stated and smiled.

"True dat. Scratch that. It'll take a lot of careful planning but ain't nobody untouchable. I'ma do some research on the U.S. Attorney to see if he has any family in the area and all that. You just be cool and let me see what I can unearth on old Greg Gamble. If we gotta smoke his ass… so be it. Just don't pull no solo, hot dog shit on me. If he gotta go, we both gon' do it. Agreed?"

"Agreed, but speaking of research and all that, what's up with your current situation? You find Doo Doo yet?!"

"Doo Doo is dead. Somebody killed him. They found him shot to death on Half Street the same day that dude and broad fired them shots at me. According to the news, his time of death was seven pm. That was before I almost got hit. So, whoever the dude and broad were, they killed Doo Doo, took his phone, and sent me that text message. Doo Doo usually called me, but I didn't think nothing of it. I fell for the okey doke and almost got got. It's cool though. I learned a valuable lesson about text messages."

"Still no idea about who they were though? The nigga and the bitch?"

I took the moment to pick my tray up and eat the rest of my food. In between bites, I said, "I been killing since I been home, so technically it could have been anybody. But my instincts tell me that it was someone who knew Doo Doo, and they knew that Doo Doo knew me. The only person that could be is somebody who's mad at us for killing Whistle and Crud. That's the only thing that makes sense to me. I'm zeroing in on Whistle's family and Crud's family. Since I don't really know where to start, I'ma take it slow. Then I'ma start a reign of terror unlike anything this city has seen in a long time. Everybody is gonna get it until I'm satisfied. Other than that, it's smooth sailing for me."

"And you still haven't talked to Mike Carter, yet?"

"I shook my head. "No hurry. I'll get around to it. Has he asked about me?"

"Naw, not lately," Quran replied.

"Good. He'll be alright. We'll talk soon."

"Why don't you want to talk to him?"

"That breakfast was good as shit, wasn't it?" I suddenly asked Quran.

Quran walked over to the trash receptacle and tossed his tray into it. He wiped his mouth again and discarded the napkin. "I guess that's your way of saying 'mind your business, Que.' I'ma respect that. Whatever it is between you and that man is on ya'll. Thanks for breakfast. I'ma go ahead and bounce. I got a few people to look for."

"A job?"

Quran nodded. "The work ain't hard and the boss ain't mean. You remember how that old ass saying goes. I'ma get up with you later. If something arises and you need me, just call."

I met Quran halfway for a departing embrace. "Remember what I said about Gamble. If he has to be taken off the chessboard, we do it together. I'ma find out how."

"Say less, big homie. Say less."

***

"Hey, Dad!" Shontay said as we embraced.

"Hey, baby girl. I need your help. Where is your laptop?"

Shontay left the room and returned with her MacBook Pro. "I need you to go online and see if there's a death announcement for two dudes. I need to know where their funerals will be held."

"Give me one name at a time. When did they die?"

"About a week or two ago."

"Names?"

"Artinis Winston. A-R-T-I-N-I-S is the first name. Winston is the last name."

"Ain't nothing been posted yet about him. What's the other name?"

"Byron Clark. B-Y-R-O-N Clark."

"There's something about him on the Washington Post website. He's being cremated, but the family is having a private memorial service at Stewart funeral home in a couple of days."

"I need all the info. That's my man. I gotta pay my respects."

Chapter 6

Greg Gamble
United States Attorney's Office
"This new bill that the City Council voted to pass would eliminate most mandatory minimums allowed for jury trials in almost all misdemeanor cases. It reduces the maximum penalties for offenses such as burglaries, car jackings, and robberies," AUSA Ian McNeely said.

"Law enforcement leaders have expressed concerns that this new bill once enacted could burden an already stretched court system. They believe that this bill sends the wrong message to residents at a time when the city is struggling with gun violence," AUSA Tabitha Kearney added.

"What is the mayor saying?" I asked my staff.

"She wrote a letter to council chairman, Allen Charles, and threatened to veto the council's vote, citing that the new bill does not make the city safer," Devin York answered.

"Allen Charles' response? Do we know what that was?"

Susan Rosenthal nodded. She shuffled through her notes. "The Chairman says that the Council will override any veto from the mayor's office. He says that the new legislation was passed unanimously by the D.C. City Council, and the city stands at the finish line of a sixteen-year process that would make significant improvements and modernize an outdated criminal code from another era. Charles and other Council members defend the bill as a necessary reform of the city's outdated criminal code."

"A bill of this caliber warrants a look from congress, right?"

"Correct," Ian McNeely stated. "The Council took issue with the mayor's criticism of the new bill, which they say can be used as fodder for members of congress who can block city legislation. Republicans in the house have already threatened to target the measure. But resolutions disapproving D.C. legislation must pass both chambers and be signed by the President. Democrats, as you know, have a narrow majority in the Senate."

AUSA Tomas Muniz typed rapidly on a laptop keyboard. He raised his hand.

"Tomas?"

"Mr. Gamble, City Council member, Phil Michaels, released a statement this morning."

"Read it to me, Tomas," I replied

"It is irresponsible for the mayor to have characterized this as a bill that doesn't make the city safer. It is irresponsible rhetoric, and it plays into folks like the Freedom Caucus in Congress who are going to use the mayor's threat of a veto and her rhetoric against us when the bill goes up towards congress."

"Besides Charles and Michaels, are there any other dissenters on the council?"

"Not that we know of," Tabitha Kearney offered. "But one councilman did say that while the new bill is more 'equitable and just', members are open to consideration for adjustments and amendments before the bill is fully implemented."

"Councilman Michaels goes on to say, 'There is simply too much good in the bill to abandon all of that work and without any back up plan from the mayor. The mayor's threat to veto this bill is a distraction given that the council can override veto from the mayor's office. This is an attempt by the mayor to foster a political theater to create a perpetual scapegoat whenever there are issues in the future. Do not believe the hype. The council is not tying the hands of our law enforcement officials or making crime worse."

I thought about everything I'd just heard. "Once this bill is enacted, violent crime rates will explode more than they already have. This bill will weaken already lenient sentencing for gun possession by reducing the maximum penalties for carrying a pistol without a license and being a felon in possession of a firearm. I think that every resident in this city should be outraged that the council has weakened the criminal justice system in a way that makes every neighborhood less safe. Their actions to pass this bill is shameful."

"Amen, brother!" AUSA Devin York shouted.

The people in the room all laughed nervously.

I joined in the laughter, but only briefly. "Seriously though, people. This new bill is going to cripple all of our efforts moving forward. I'm going to meet with some people and see if I can persuade them to see things our way. Anything else on the table that I need to know?"

The door to the conference room opened and in walked Ari Weinstein.

"Greg, sorry to disturb your meeting but I need to know what you decided about Nykemia EVerett. His custody hearing is set for 1 pm, and I'm on my way to Superior Court to give our appearance on a few cases. I'm good on every one of them except the Everett case."

"If my memory serves me correctly, Nykemia 'Bey' Everett was indicted with Malik Hewitt for a murder in Southeast about six years ago. They went to trial and lost on all counts. Then an appeals court overturned their convictions last year. The witnesses against them refused to testify a second time in a new trial, so Everett and Hewitt were released to the streets, for reasons unknown. At this time, Nykemia Everett went to Wahler place in Southeast and allegedly shot and killed Hewitt in front of his baby's mother and his son."

"Everett was not wearing any type of disguise."

"The shooter was wearing a mask," Ari Weinstein explained, "But Hewitt's son recognized an article of clothing that Everett was wearing hours before Hewitt was killed. Metropolitan police executed a search warrant on Everett's home and found a Helly Henson jacket that matches the description given by the teenager. Everett was arrested and has been at the DC jail for about ninety days "

"Didn't we just have a case similar to this one?" I asked.

Ian McNeely spoke up. "Yeah, boss. The Merkel Michell case. Different people, same case. Dalvin Thomas was co-defendants with Markel Mitchell on a murder charge. They beat the case, but Thomas found out that Mitchell made statements while in custody. Thomas was sent to Virginia to do time. When he got back to DC, he killed Mitchell."

"The cases are definitely similar," Ari Weinstein admitted, "but so far, we don't know why Nykemia Everett killed Malik Hewitt. If ... he did it. As you all know, we're going to need a lot more than a jacket to get a conviction in this case."

"So, what do you need from me, Ari?"

"Permission to offer Everett a pre indictment plea. Something sweet like seven or eight years with a cop. We can call it manslaughter. Hewitt was a career criminal with several sex offenses on his record. The community is a better place without him."

"Permission granted, Ari. Get it done."

Once Ari Weinstein was out the door. I asked the remaining people, "Is there anything else that requires my attention before we break?"

"That's all I have," Tabitha said.

"Nothing else for me," Ian Mnneely said and stood.

"I'm done," Tomas Muniz answered.

"My stomach is growling. I need an early lunch," Devin York chimed

"Or a late breakfast."

"Thanks for the clarity, Tomas."

As everybody filed out of the room, Susan Rosenthal hung back. After making sure that we were the only two people left in the room, she said, "Are you still on board with what I suggested the other day?"

Rising from my seat, I gathered my things without looking at Susan directly. "I am."

"Good. I'm just checking. I'm approaching Maryann Settles tonight. She works at a Kaiser Permanente off Woodyard Road in Clinton. Her shift is the two until two in the morning shift. When do you think you'll be able to talk to the husband, Christopher?"

"If you're confronting Maryann today, I'll have to see the husband today as well. He works the seven to three shift at Metro. He's stationed at the Foggy Bottom site. He shouldn't be hard to find. I got some things to do, and then I'll leave and head that way."

"Okay. keep in touch and let me know what Christopher Settles says," Susan said and left the room.

***

"Christopher Settles?"

"Who's asking?"

The man standing in front of me was a little taller than me and slender. He was older. His salt and pepper beard was neatly trimmed, his head was bald. Christopher Settles reminded me of the handyman character Overton from the comedy show, *Living* Single comedy from back in the day. The navy blue Metro uniform hung loosely from his frame. I smiled to lessen the possible tension.

"My name is Greg Gamble. I'm the …"

"U.S. Attorney for D.C. I know who you are."

"Good, because I know who you are, too. Christopher John Settles, born on August 4th 1958. Born and raised here in Southeast, Washington D.C. to Doris and Craig Settles.

You have six siblings. Only two of which are still alive. Your brother, David, is incarcerated in the BOP. He's doing life for a double murder in Maryland. Your sister, Deborah Louise, works for the Department of Housing and Urban Development. You have three nieces who live here in Washington. They live mixed lives. Your wife, Maryann …"

"Signed some stuff… on affidavit to correct a wrong from years ago. What does any of this have to do with me? Why are you here talkin' to me?!"

Slowly, I reached into my pocket and pulled out a pack of Doublemint chewing gum. I unwrapped a piece and put it in my mouth. "I'm here because your life is about to change …"

"Change?" Christopher Settles repeated. "Change how?"

"The past, Christopher, is always better left in the past. That's why it's called the past. The situation with Michael Carter back in 1995 was a necessary situation. Michael Carter was and is still a menace to society. We did … I did what needed to be done to make the city safer. And we did that with your wife's help. I read her affidavit like twenty times since I received it. After all these years, she's decided to come forward and undo all we did years ago. Why?"

Christopher Settles' eyes dropped to the neon vest that the other Metro workers wore while on duty. He picked it up and put it on.

"Again, I ask you, why are you here talking to me about this? If you read the affidavit twenty times, you know the answer to your question. You coerced her into lying on an innocent man. She wants to correct her mistakes."

"I got that part, but why now? Why almost seventeen years later?"

"I think you're asking the wrong question, counselor. That's what they call lawyers in court, right? Counselor? You're asking the wrong question, and you're asking the wrong person."

"Humor me, Christopher. What is the right question?"

"The right question would be, why not now? Hasn't that man been in jail long enough for a murder that he didn't commit?"

"Who said he didn't commit it? Just because your wife didn't really see him do it doesn't mean that he didn't kill Dontay Samuels."

"Well, if he did do it, you wouldn't have needed Maryann to lie, now would you?

"Drastic times call for drastic measures. Sometimes the truth is packaged inside of a lie,"

Christopher Settles snorted. "You come here to give me oxymorons?"

"No, Christopher, I came here to warn you. Talk to your wife. Get her to abandon these aspirations of getting sanctified. I don't know if her miraculous conversion from drug user to dealer and prostitute."

"Oh ... she never told you about those charges, huh? Go home tonight and talk to your wife about everything. Everything. There's ..."

"Wait a minute, wait a minute. Earlier you said that our lives were about to change. Now you're saying that you are warning me. You started all of this talking by pointing out that you did your research on me, my family, and all that. But let me tell you something you must don't know. I'm not a scared muthafucka. I'm not a sucka. I'm not a bitch on no level. I'm from the hood. The real hood. Not this watered down shit you call a community in D.C. now.

I'm anti-rat and had I known that my wife did that hot shit when I met her, I would have never married her. I hate cops and I like prosecutors even less. You speak of change. My life changed the day I found out that my wife was in the same category of Rayful Edmonds. And as for your warning, stick it in your ass. Don't ever come to my place of business again talking tough. Don't ever come and approach me again. Fuck outta here."

I stood riveted to my spot as I watched Christopher Settles walk away. The smirk on my face told the story of how I felt. In a perverse kind of way, I was turned on by what the man had said. I pulled out my cell phone and called Susan.

"Hey, Greg. What did Christopher Settles say?" Susan asked.

I watched Christopher Settles recede and disappear. "Tough nut to crack. Hope you have better luck with Maryann. Call me after you talk to her. I got another person that I need to see."

I disconnected the call with Susan Rosenthal and made another.

"Hey, it's Greg Gamble. I need to talk to you. Today. Within the next hour. Alone. In private." I listened to the man on the other end of the phone. "Good. I'll be there in an hour or less. Depending on rush hour traffic."

***

"Gregory Gamble. It's a pleasure to see you again."

Ignoring the facetious nature of Allen Charles' greeting, I walked past him and his outstretched hand. Allen Charles was the only Caucasian member of the city council in DC. he was also the longest tenured councilmember, thus his title of council chairman. I found a seat in his office that I liked and sat down. Allen Charles was close to sixty and gave me George Clooney vibes. His suspenders were paisley, his shirt white. His pants were starched and impeccably tailored. The wing tipped shoes were polished to perfection. The silence in the room was intentional. I watched as Allen Charles walked behind his desk and sat down.

"Mr. United States Attorney, what do I have the pleasure of this impromptu visit? On the phone you said it was important. I rearranged my schedule to accommodate you. What can I do for you?"

"The new crime reform bill that you're campaining is going to make my job a lot harder."

"I disagree, but please continue."

"You've heard all the reasons why it shouldn't be enacted, so I won't waste time beating a dead horse."

"Thank you."

"Do you like history, Allen?"

"History? What aspect of history are you referring to?"

"You pick one, anyone. But here's why I ask that. Me, I love history. I consider books on certain hysterical figures my greatest possessions. The stories about Joseph Stalin, Vladimir Illich Lenin, Che Gueverra, Mussillini, Julius Censer, Ghengis Khan, Hannibal, Idi Ameen … fascinating. But one of the most polarizing historical figures that I love is J. Edger Hoover. Why? Because one man controlled the nation's greatest law enforcement agency for decades. The power that he possessed was unmatched by anyone in the history of this great nation. No one could cower J. Edger Hoover. No sitting president or politician. No military figures. No other law enforcement person. No businessperson. No one. Do you know why that is, Allen?"

"Uh, can't say that I do. I'm not really a J. Edger Hoover aficionado. Do you know why he wielded such power, Greg?"

I nodded and rose from my chair. I walked closer to Allen Charles' desk. "J. Edger Hoover's power lay in the fact that he knew everybody's secrets. He compiled a dossier on everybody, Allen. Big or small. Actors, actresses, business execs, politicians, sports figures, celebrities from every walk of life, lawyers, judges, police officers, security guards, crossing guards, educators, gang leaders, clergymen, everybody. No one could match his plethora of knowledge about people. All people. He remained in power in Washington until he died. There was no other man like him …"

"And your point is, Greg?"

"My point is, Allen, that I am a student of history. All men have secrets, and I know yours."

"I beg your pardon!!" Allen Charles bellowed as he shot up out of his seat.

"You heard me," I answered, then turned around and retrieved my briefcase. I removed a manila envelope from the briefcase. I tossed that envelope on Allan Charles' desk. He eyed it as if it was a poisonous snake.

"What the hell is this?"

"Open it and see."

Allen Charles opened the envelope and extracted a sheaf of papers and several high quality 5x7 photographs. He eyed the photos one by one, and the color drained from his face. Lastly, he read through the papers. "Where … where did you get these? How did you …?"

"It doesn't matter, Allen. What matters is that I have several copies of everything in your hand. And if … Well, when the mayor vetoes the new bill the council passed, if you or the council overrides that veto, every news outlet in the city will receive a copy of it."

"And if I do what you ask, not override the veto, how do I know that you won't use this against me again whenever the council passes legislation that you don't like? What assurances do I have that this won't ever happen again?"

"None. enjoy the rest of your day, Allen."

Chapter 7

Susan Rosenthal
Kaiser Permanente Medical Center
Woodyard Road

"Window sitting, way up high / I can't look up enough to see the sky / ain't no good lying here below / death row / don't want no preacher man to come around / I don't need him laying my burden down / I already told Jesus everything I know / death row / when it's time for my last request / tell my momma that I did my best / tell my baby that I love her so / death row / got a calendar on my wall / marking days until I get the call / til it's time for me to go / death row / death row …"

When I turned off the engine of my car, the morbid music sung by Chris Stapleton went with it, and I was kind of relieved. His music had a way of making me too reflective and a little melancholy. I sat behind the wheel of my Mercedes and thought about my life. It was never supposed to be like this for a white woman born a precious white girl right outside of Muncie, Indiana. Nobody from Herbertsville had ever accomplished more than being a factory worker in the auto plants. Since I was a child, I knew that I was bigger than Herbertsville, Indiana, I was better. I made my way to Indiana University and fell in love with law. After four years of college and three years of law school, I passed the Indiana

State bar exam. But that wasn't good enough. There were no real powerful people in Indiana. Real power lay east in Washington, D.C. I landed in the nation's capital in 1995 with nothing more than a few bags of luggage and a meager amount of money. Finding a room to rent was quick. Getting accepted at the United States Attorney office took longer. I never dreamed about being a prosecutor. But I had to make my bones somewhere. My first week at the 'Triple Nickel' as it was called due to its address being 555 Fourth Street, I met Greg Gamble. He was just a lowly assistant prosecutor back then. He was nice to me, and I found myself attracted to him. That scared me because I had never been attracted to black men before, but it was something about Greg Gamble that exuded power, charisma and strength. His intelligence on criminal cases was undeniable. His edge was like a hot cup of coffee on a dismal, cold morning. I was drawn to his poise, his gentle manner, his confidence. In a room with him, I hung on to his every word. I fetched his coffee. I did whatever I could to help him. I just wanted to be near him. At home in my rented room, I fantasized about him. I imagined him doing unspeakable things to me in every unspeakable way. I remember all the times I rubbed my wet center thinking about Greg Gamble inside me. I was twenty five years old and very impressionable. Twenty five years old and green as hell. The day that Greg Gamble came to me with the Michael Carter case was the first time that I'd even heard of it.

United States Attorney's Office (1995)
"Susan, can I talk to you for a minute?"
"Sure, Greg. What's on your mind?" I asked.
"There's a case I been working on and it's about to go to shit. Both of my witnesses are now unavailable. That means we'll have to dismiss the case, and I can't do that. Don't want to do that. This guy I'm prosecuting is a menace. A psychopath. He's a serial killer that has to be stopped. I have

to stop him ... we have to stop him. Have you ever heard the saying about truth and justice is sometimes wrapped inside a lie?"

"Uh ... no. I don't think ... "

"I know that you've heard the term drastic times call for drastic measures."

"I have heard that one, but I'm confused ..."

"Don't be, Susan. I'm asking you for a favor. One that will bear a ripe return."

"Sure, Greg, I'll do whatever you need me to do, but I'm a little unclear as to what it is that you need. What's the favor?"

"Before I tell you what it is, let me ask you a question. What kind of a prosecutor do you want to be, Susan? One that gets things done? Or one that just wants to get by until better things come your way?"

"One that gets things done. Why? Where are you ...?"

"Going with all of this? Let me ask you a different question. Are you a good girl from the Midwest who's always gotta do things the right way?"

"We all have to do things the right way, right? No matter where we're from, right?"

"Wrong. Sometimes in life, Susan, we're confronted with life's conundrums that call for hard decisions to be made. Even when something wrong brings about something right. Does that make sense?"

"A little ... yeah, I guess."

"In the history of our great nation, the people in power did bad things to bring about good results. When those in power make decisions, those decisions affect you and me and everyone in the United States. And sometimes those people in power have to go around the U.S. Constitution. Everything is done off the record. Bad things are done to bad people to effect change for the benefit of all people. For instance, the CIA sends men, paid mercenaries, to kill elected officials in other countries. The people in the CIA understand that certain dictators or leaders are bad for their own countries and ours. The country or region must be stabilized in order to benefit the U.S. That's the position I find myself in, Susan. The community as a whole needs to be protected from Michael Maurice Carter. You and I are the people in power. I had to make a hard decision about what to do in his case. And I've made that decision. I need your help to make it happen. When the time comes, I am going to ask you to meet with someone and then do something else for me. But what I need to know now, right now is, are you with me on this?"

"Well ... if you need me, Greg. Of course, I'll help you. Anything you need from me, I'll do it."

Then three months later, Greg Gamble approached me again.

"Remember the conversation that we had months ago?" Greg asked me.

"About doing something wrong to accomplish something good?"

Greg nodded. "Exactly."

"I remember."

Greg closed the door of my office, walked up to my chair, and leaned against the wall.

"Well, the time to act is now. I need you to help me now."

"Help you, how?"

"There's a woman in central booking right now. Her name is Maryann Dunbar, but she goes by the name Settles, Maryann Settles. I think she'll be better off talking to a woman. Here's what I need you to go to her and say."

My dumb ass ate up every word Greg Gamble had fed me. I couldn't believe I was that gullible as a rookie at the U.S. Attorney office. I thought about exactly what I had said to Maryann Settles, and how I had coaxed her into going along with Greg Gamble's plan to implicate Michael Carter in Dontay Samuel's murder. I remember the day that I introduced Maryann to Greg. I became complicit in the whole scheme to bury Michael Carter. Now, seventeen years later, the whole thing was about to blow up in our faces. Unless … I could convince Maryann Settles to go back in the shadows. I was prepared to beg, grovel, and plead. If all of that failed … the thought of what would happen next, what had to happen next, shook me to the core …

"Drastic times call for drastic measures …"

***

The woman grabbed the clipboard that had the paper I'd just filled out on it. I recognized her instantly. Her features had matured with time, but basically, Maryann Settles, still looked the same. Her skin was caramel with sheen and a certain glow to it. Her makeup was flawless. She'd gained a few pounds, but even the excess weight accented her. The hospital scrubs she wore hugged her curves. The woman looked much better than she had in 1996 while addicted to drugs. Maryann Settles looked at the paper, then around the room until her eyes settled on mine. Our eyes locked for what seemed like an eternity.

"I remember you," Maryann Settles said.

I got up out of my seat and walked up to her. "I need to talk to you, Maryann. It's very important.

"Is this about the affidavit I sent to his lawyer?"

"His being Michael Carter?"

Maryann Settles nodded.

"It is, but I really need you to listen to me, Maryann. Can we go somewhere and talk privately?"

"I don't know what for, but I guess we can. C'mon, there's a room we can use for a few minutes. I can always act like I'm taking your vitals."

Inside a small examination room, Maryann closed the door completely.

"If you've come here to try and dissuade me from …"

"Maryann, why are you doing this? Why after so many years? Why are you coming forward with … with …"

"The truth? That's what it is, isn't it, Ms. Rosenthal?"

"It's Mrs. Rosenthal. I used my maiden name, but I'm married now."

"So am I. But you already know that given that Greg Gamble has already talked to my husband, attempted to warn him Whatever that means. But it will do you and him no good. Almost seventeen years ago, I implicated a man in a murder that he didn't do. The streets talk, Mrs. Rosenthal. I listened, but it was too late. I had already sold my soul to the devil."

Michael Carter didn't kill Dontay Samuels. Somebody else did. A friend of his named Quran. Quran Bashir whose father, Ameen, was my first crush ever. I knew back in 1996 that Michael Carter was innocent, but I was afraid to go to prison for my third drug charge. I was in no shape for jail."

"But now you are? Is that what you're telling me? Because perjury will get you five years in prison. You know that, right?"

"I do, but God got me. I'm not afraid anymore. It's the least I can do to correct what I did in '96. That shit has been haunting me for too long, and it's time to let it go. I said what I said in the affidavit, and I'm ready to testify on the stand. I have to make amends for what I did."

"Making amends doesn't have to mean you get on a witness stand and spill your guts about me or Greg. You did a good thing by helping to put Michael Carter away. He was a killer, Maryann. Even if he didn't kill Dontay Samuels."

" It does matter if he didn't kill Dontay. I lied and said that I witnessed that man kill Dontay Samuels, and I never witnessed that. I need to… I have to do the right thing. If that means exposing you and Greg Gamble, then so be it," Maryann Settles said with emphasis and finality.

"And there's nothing I can say or do to change your mind?"

"I'm sorry, but no."

"No, Maryann. I'm the one who's sorry."

"You should be. You damn well should be."

***

Outside in the parking lot, I made two calls. One was to my husband Grant to tell him that I'd be late getting home. A the other was to Greg Gamble.

"What did she say?" Greg asked.

"In a nutshell, she told us to go fuck ourselves. She says that she doesn't care if we charge her with perjury. She comes off as a defending angel of right and good. Says that she's been grappling with regret for years over what she did to an innocent man. She in it to win it, Greg. She's not backing down and according to her, what she's doing … the affidavit … is the right thing to do."

"Okay," Greg Gamble acquiesced. "What now?"

"Plan B. Talk to you soon."

***

Carlos mixed a drink behind the bar in his study. He rarely drank hard liquor. I sat on the couch across from the bar with my feet tucked underneath my legs.

"Are you one hundred percent sure that these people have to die?"

I let Carlos's words sink in all the way before answering. "What other choice do I have? Do we have? As the second highest ranking prosecutor in the city, I basically work for you. I have always done whatever you asked me to do for you and your organization. If this gets out … and I'm implicated in it, which is exactly what Maryann Settles plans to do, I'm out at the U.S. Attorney's office. This scandal will finish both Greg and I off. We'd be out of there before you could say 'cheese' in Spanish and English. It would be our word against hers, but if she somehow retained the stubs from the checks and vouchers, that strengthens her allegations. After that, out comes the allegations made against me in the Kareemah 'Angel' El-amin case when I destroyed those DNA samples and told you where Fatima Muhammad was being held while on witness protection. All of this is a lot of shit that needs to stay buried in the past."

Carlos Trinidad sipped whatever was in his glass before walking over to a cushy sofa across from mine and sitting down. "Everything with me, Susan, is on a need to know basis and before now, you didn't need to know what I'm about to tell you, but now you do. I haven't always been completely honest with you. The main reason being that too much information is never a weapon to hold in your position. Don't misunderstand what I'm saying. I trust you with my life and my comrades' lives. Your dedication and commitment to me and this organization is undeniable and without question. But compartmentalization is always necessary. Michael Carter was a part of my organization in the nineties. He was introduced to me by a friend of mine named Ameen Bashir …"

"Ameen Bashir. That's the second time tonight that I have heard that name. Excuse me. Please continue."

"Ameen Bashir has roots that go back to Newark, New Jersey to people I knew, but that's a different story entirely. Ameen Bashir did contract killing for me. He did the dirty work that needed to be done when Hispanic men could not get into certain places. I grew to love him for his skill, loyalty, and respect. He was a father to three sons. Quran, Jihad and Khitab. Married to a woman named Khadijah. Michael Carter was Ameen's best friend and comrade. I took Michael Carter in at Ameen's behest. To prove himself worthy, he had to kill a man for me. Victoriano Martinez. He did that, and I rewarded him by making him rich. But then something happened. Someone killed Ameen Bashir. The streets never revealed who his killer was. That infuriated me. I wanted to exact revenge on whoever was responsible for Ameen's death. To me, it seemed that Mike Carter was complicit in some way or vaguely responsible.

So, in 1995 when he was arrested for murder, I never intervened in his situation. I knew ... Well, let me be clear. I never knew about your involvement. Even though you and I hadn't met yet, all I knew about was Greg Gamble. I didn't know the specifics of the case, but I was aware that there were two witnesses. Thomas Turner and Maryann Settles. I could have had both witnesses killed at any time. I had information on both of them. And although I hate rats, I allowed Mike's situation to play out the way it did. When he lost in trial, I felt nothing. I was still upset about Ameen Bashir's death and Mike's possible hand in it. It's been almost seventeen years, Susan. I still never found out exactly what happened to Ameen, but I have forgiven Mike Carter for whatever his role may or may not have been in it. I believe that it is time for Mike Carter to be a free man. He didn't kill Dontay Samuels ..."

"We know that, Carlos. Ameen Bashir's son, Quran, killed Dontay."

Carlos smiled, then finished his drink. "Having too much information can be dangerous, Susan."

"Some things are learned behavior. Maybe I've been around you too long," I replied and returned the smile.

"Where is the affidavit that Maryann Settles drew up and signed? Let me see it again."

I got up from the couch and retrieved the three page copy of Maryann Settles' affidavit. I handed it to Carlos.

Carlos quietly read all three pages. "Killing Maryann Settles and her husband is not going to happen, Susan."

"But, Carlos ... you know ... I've told you the damage ..."

"Let me finish, chica. Listen to me. I just told you about my association with Michael Carter for a reason. As I said earlier, he didn't kill Dontay Samuels, and I think it's time for him to be freed. That's number one. Number two, Greg Gamble has been and always will be a thorn in the men of my character's side. It's time for him to go as United States Attorney. It's time for you to take his place. You will be in the best possible position to help the organization and yourself. It's your time. You've been at the U.S. Attorney's office for eighteen years. I'm going to have a talk with Maryann Settles and her husband. Things will proceed how they will, but you will be taken completely out of the equation. There'll be no mention of you anywhere. If this situation is as bad as you say it is, it should only cripple Greg Gamble and remove him from office. Once it takes full steam, you'll turn against him and advocate that he be prosecuted. That way, we all win. You, me, Maryann Settles, and Michael Carter. "How does that sound to you?"

"Sounds like you have some sort of an invested interest in Michael Carter."

Carlos smiled again to disarm me. "Got me there, chica. The same as always. You have an uncanny ability to sniff out my bullshit. Individuals inside my organization have never lost contact with Michael Carter. I respected the fact that he never got weak enough to mention me or my organization to the cops. With Luiz's guidance, Mike Carter started a murder for hire business from the BOP. He' has run it for almost ten years."

"A murder for hire business? He employs killers for hire?" I asked incredulously.

Carlos nodded. "I owe a friend a favor, and he asked that I help Mike Carter. So, I have more reasons than one to want Mike Carter free. I'm going to visit Maryann Settles and her husband. The affidavit that you have will change ..."

"I think Jonathan Zucker might've already filed the motion with that affidavit ..."

"He hasn't filed his motion yet."

"How do you know that?"

"Do you really have to ask that?"

"I see, and one more thing. Do you know who Michael Carter employs in the city to do all of his killing?"

"Of course, I do. And I think you know who it is too. That's why you decided to ask me that question. Take a guess."

"Quran Bashir."

Carlos nodded.

Chapter 8

Zin
Lose A Pound Fitness Studio
1200 Lebaum Street SE

"Welcome back, Zin. it's been what?" Tina Grover asked as she prepared to get me back into shape.

"It's been about seven months, TG," I replied while stretching. My yoga pants felt a little snug suggesting that I had gained some weight. Panic struck as I tried to remember my last period. I couldn't. "Shit!" I muttered to myself.

"Shit is right," Tina said. "I'm gonna make you pay for the layoff. So, get ready, sis."

"Come on with it."

"Lie on the mat on your back," TG said while handing me a five pound dumbbell. "Put the weight in your right hand and hold it directly over your chest, right knee bent."

I lay back and held the dumbbell, doing exactly as Tina instructed, but my mind was elsewhere. I couldn't believe I had been so reckless. I thought about the marathon sex I'd had with Quran for the last two nights and how using condoms wasn't even a thought.

"Press the bell forward and up, propping yourself onto your left elbow like this. Good, pause. Now push your torso off the floor. Pause. Now, return to the starting position. Do five sets on each side before pausing again."

There was no way I could be pregnant. Could it?

"Never take your eyes off the dumbbell. That helps you keep the bell and your shoulder stable and aligned right. A'ight ... now, our next exercise. You with me, Zin?"

"I'm here. Let's go."

"Drop the dumbbell. Now lie back, hands touching your head, feet together. Now sit up and simultaneously bring your left knee towards your chest. Try to touch it to your right elbow. Pause. Squeeze your core, then return to start. That's rep one. Repeat on the other side."

***

"Ms. Carter, I'd like to thank you again for giving me a chance to work for you. I promise that I will always do the best job I can, "Demiyah James said.

"Demiyah, as young black women we gotta look out for each other, right?"

"You better believe it, but still ..."

"But nothing. You're more than qualified, and it's just a step towards your real goal of becoming a lawyer. Besides, you're beautiful and intelligent. So, you make a good secretary slash paralegal slash assistant. I'm gonna be out of the office a lot, so I need you to really take care of this place. Okay?"

"You got it, Ms. Carter. Don't worry about a thing."

"Good, and Demiyah, Ms. Carter is my aunt Linda. Call me Zin, please."

"Got you. Okay, so before you walked in, you got a call from a Mr. Zucker, he says that he called your cell phone a few times ..."

"I had the phone off while I was working out."

"I need to work out... but anyway, he needs you to call him, and you have a seminar of some kind at Howard University Law school. That's at 1 pm. Then you have a hearing scheduled for 3 pm in front of Judge Silas at

Superior Court in reference to a client named Marquee Venable."

"Damn, I forgot about that. I'll be in my office if you need me."

Inside my office, I removed my heels and got some work done before deciding to give Jonathan Zucker a call back. I called him from my cell phone.

"Hello, Zin. How are you?"

"I'm good, Jon… and you?"

"Getting older, but also getting better. I got some news for you about your father's case. I can give it to you over the phone, or we can meet later. Your choice."

"Good news or bad news, Jon?"

"Neither. Just a few new wrinkles. You wanna hear them?"

"Yeah, why not. Shoot," I told Jon.

"I got a call from Gary Kelman. Maryann Settles called him. He gave her my number. Apparently, she's revised the affidavit. It's all basically the same recantation, but for some strange reason, she omitted everything about Susan Rosenthal. She faxed me a copy of the new affidavit. It's still three pages, but like I said, it's more about Greg Gamble."

"Susan Rosenthal was removed from the affidavit. That's strange. Wouldn't you say?"

"Definitely. But we can ask her why when I … or we depose her in a week. After I've filed the motion. Which is ready to be filed, I should add."

"That's great news. The filing and Maryann Settles not recanting her recantation. I think there are unknown forces at play behind the scenes here. Get that motion and the new affidavit filed as soon as possible, Jon."

"I'm filing it today. In an hour or so."

"Good, and do me a favor. Fax me the new affidavit so I can read it."

"I'm doing it now, Zin. Anything before I go?"

"Yeah, have you talked to my father lately?"

"No. Tomorrow is Saturday. I'll set up a call for Monday and tell him everything. Need me to tell him something?"

I thought again about the fact that I might be pregnant. "No, I just asked. I'll send him an email on Corrlinks. Thanks, Jon. Talk to you later."

"Bye, kid. Have a good day."

Ending the call, I decided to make an appointment with my gynecologist as soon as possible. If I was in fact pregnant, I needed to know it immediately.

***

Howard University Law Center Auditorium

"Although it's almost invisible to the public, the use of criminal informants is everywhere in the U.S. justice system. From street corners to jails to courthouses to prisons, every year the government negotiates thousands of deals with criminal offenders in which suspects can avoid arrest or punishment in exchange for information. These deals typically take place off the record, subject to few roles and little oversight. While criminal informants ... often referred to as 'snitches' can be important investigative tools, using them has some serious costs. Informants often continue to commit crimes while the information they provide is infamously unreliable. Taken together, these facts make snitching an important and problematic aspect of the way America does justice. The practice of trading information for guilt is so pervasive that it has literally become a thinking business. Jailhouse informants are participating in a for profit snitching operation in most federal prisons. As part of the ring, prisoners are buying and selling information about pending cases to offer to prosecutors to reduce their own sentences ..."

"Here in D.C., we call that jumping on people's cases," I muttered to myself but went back to listening to Tawana

Gavin, chairwoman of the Black Defense Lawyers of America, speak. Criminal justice reform was a hot button issue all over America.

"When police rely on criminal informants, innocent people pay a heavy price. The significant costs and dangers of this practice have remained almost overlooked. The deals between criminal suspects and the government tend to remain undocumented and unregulated. There is very little public data about the ways that police and prosecutors wield their immense discretion to create, forgive, and deploy informants. It's way past time for these practices to change. The use of 'snitches' is an important public policy that determines the outcome of thousands of investigations and cases every year. Costing millions of dollars and affecting millions of lives. It should no longer be permitted to operate off the record as it is."

The auditorium was getting a little warm, so I removed my suit jacket. I folded the jacket and draped it across the back of my chair. I thought about the new affidavit that Maryann Settles sent to Jon Zucker. The old affidavit and the new one were almost identical. Except for the paragraphs that referenced Assistant U.S. Attorney Susan Rosenthal. For the life of me, I couldn't figure out why Maryann Settles would do that. Had she been mistaken about who had approached her for Greg Gamble? Who had made the payments to her? Or had Susan Rosenthal gotten to Maryann Settles? If that was the case, wouldn't Susan Rosenthal have coerced Maryann to recant her entire recantation?

"The heart of snitching is the deal between the government and the informant. The government permits the informant to avoid potential criminal liability or punishment in exchange for information. Not to be redundant, but I have to be emphatic when I say this. Anyone can be made into an informant if they are not already one regardless of the nature of their offense. Nearly anything can be traded. Including sex with a partner, gifts given to family members, and money.

For example, informant Amy Geffert worked off her drug charges by posing as a prostitute and having sex with a suspect that the government was after. In exchange for cooperation, informants can earn forgiveness for every kind of crime. While the most common snitch deals typically involve drug offenses, there are many other categories of snitches who earn leniency for less serious and more serious crimes. In other words, no crime is off limits. Snitches with defense counsel tend to get better determinant deals. By contrast, unrepresented snitches who negotiate directly with police, typically street and drug snitches, are essentially at the government's mercy. They rely on the unwritten law of the street that information and cooperation will eventually be rewarded. In other words, while the basic contours of the snitch deal remain the same, every case has its own distinctive character …"

My cell phone vibrated suddenly. I reached into my purse and pulled out the phone. The caller was my father. I hesitated before answering the call.

"Hey, dad. What's up?"

"We been on lock down for a minute. I'm just checking on you …"

I listened to my father talk as I got up and walked out of the auditorium. I wanted to focus on whatever he had to say.

Chapter 9

Michael Carter
USP Canaan
Waymart, Pennsylvania

"We been on lockdown for a minute. I'm just checking on ya. They got us on this modified shit where only one tier comes out at a time, but I'm hoping that they give us some yard soon. I think I'm getting cabin fever from being in the cell so long. Where are you? Were you busy?

"Not really," Zin replied. "I'm at Howard University listening to a criminologist speak about informants.'

"Informants?"

"Yeah, informants. I'm learning some shit I never knew about how the government operates with their snitches. And speaking of snitches, Maryann Settles changed her story."

"Changed her story? She took her recantation back?"

"No, dad. She just amended her statements for some reason. I won't get into the specifics here on this monitored phone. Jon Zucker is going to call up there on Monday. He'll tell you everything about it, but I can tell you that he filed your 23-110 today. So, the ball is rolling."

"That's good news. Other than that, how you?"

"I'm good, dad. Just hired an assistant and office manager. I'm about to move into my new place. "

"New place? Is Jerome moving with you to the new place?"

"His name is Jermaine, dad, and no he's not moving with me. It's over between us. I'm moving to my new place alone. Just me. Aunt Linda is good. We're good. How are you doing in there?"

"Other than the cabin fever, I'm good. Taking my blood pressure medic…"

"Which medicines do you take again?" Zin asked.

"Lisinopril and Amlodipine," I replied.

"Same thing Aunt Linda takes. I guess hypertension runs in the family, huh? "

"Guess it does. Have you had your pressure checked lately?"

"If my blood pressure is up, it's because of you. Me, worrying about you and your case."

"I worry about you, too, baby girl."

"No need. I'm good, dad. Really."

"Okay. Well, I'ma let you go back to your seminar. I love you, Zin."

"Love you, too, dad. Take care."

"I will, baby. Goodbye."

"Bye, dad."

I replaced the phone on the hook and walked away from the wall phone. Cutting across the unit, I was met by a homie named H-Mob.

"Mike, what's up, big homie?" H-Mob asked.

Giving the young boy a pound and a soldier hug, I replied, "I'm good, young H-Mob. What's up with you?"

"Ain't shit, but I gotta see what's up with the big homies next door."

"The big homies who?"

"Fat Boy and D.C. niggas keep whispering about some 'hot shit' that my men 'nem did. Some nigga just got off the bus named Demo."

"He's the one that been pushing some shit that niggas say is on the computer. The homie just signed to me on the window and said that Big and D.C.'s gonna cook the dude.

So, I'm tryna see what's up. Because if they roll, I roll. You already know I'm on my Wellington Park shit super hard."

"Where's Demo at? What unit?" I asked.

"He's in D-2," H-Mob replied.

"That means that they have to see each other on the yard."

H-Mob nodded. "And the calling yard tomorrow. Early. This shit is about to go back on lockdown."

"Shit!" I mumbled and shook my head.

***

The next morning...

"Who is that right there with Big and 'nem?" Henny 'Lil Man' James, my celly, asked.

I looked across the yard and spotted six men moving towards three men on the other side of the field. "That's Mike Mike, Black Boy, and Toonchi. Demo got Gene Braxton and Keke Starr with him. It looks like it's about to go down."

Minutes later, it went down. Fat Big, D.C., H-Mob and the rest of the Wellington Park dudes mauled the Valley Green homies. I watched Demo run around the yard as D.C. and Fat Big chased him and repeatedly stabbed him on the other side of the yard. H-Mob and company feasted on Gene Braxton and Keke.

"ALL INMATES ON THE YARD GET DOWN ON THE GROUND! OR YOU WILL BE SHOT!" the loudspeaker called out in English and Spanish.

"Here we go again, " I mumbled as I slowly got on the ground.

***

Inside the cell, I pulled off my boots and laid on the bunk. My celly paced the cell floor. I folded my arms and rested the back of my head on my palms.

"This shit is crazy, slim."

Lil' man stopped and said, "All this 'hot' shit is getting out of control. I'm confused by all this shit nowadays. There's too many definitions of what's hot and what's not. You got good men on the yard out there butchering each other about the way words are interpreted. Situation after situation. You heard about the 'Poochie situation', right?"

"What Poochie? Alphonso White?"

"Yeah, Conrad. About the cellphone shit up Allenwood."

"I heard about it," I told Lil' Man.

"Did you read the SIS report that niggas got here?"

"I did."

"So, what do you think about Poochie's statements?"

"The people had other niggas on the beef that told about the phone. That's how the homie got caught up with it in the first place. When the people got the numbers out of the phone and rounded dudes up, a couple niggas told everything off the break. So, the people knew the business already from what I read Poochie acknowledged using the phone and said he paid some commissary to use it. Is that hot to me? No. But I think he shouldn't have never met with SIS from the beginning. He should have done what a couple other men did and not say shit. Niggas is saying that he hot because he said he used the phone and he paid to use it. I don't agree."

"Okay, but what about the Cardo situation?"

"Cardo and Lil E Rock?"

"Recardo Curtis, yeah."

"Their case is a little different. E Rock went to trial and the government said, 'We are going to present to you, the jury, Recardo Curtis who's going to tell you that he gave Eric Ginyard a gun on September 11, 1998' They said that in E Rock's trial at the opening statement ..."

"I'm hipped, but Cardo never testified."

"He got on the stand and took the fifth."

"So, is he hot for that?"

"To me, yeah. Why? Because he was a government witness. Even though he took the fifth, he got up there for the government. He had to have told them people something to make them put him up there. Them prosecutors aren't dummies. They could've lost the case on a tech if they had lied on Cardo. When they said in their opening that they were gonna put Cardo on the stand, they believed that he was gonna say that he gave E Rock a gun and that E Rock shot somebody."

"But... if he told them that they would have confronted him with his prior statements. They didn't do that."

"From what I read, I'm saying he's hot."

"What about Tweet on that kidnapping case?"

"Tweet copped to thirty years to free Rick. Naw, he ain't hot."

"But he said... he copped and said it was three of them..."

"I read the whole case on the computer, and I talked to Rick personally. He said that Tweet ain't hot. I agree."

"Swamp?"

"Hot ass shit!"

"Dominic Gibson and Maurice Douglas?"

"Demo and Moe on that police killing? Both of 'em hot as shit."

"Why? Because they blamed each other as the shooter?"

"Yeah, but Domo fucked up on some other shit, too."

"Melvin Thomas?"

"Beast?"

Lil' Man nodded.

"Hot as shit!" I emphasized.

"Cornell Thomas?"

"Scorching."

"Black Marco from 58th and Field Place?"

"He said some wild shit to his grandmother on the phone and the people got the call and used it against Foots and 'nem. I'm on the fence about that one. You know Foots went home and came back in on a conspiracy. He running around saying that Buck …"

"Buckey Fields?"

"Yeah. He saying that Buck called him from the jail phone at D.C. jail and said something about Foots having a key or some shit. Foots is saying that the ATF got on his line because of Buck's call. Is that hot to you?"

"Fuck no! Or that shit he supposed to have said about everybody having keys. He never implicated nobody about no guns or drugs."

"A'ight. What about the Mario and Izzy beef?"

"We ain't even about to get into that one," Lil Man said and smiled. "I'm confused about a lot of that shit. Let me ask you this, what's your take on the Greg Bryce and Skinny Pimp joint?"

"Slim, that coward nigga, Skinny Pimp, running around spreading that shit about Greg. He ain't never produced no paperwork. Their joint is similar to Buck's joints, to me. Two codefendants beefing with each other. I'm with old Bryce-Bey. Why? Because Greg is defending that wild shit and Pimp just talking. Slim barbecued Skinny Pimp up the jail about that shit. Almost killed his stupid ass. Greg been crushing niggas about that shit for years. He cooked a nigga out California …"

"About that slander?"

"Naw, some other shit, but that's my point. Just like Buck, he gon' nail niggas asses to the ground if he hear you said that shit. A good man come out of ADX and told me that Greg is chasing that nigga Randy Shaw all over the federal system about that shit."

"Andre Richardson."

"Carey Moore's brother, Dre?"

Lil' Man nodded.

"Slim hot as cayenne peppers."

"Bubbles."

"What Bubbles? Ronald Fraizer?"

"Yeah, Bub."

"Mike Boone been showing the paperwork. Bubbles wicked as shit. He been getting checked in all over the feds. Twin and 'nem checked him in here, Down B-1. Look, slim, I'ma fall back and take me a nap. I'ma holla back in the morning."

"A'ight, slim."

Chapter 10

Jihad
Parking lot of Bliss Nightclub
"I told Quran what I'm about to tell you. I'm serious about this situation, lil bruh. I been all over the country performing. One thing I learned from touring is this. In all major cities ... Charlotte, Miami, Mobile, Memphis, New Orleans, Atlanta, Dallas, Houston, Louisville, St. Louis, Detroit, Cleveland, Buffalo, Little Rock, Omaha, Indianapolis, even Baltimore, when niggas come to town to perform, they gotta check in with the real niggas in every city. You gotta pay them niggas for security. Just to make sure you and your men keep y'all jewelry and money after the club lets out. Y'all need weed, pills, lean ... whatever, . y'all gotta cop that shit from them niggas. But here in D.C., we don't do that. We let these rap niggas come through and act like we grew up with these niggas. Shit sickening, slim. Niggas in D.C. be actin' like straight groupies when niggas come here. We getting on the Gram making ourselves look stupid as shit welcoming The Migos and Gucci Mane 'nem in our hoods and not making them niggas pay homage. It's time niggas get together and make them industry niggas check in. Think about what I'm saying Jay," Anwar 'Big G' Glover said.

"I hear you, slim," I replied as Big G walked off in the direction of the club's entrance.

"Aye, slim, what's really good with that nigga Big G?" Bo asked. "Niggas be saying all kinda shit about homie. Is he fucked up or what?"

I shrugged my shoulders. "I met slim through Quran. And you and I both know bruh ain't fuckin with no rats."

"True dat, true dat. I was just curious though because slim got his own shoe out here. And everybody wearing them. He on T.V., and he in movies, …"

"On the radio. I already know. Ain't nobody never seen no paperwork, so, I guess he's official until he ain't. And on some real shit, I feel him on all that shit he was saying. Out of town niggas come to D.C. and do whatever they want. Ball players, celebrities, street niggas … ain't nobody paying no dues."

Bo started walking towards the club. "I'ma tell that to Moneybagg after I get through partying with him and all them country ass bitches he got with him."

Pulling the two guns off my waist, I put them under the driver's seat and followed Bo inside Bliss.

***

"I thought a broke nigga said sum. Talkin' shit but they still ain't saying nothing. I trapped this bitch out 'til the feds come. Run it up run it up. I thought a broke nigga said something. How it go when I'm talkin', you listen. Cut her off 'cause she spoke on the business. Hundreds and fifties. Can't swap a dime for a penny. You know that's a stupid decision. Heads first with it. I shot a shot at my niggas. Really didn't think before I did it. Make it make sense."

"Aye, bruh, I let me see that picture you have of the dude Baby E from Clay Terrace," Bo tapped me and said.

I pulled my phone out and showed him the photo. "Bruh, you know my shit is twenty twenty vision. I'ma bloodhound when it comes to spotting an opp. Look over there in the VIP section. Ain't that the nigga Baby E popping the bottles at the table to the far left? The light brown-skinned nigga with all the jewels on?"

I looked exactly where Bo had directed me to. I glanced at the phone and then the dude in the VIP section. Sure enough, the man was Baby E. Ever since receiving the order to hit Baby E, Quran and I, or Quran alone had drove through the Clay Terrace neighborhood looking for the doomed man. And on the one night that I hadn't been looking for him, he appeared out of nowhere. "Yea, that's him, slim."

"Hit Quran and…"

"Hit Quran for what, slim? I can handle this. Me and you."

"Say less, bruh. Say less."

***

Bo was behind the wheel of the Buick Lucerne Sedan. I sat in the passenger seat and checked to make sure the ACP was ready to deliver death to my target. The ACP mini stared back at me as if to say, "You already know how I get down."

"I do know," I mumbled.

"What did you say, bruh?" Bo asked with his eyes on the road.

"I was talkin' to myself, slim," I replied. "Don't lose him, Bo. I wanna finish him tonight."

"Chill out, bruh. Let me get my drive on. I got him. Fall back."

We were following a black Mercedes S550 and a silver Genesis. Baby E was in the passenger seat of the Mercedes. A man was behind the wheel driving. The second car, the Genesis, had two men inside it as well. The chances that all four men were armed was great.

"What's the plan?" Bo asked.

"Let's just stay a distance back and see where they're going. If they head to Clay Terrace, we gotta engage before they get there. I'm sure there will be other shooters outside somewhere. Getting Baby E in the hood would be suicide. Maybe they will split up once they hit the highway. If not, it's all good because the element of surprise is on our side. What you got on you?"

"A Glock 26 with the switch that's extended."

"That's it?" I asked incredulously.

"Yeah, that's it. I thought it was party time. The Glock was a just in case joint. Had I known we'd be hunting, I'da brought out some tall shit."

"Well, hopefully this ACP, my Ruger, and your weak ass Glizzy will be enough."

The two cars didn't hit the highway like I thought they would. They took the long way to wherever they were headed. Once they hit Benning Road near Hechinger Mall, I realized their destination.

"They're headed to Clay Terrace," I said aloud.

"I'm hip," Bo replied. "What you wanna do? Abort?"

"Naw, not yet. Just keep following 'em. See if I'm wrong. I can't abort the mission. I'm geekin' like shit to get this nigga. I ain't fucked a nigga around in a minute. If they're heading to their hood, I'ma have to jump out and try and get him at a light or something."

"A'ight, bruh. Whatever you say. I'm with it."

The two cars took Benning Road straight out. At the Minnesota Avenue and Benning intersection, I waited to see what they would do. Both cars sped through and continued down Benning Road headed towards East Capitol Street. I told Bo to hit the signal to turn left onto East Capitol, but the cars did something unexpected. They kept straight through the light and turned into the BenCo shopping center.

"Got their ass," I muttered as my excitement rose. "Don't turn into the shopping center, slim. Pull down by the laundry mat. There's an alley. We'll get out there."

The streetlights illuminated the area, but it was early in the A.M. and basically desolate in the shopping center. There were only three establishments open. The Subway sandwich shop, America's Best Wings and the Chinese carryout. The two cars parked in the lot and all four men exited the two vehicles.

"Let's go, slim," I ordered as we exited the Buick.

Only three of the dudes went inside America's Best Wings and stood at the counter. From the distance I could see the lone man leaning on the hood of the Genesis. He fired up a cigarette or blunt. Baby E was inside the wing spot. I hid the mini under my coat as I hid beside the entrance to the laundromat. Bo by my side, I looked to my left. His Glock was out and down in front of him. The wait was on. I needed the three men to exit the wing spot before I could crush their asses. Ten minutes later, that happened. The three men were preoccupied by their food as we ran out of the darkness, but the fourth man, who'd stayed behind, saw us coming.

"Get down! It's a hit!" he screamed before pulling two guns and sparking at us.

I let the ACP with the seventy five 3.56's rip. The dude shooting the two guns went down, and I expected to get closer, but other guns entered the fray. I stood my ground and tried to deliver death to the four men. Hiding on the other side of the cars, the men managed to get inside their vehicles. My bullets ate at the metal like paper. Windows shattered. Somehow, the two cars managed to back away in an attempt to pull off. I ran up closer. The men returned fire, and I felt the searing pain of a bullet in my leg and side. I turned to run and that was when I saw Bo. He was down, laying in a pool of blood. I stood over him and my tears came. Bo was gone. The neat little hole in his forehead told me that. I grabbed Bo's Glock, and quickly limped back to the Buick. I could hear sirens in the distance. Bo had left the car running. I leaped in the driver's seat and sped through the alley. I came out on Bass Street and parked the Buick near J.C. Neal Elementary School. Blood stained my jeans and Hugo Boss sweatshirt. I didn't know how bad I was hit, but I knew that

I couldn't be out on the streets driving. The cops would stop every car they saw in the area.

I pulled out my cell phone and called Quran.

Chapter 11

Quran

Finding the Buick was easy. The directions Jihad gave were good. I double parked on 51st Street and jumped out of the truck. I ran over to the Buick and pulled the driver's side door open. My adrenaline was pumping, my body full of fear. Jihad was laid out on the backseat. I opened the rear door and tapped Jihad.

"Jay … Jay, wake up, Jay!!" I put my hand on his chest and felt a heartbeat. "Let's go, baby boy! C'mon … get up."

When Jihad didn't move, I said, "'Fuck it" to myself and got in the driver's seat of the Buick. I left the truck in its spot and sped off to the nearest hospital, United Medical Center.

***

"A few more minutes, and your brother wouldn't have made it, Mr. Bashir. He's not out of the woods yet, but he's responding well to the surgery to stop the bleeding in his stomach. The bullet wound to his leg is less serious. The bullet apparently went straight through and exited. There's some muscle damage, but again … nothing serious. We had to do an abdominal entry. Your brother is going to look a little different after this. There are internal and external sutures that are keeping the wound closed. He's lost a lot of blood, but we replaced it and stabilized him. Your brother is still fully sedated. He's been given pain meds and antibiotics.

I suggest that you go home and get some rest. You'll be able to see him tomorrow."

"Thank you, doctor. Can I pay cash for his bill?"

"That's not my department, Mr. Bashir. I just do the miracle part. Good day."

The doctor turned to leave but turned back to me. "Metropolitan Police detectives are waiting to talk to you."

As if on cue, two plain clothes detectives appeared and headed my way.

"Mr. Bashir?" the lead detective asked. He was a young, white dude with a military haircut.

"What's up?" I replied.

"Quran Bashir?" the second detective said. He was an older black dude that looked like Chris Rock.

"Yeah, what's up?"

"Jihad Bashir, the shooting victim, he's your brother, correct?" the white detective asked. "We were told that he's your brother."

"Yeah, that's my brother," I replied.

"Do you know what happened to your brother?"

"He got shot."

"I know that, Mr. Bashir. What I'm asking is do you know how he got shot, or who shot him?"

"The answer is no to both questions. All I know is he got shot."

"Are you the person who transported him here?" the black detective asked.

"I am."

"Where were you when the shooting occurred?" This came from the white detective.

"Were you with your brother when he was shot, Mr. Bashir?" the black detective asked.

"No, I wasn't there. I was at home. I got a call from my brother and he said that he was injured. Said that he couldn't make it to a hospital at all. Listen, I'm not a witness to anything, so I resent this interrogation. I'ma make this short and concise, then I'm not answering any more questions unless I have my lawyer present. I was at home asleep. I got a call from my brother saying that he'd been injured … shot and that he needed help. I jumped into my car and went to the Bliss Nightclub. My brother was about two blocks away. He said that he'd been inside the club and got into it with some dudes. In the parking lot of the club, he was approached and shot immediately. He was able to run away and call. Me. That's all I know. I picked my brother up …"

"And drove him to UMC?" the white detective asked. "Why? Wouldn't Howard University hospital have been closer?"

"I'ma a Southeast dude. Born and raised. My instincts were to bring my brother to a hospital closer toSoutheast. To me, it was smart because whoever shot my brother would know that he'd go to Howard, and maybe they'd want to finish him off there. So, I brought him here."

The black detective pulled out a business card and passed it to me. "Okay, Mr. Bashir, that's all we have. If you want to share anything else about your brother and who may have shot him, please feel free to call me. Okay?"

"I'll be sure to do that, detective," I told him.

Once both detectives had left, I flicked the card into the air and walked out into the parking lot.

Minutes later, Zin's Infiniti appeared. I hopped into her car and told her everything I knew."

***

Two days later…
Sitting across from Jay's bed, I had my feet up on the table near the bed. I was reading a book called *Cruddy Buddy* by a dude named Ducksauce. The book was a relic from another era, but it was funny as shit. There was some street shit in the book that I could identify with. My cell phone vibrated; the caller was Kiki Swinson. "Hello?"

"You did that shit on purpose, Que! That was fucked up!" Kiki spat into the phone.

"Kiki... we talked about this already," I replied.

"And you denied answering the phone while we was fucking that day."

"Look, baby girl ... I ain't got time for this shit. I'm dealing with a family emergency."

"You foul, Que. and that's fucked up because I always been good to you. I fucked with you ..."

Something inside me snapped. "Check this out, baby girl. You right. I did answer the phone. I was on some bullshit because you never told me that you had a husband named Juice. I got a man who was in Petersburg with the dude. I got a man down there with him right now that I talk to. He confirmed that your husband, Julius Seay, is in the bin. Instead of you just keeping it one hundred, you lied. "

"I never lied to you, Que..."

"You lied by omission. You never told me that you had a husband. I found out a few days before you came to D.C. So, when I saw that your phone kept ringing and the caller was Juice, I hit the five and let him hear us. I'm sorry if I broke up your happy home, but I was fucked up about it when I found out I been fucking a married woman. I was on some bullshit. I acted like a sucka. My bad. I apologize."

"But you got other bitches, Que and I never said shit," Kiki whined. "I never paid that no mind. When we were together. It was just us doing us. Nobody else mattered."

"Until it did matter. Like now. You should've told me, Kiki, and let me decide if I wanted to be in a triangle with you ..."

"Triangle? Juice is locked up. I can't fuck him. How is that a triangle, Que?"

"It's semantics, Kiki. Either way, I did what I did. On some real 'G' shit, I apologize. I shouldn't have did that wild ass shit."

"I agree, but it's done. So, I guess it was meant to be. He... Juice knows that I'm a freak, and he been in jail for almost ten years. He had to know I was out here fucking. I lied and said I wasn't, but he had to know I was lying."

"So, what's the hook? He tryna divorce you?"

"Fuck no. that crazy ass nigga love me too much. He forgave me."

"For real? Slim is a good nigga. You gotta keep him."

"What about you, though?" Kiki asked.

"What about me?" I replied.

"Can I keep you, Que?"

I had to laugh at that. Women were some bewildering creatures. "Sure, you can, baby girl. Sure you can."

"Good. I gotta go to New York in a few days. Can I pit stop in D.C. again?"

"For sure. Just let me know when."

"A'ight, Que. Deal with your family emergency. I'll be in touch."

"A'ight, baby girl. Later."

Just as I put my phone up and opened the book back up, I heard, "You are a foul nigga." I looked up at Jihad. His eyes were open. On his face was a smile.

I tossed the book and got out of the chair. I leaned down and embraced my brother. "You had me worried for a minute there, Jay."

"Worried? For what, big bruh. A couple bullets can't stop me. I'm superman."

"Yeah, a'ight, superman ..."

"Bo... what happened?"

"Bo's dead, Jay. it was all over the news yesterday. Bo died and so did some other dude that got hit at the BenCo center. What happened out there, baby boy?"

"We was at Bliss, and we saw Baby E. Bo spotted him. I confirmed that it was him. I made the decision to get at him. Baby E had niggas with him. They left in two cars. We followed them to the BenCo. We tried to get Baby E, but one of his men saw the move and called an audible …"

"There was a shootout between y'all and them. Bo got hit, the dude, and you."

Jihad nodded. "I ran …" Tears formed in Jihad's eyes and rolled down the side of his face. "I saw that Bo was hit bad. I ran to the car and pulled off. I knew that I was hit bad. That's when I pulled over and called you. I fucked up, Que. I shouldn't have went after him. I should've waited …"

"Jay, don't blame yourself," I cajoled. "You made a business decision and things went bad. It happens. I know you fucked up about Bo. Shit, so am I. He was my lil' man and your right hand. But he knew the risk. He lived the life. He died how he lived. By the gun. That's what Bo signed up for."

"I know, but," Jhad stated but got too choked up to finish.

"Ain't no buts, baby boy. It is what it is. Bo was a part of the game. Like I said, he knew the risk. Besides, we got other shit to worry about. The cops were here. They're investigating your shooting. They questioned me. I told them that you got shot in the Bliss parking lot, and you ran. I said that you called me, and I picked you up a few blocks away from Bliss. Then I brought you here. I tried to put you away from the scene at BenCo. But my story won't hold up, and they will be back. If the cops view camera footage from Bliss and don't see no shooting, they're gonna know that I lied. They are also gonna see you entering and leaving Bliss. You and Bo. They'll see that y'all got into the Buick and drove off. If the BenCo has cameras … which I think they do … they will have you and Bo in the parking lot shooting guns. Two people died, Bo and the other dude. If they match the bullets in Bo's body to the bullets taken out of you, that puts you at the BenCo scene. It's enough to get a judge to sign off on an arrest warrant. You know what happens after that."

"Damn, bruh … I fucked up, huh?"

"Don't even sweat it, baby boy. We gon' get through it. If worse comes to worse, you gon' have the best lawyer in the city."

"Who? Brian Mc Daniels?"

"Naw, nigga. Zinfandel Carter."

"Cool. That's what's up. The car ... what happened to it?" Jihad asked.

"Gone. The car, your coat, the ACP, and the Ruger you had on you. I also took the shirt you had on and got rid of it. Your phone, too. And the Glock I found. All gone."

"Damn. Thanks, Que."

"Don't mention it, baby boy. What are big brothers for?"

The door to Jihad's room opened, and Tosheka appeared in the doorway. She had fresh tears in her eyes. She looked from me to Jihad.

"I guess that's my cue, baby boy," I told Jihad.

Tosheka walked into the room. "My showing up is not your cue to leave, Que. You don't have to go because I'm here."

Ignoring Tosheka, I leaned down and hugged my younger brother. I kissed his cheek and said, "Don't worry about nothing, Jay. You just get better. And if you need me for anything, call me."

"On what? My phone's gone, remember?"

"Use the landline phone on the table."

"A'ight then. Assalamu Alaikum."

"Walaikum Assalam."

I walked around Tosheka and left the hospital room with death on my mind.

***

The person that was killed at the BenCo market wasn't Baby E. The man's name was Denico Autrey. No other names had been released, but there was an ongoing investigation . Baby E was still alive, and I needed to change that. I needed to find him, Jojo Morris, and Kendra Dyson. Once that was done, I decided that a vacation was in order. As I increased the volume of the music playing in the truck, the last person I thought about was Tosheka Jennings. I couldn't figure out why, but her face wouldn't leave my head. I had convinced myself that I didn't love Tosheka and that I didn't care about her being with Jihad. I convinced myself that she was just a thot. A piece of pussy to hit when the need arose. I convinced myself that I didn't care about her. I convinced myself that she meant nothing to me. So, why couldn't I get her out of my mind?

My cell phone vibrating broke my reverie. I looked at the screen. The caller was Sean.

"Assalamu Alaikum, . What's good?"

"You busy, youngin?" Sean asked.

"Naw, why? What's up, old head?"

"I'll tell you when you get here. Meet me at Minnesota Seafood in thirty minutes."

"Bet. I'm on my way." I disconnected the phone call.

I headed for the other side of the city and knew that it was work call time. I listened to Queen Naija sing as I drove. I thought about Kiki. I thought about Zin. I thought about Tosheka.

Chapter 12

Tosheka

The tears in my eyes confused me. I couldn't decide whether I cried because Jihad was hurt, or if I cried because Quran was hurt because his brother was hurt. I stood in front of Jihad's hospital bed and wiped my eyes.

"Don't cry for me, I'm good. Hurt a little, but still good."

"Word around town is that you and Bo got into it at Bliss. What the fuck happened, Jihad?"

"We'll talk about it another time. You look good as shit, Tee."

I did a little pirouette and smiled. "I do, huh?"

"Stop faking. You know you a bad mutha …"

"Shut your mouth," I finished the statement and laughed. "I'm really glad that you're alright, Jay. When I heard about Bo and that you was with him, I was worried sick."

"Is that right? C'mere. Tell me what you was worried about."

Walking closer to the bed, I reached under the covers until I had Jihad's dick in my hand. I was worried about you and him." Jihad's manhood grew in my hand. I stroked him gently.

"A-A-r-r-gh, shit!" Jihad yelped. Then he laughed. "It hurts when my dick gets hard. That's crazy!"

I released him from my grasp. "Well, don't let your dick get hard."

"How can I not? The way you just sprint around and showed me that phat ass in them jeans. Your coat open and your shirt ain't doing shit to hide them tig ol' bitties. You done came in here with that lip gloss on your lips that I like… aarrgh… shit. Damn!"

All I could do was laugh at Jihad. Not his pain, just his horniness despite his circumstances. I leaned over him and kissed his lips. Then I reached under the covers to rub his dick again. His dick responded to my touch just as he moaned in pain again. Suddenly I felt frisky. I felt adventurous and nasty. I turned and walked away from the bed.

"Where the hell you going?"

"Chill out. I'm just locking the door for a minute." I locked the door and walked back to Jihad.

"Locking the door? Locking the door for what?"

I moved the covers to reveal Jihad's hospital gown. I lifted the gown until his hard on was visible. "It would be a damn shame to let all this dick go to waste." I leaned over and put Jihad in my mouth.

***

"You got staples in your stomach."

"Inside and out. It's from the surgery."

"It's all good, boo. Scars can be sexy, too. Even Thor had scars."

"Thor? What the fuck? You like comic books?"

"Comic books, no. Good movies, yes. I like the *Thor* movies. And pretty much all the Marvel movies. *Iron Man, The Incredible Hulk, Dr. Strange, Black Widow* … that's my shit. I really hope you learn a lesson from this, Jay. You need to slow your mannish ass down. Leave all that super thug shit to your big brother."

"Is that right? How do you know that I'm not the super thug instead of him?"

"Duh? Because I been around the both of you for years."

"The both of us. The both of us. Why are you with me, Tee?"

"Jihad, please. You know why I'm with you. Don't start acting …"

"Acting what, Tee? Crazy? Sentimental? Like a sucka?"

My emotions were out of whack. My thoughts ran rampant inside my head. I wanted to tell Jihad the truth, but I couldn't. I couldn't tell him what I knew and what he already knew. "My friend's brother got killed. They're having a memorial for him. I promised her that I'd come. I have to go, Jihad."

"Well, go then," Jihad said and closed his eyes. "Go."

I turned and left the room as fast as I could. My lust and my lies followed me the entire way. I had already told Jihad why I was with him. I never hid that from him. So, why ask me that again? Did he have a head injury, too? I walked through the hospital praying for his speedy recovery and thinking about Lil Bo, who had been killed. Life was too short to be playing games. I decided then that I needed to figure out my life and figure it out fast before lies, betrayal and hurt buried me in more than just dirt.

Chapter 13

Brion 'Blast' Clark
Stewart funeral home
Benning Road, N.E.

"Say goodbye to what we had. The good times that made us laugh outweigh the bad."

My mother's cries were the loudest I had ever heard. No matter how I moved or which way I turned I was assaulted by these screams. I had never heard my family in so much pain. The tears that I tried to hide from the world were now on full display, for all to see. I sat in the front row of the funeral home and tried to avoid the 10 x 13 photo of my brother Crud. I avoided the obituary in my hand that was inundated with photos of him with various women, and his children. I looked around the room at my family, then at my niece and nephew. They would never see their father again, and I'd never see my big brother again. A controlled rage built inside me and festered. I had promised my sister that whoever was responsible for my brother's death would be found and dealt with, but I hadn't been able to keep that promise. Sean Branch had proven hard to find. Even finding his sidekick, Quran, with the grey eyes was hard to do. Bionca gave me some info on both men, but I still couldn't find them. It was as if Sean Branch was a ghost.

"I don't know where this road is going to lead to. All I know is where we've been and what we've been through. It's so hard to say goodbye to yesterday, and I'll take with me the memories / to be my sunshine after the rain..."

I thought about snatching the girl named Tosheka and getting her to lead me to Quran. Then I would use Quran to lead me to Sean Branch. But at the moment, Bionca was against that. She knew that in the aftermath of whatever happened, her friend Tosheka would have to die. My older sister wanted to avoid that.

"Tosheka's only sin is messing with the grey eyed nigga, Quran. Besides, he's not the one who killed our brother according to Doo Doo. Sean Branch did. So, involving Tosheka is out of the question right now," Bionca had said when I suggested the plan to grab her friend Tosheka.

I'd been all over Northeast looking for Sean Branch. I went to Montana Avenue, Brentwood, Saratoga, Longdon Park, South Dakota Ave, Riggs Park, New York Avenue, Rhode Island Avenue. I looked on Tenth Street, Twelfth St., Fort Lincoln, Tacoma Park, Michigan Park, and Eastern Avenue all the way out to the Maryland side. I'd been to barbershops, pool halls, rec centers, shoe stores, restaurants, carry outs, clothing stores, everywhere. But still nothing.

"My brother Byron was an athlete. He was intelligent. He loved to dress nice and look fly. Boy, did he like to wear foreign clothes."

My sister Brechelle was on the platform in front of the funeral home talking. "He was always there for me. He helped me out with everything ... I can't ... I can't ... I can't believe that ..." That was as far as she got before she broke down in a fit of tears.

I leapt out of my seat and went to her. We all did. Before we knew it the platform was filled with family members surrounding my little sister.

***

"Bae, I'm tired, and I'm hungry as hell," Ren told me.

"Me, too. C'mon, let's bounce. I'ma holla at my people and let them know that we out. We gon' skip the repast and go home. We can stop and get food on the way home."

Ren hugged me and kissed my lips. "I'm really sorry about your brother, bae. This shit has really torn the family apart."

"I'm hip, but bad times don't last. Strong people do."

"That's right. Talk that shit to me, Farrakhan. I love it."

"Go 'head with that, Ren. You crazy as shit."

"Crazy about you. I'ma go to the bathroom right quick. I told your ass that I might be pregnant. My stomach queasy as hell. Go ahead to the car. I'll be there in a few minutes."

"A'ight. Don't be long."

My mother and sisters were in a huddle with other family members when I approached them. I pulled my mother and sister, Bionca to the side.

"I'ma bounce. Me and Ren. She ain't feeling too good and neither am I. Y'all enjoy the repast as much as possible, and I'ma come through tomorrow."

I gave Bionca a furtive glance that she caught. "I gotta take care of some stuff immediately after I leave the house."

"I love you, Brion," my mother said as she hugged me. "You be safe out here. Call me later once y'all get home. Where's Ren?"

"In the bathroom. She's gonna meet me at the car."

Bionca grabbed me and then hugged me tight. "Love you, baby brother. Call me later." She kissed me on the check.

"I will. Love y'all. Bye."

***

I left Stewart's and walked down Benning Road. At the corner, I made a left in route to the parking lot behind the funeral home. My mind was all over the place as I made my way to my Lexus. Then something happened that I never expected. A man appeared out of the shadows; his beard unmistakable. A gun appeared in his hand as he raised it.

"The situation with your brother was business. You just made it personal. Now, I'ma kill your whole family, too."

That was the last thing I heard before the sparks from the gun faded my whole world to black.

Chapter 14

Ren Tyler

The feeling in my stomach was like I ate something spoiled. After trying to use the toilet in both ways, I tried to make myself hurl. But nothing I did settled me. I sat down on the toilet and reached into my purse. The box with the home pregnancy test inside it was bulky but advertised to be effective. Opening the box, I removed the test and read the instructions. All I needed to do was add a few drops of urine to the applicator and then wait five minutes for the results. Light blue minus sign if negative, light pink plus sign if positive.

"Here goes nothing," I mumbled to myself as I put the test inside the toilet.

Seconds later a stream of urine coated the applicator. I held it out to await the results. Feelings of trepidation washed over me. I didn't know whether I wanted to be pregnant or not. I knew that I loved Blast with all my heart and soul, but being a twenty four year old mother wasn't exactly compatible with the lifestyle I was living. I thought about the three men I'd killed in the last week. Miguel Harris, the dude with him, and Doo Doo. I thought about the third man I'd shot who was on Orleans Place with Miguel and the other dude. As far as I knew, he was still fighting for his life at the hospital. If he lived or died made no difference to me. Killing people was second nature to me. A skill taught to me by my father. Von Tyler had always wanted a son. A male child that he could pass on everything he knew to. But as fate would have it, he wasn't that lucky. My mother Dorenda pushed out a seven pound baby girl and named me Rennausance. My father was a student of the game and made a great teacher. Growing up in Northeast D.C. near Ivy city. I learned all there was to know about everything there was to know. Gambling, drugs, sports, guns, boys, and self-defense.

"Don't ever be a victim, Ren. never. You're a Tyler, and Tylers are never victims. We never forgive and we never forget. If somebody hits you, you maim them. If they hurt you or maim you, you kill them. Simple as that. Man, woman, animal, or child. D.C. is a few years removed from being the murder capital. It's always been that for a reason. You are not like regular girls, Ren. You're me manifested into a female form. When you were a toddler, I sat you down in front of two thangs. A Barbie doll and an empty gun. A .380. I wanted to see what would interest you more. You got up and grabbed the gun. That's when I knew. You'd become a natural born killer. Just like your father. "

When I was thirteen years old, the boy who lived next door to me, Christopher Williams, lured me to his house to play the Dreamcast. He was two years older than me. After several games of Madden football, he raped me. The very next day, I lured him into the woods and killed him. That was the very first time I'd even had sex. It was the first time I' got pregnant. I told my father what happened. Without showing any emotion, he and my mother took me to Hillcrest to get an abortion. Three days after that my father killed Christopher's mother, grandmother, and both of their pit bulls. I snapped out of my stroll down memory lane and looked at the applicator. The results were in. The pink plus sign was unmistakable. I thought about something that Blast had said to me days ago inside of the Carolina Kitchen restaurant. I thought about the conversation we had ...

"Well, what would you like to eat?"
"I'ma get the crab cakes, fried fish, the mac and cheese, and the fried cabbage. Let me get some potato salad on the side, and banana pudding for dessert."
"Got damn, baby! You ain't bullshittin' when you say you hungry, huh?"
"I think it's the weed, boo. Or I might be pregnant."
"That wouldn't be bad at all. A life taken, a life given ..."

"A life taken, a life given ..." I repeated as I pulled up my clothes. At the sink, I washed my hands, then dropped the pregnancy test into my purse. I couldn't wait to show it to Blast. I left the bathroom in a hurry, a smile etched across my face. Then suddenly I heard gunshots. "Blast." I said to myself and rushed out of the funeral home door. My heels I wore were impeding me, so I stopped to take them off. Purse in one hand, heels in the other, I ran down the street and turned the corner. A foreboding washed over me.

I know exactly where Blast's Lexus was parked. It was there. I could see it. As I ran up closer to the car, I stopped immediately. I could smell the gunpowder in the air. I could see two feet on the ground. Instantly, I recognized the Louis Vuitton black suede loafers that Blast had worn to the memorial. "No ... please God ... no ..." I prayed, but my prayers wouldn't be answered. Blast lay on the ground next to his Lexus, with bullet holes in his face and head.

"No!--! No!-" I dropped my knees and grabbed his bloody head. My tears coating him in death.
"BLAST!"

Chapter 15

The News

"A district man who fatally shot an acquaintance who was walking his two children to school last year was sentenced to life in prison today. James Harris pleaded guilty to second degree murder in the 2012 fatal shooting of Cinquez Miller. Miller was dating Harris's sister. Prosecutor Ari Weinstein said the two men had an ongoing dispute. Miller was holding the hands of his four and five year old children when the incident occurred. Harris fired seven shots, striking Miller five times in the face and upper body. Neither child was injured. Harris, who was on probation at the time of the shooting for a gun offense, was arrested three months after the shooting. Harris was charged with first degree murder while armed, but as a part of his plea agreement, prosecutors agreed to spare him a possible death sentence.

United States Attorney Greg Gamble had this to say today.

"This was an especially tragic crime. Video footage from a nearby home depicted images of the defendant standing over the decadent and continuing to fire multiple rounds. This is an egregious crime on the morning of a school day where Cinquez Miller was walking his two children to school. This incident should never have happened. I can only imagine the traumatization that those two children will face as they grow up."

Despite being sentenced to thirty five years to life in prison, Harris expressed remorse and apologized to his family and Miller's.

"A twenty seven year old man has been charged with murder today. Christian Pual was arrested by the capital area joint fugitive task force and charged with the 2013 murder of Alex Vinson. Pual of Temple Hills, MD. is accused of killing Vinson in Bladensburg, MD. over a dice game gone wrong. He's being held at the Upper Marlboro Detention Center without bail. About 3:10 a.m. on May 15th, officers responded to the 5600 block of Annapolis Road for a reported shooting in a parking lot. They found Alex Vinson suffering from gunshot wounds. He died at the scene. Prince George's County police said in a news release that they identified Paul as a suspect in the shooting through the course of the investigation and information provided to the county's crime stoppers program. An attorney representing Christian Paul could not be reached for comment. A double murder trial is set in the district. The broad contours of what happened in a dark district of Columbia parking lot nearly two years ago is now known. An off duty police officer, Jayden Beavis, walked out of his condo building at 5 am. He spotted a suspicious looking vehicle, went to investigate, and ended up confronting the vehicle's three occupants. As the men drove past and away from Beauvis, the officer fired five rounds, fatally hitting two of the three men from behind and barely missing the third in a case that drew outrage in the community. Now, with Beauvis's double murder trial set to start Monday, the forty one year old is poised to publicly speak about the encounter for the first time. Beauvis was a sworn member of the Pentagon Police Force at the time of the encounter. He was off duty and not in uniform that morning in NoMa, according to his attorneys, but tried to make a citizen's arrest after seeing the men breaking into a work van. His attorneys think his testimony will convince a jury that Beauvis was defending himself when he saw the car come at him. The case about to start next week in the District is extremely rare in itself. A one-time police officer being charged with two counts of first degree murder. Evidence and testimony are expected to swing from deep emotions to specific debate over laws governing self-defense. Prosecutors Susan Rosenthal and Ian McNealy plan to lean on surveillance video, which they say show the driver of the car trying to avoid Beauvis. The car went around the officer and then drove away. Assistant United States Attorney Susan Rosenthal, the second highest ranking prosecutor at the U.S. attorney's office, had this to say earlier…"

"The video will show the former officer taking a position behind the vehicle after it passes him, and he fires into the back of the vehicle. You see the muzzle flashes. The evidence shows that a bullet pierced the back of the car, and the two men were shot in the back. Officer Beauvis shot at the car not because the men posed a danger to him, but because the men disrespected him. They hadn't done what he told them to do. They didn't stop. He was on that day a self-appointed vigilante because the crime took place where he lived. The shooting killed Dominique Williams, 32, who was in the backseat of the vehicle and thirty eight year old James Johnson, who was in the front passenger seat. "

"McNealy and Rosenthal are expected to call Michael Thomas, the driver who survived the shooting, as a witness. While doing so would open him up to rough cross examination, Thomas has shown a knack for candor that jurors may find appealing. In other news today, D.C. police identified a man shot and wounded by an officer in Southeast Washington on Friday. That man has been identified as twenty eight year old Stephen Simms. They also confirm that Simms was not connected to an assault the officer had been called to the area to investigate. The officer, who has yet to be named publicly, was called to the 1300 black of Good Hope Road shortly after 10 a.m. Friday for a report of an assault in progress. The officer located a female victim who had suffered injuries not thought to be life threatening. An investigation revealed that someone had allegedly struck the female victim with a metal object of some kind during an argument. The attacker fled before officers arrived. During a search of the area, a police officer saw SImmes, a resident of Northeast, enter the passenger side of a vehicle and thought he might be the perpetrator of the assault. The officer gave Simms numerous commands to exit the vehicle and to stop reaching, but Simms didn't comply. At that point, the officer fired a single shot striking Simms. D.C. police found what was believed to be cocaine on Simms … wait … I'm receiving breaking news out of Northeast, Washington … We will now go live to the 3900 block of Benning Road where a man attending a memorial service at Stewart's funeral home was just gunned down in the funeral home parking lot … Anijah?"

"Good evening, Maria. I'm reporting live from Stewart's funeral home where a memorial service for a man named Byron Clark was just ending. Our viewers will recall that Byron Clark was one of two men killed inside a home on Third street in Southeast almost two weeks ago. The family of Byron Clark had to have a memorial for their loved one instead of a wake and open casket funeral due to the fact that Byron Clark had been completely decapitated. As mourners for Mr. Clark left the funeral home, Byron Clark's younger brother, Brion Jermaine Clark, was gunned down as he walked to his vehicle, about an hour ago."

Chapter 16

Sean Branch

"Once I put my thinking cap on, it wasn't hard to figure out that the dude and the bitch that tried to ambush me on Naylor Road was connected to either Whistle or Crud. Since they tried to move on me and not you, I zeroed in on Crud. I found out days ago that Doo Doo was dead. His body was found down by the old Eastside nightclub on Half Street. Not too far from the new stadium they built for the soccer team D.C. United. Once I knew that Doo Doo was dead, I put two and two together. Whoever knocked Doo Doo off knew him. They talked to him, and he told them that I killed Crud. Probably told them that you killed Whistle. Under duress, Doo Doo had to have admitted his relationship to me. That's how Crud's brother knew to use Doo Doo's phone to send that text. Once I was sure that it was somebody connected to Crud or Whistle, I got baby girl to search online for death notices. She found one for Crud. I was outside of Stewart's for hours watching the entrance to that joint. Eventually, I recognized the dude who fired at me on Naylor Road."

"What about the broad?" Quran asked.

"He had a bitch with him, but I couldn't be one hundred percent sure if it was her from the angles I had. The bitch with him today looked similar, but her hair was , a different color. I was gon' torch her ass too, but for some reason, she didn't leave the funeral home with the dude."

Quran cracked open a crab leg and dug the meat out. He dipped the meat into a dish of melted butter and cocktail sauce, then popped it in his mouth.

"Big homie you wild as shit," Quran said suddenly and laughed. "You don't give a fuck. You got us sitting in a seafood joint eating crab legs and shrimp and shit three blocks from where you just committed a murder. Of all the places to lamp at, why the fuck are we here? We're in this 'hole in the wall' ass joint chilling like the whole 6th D police department ain't two football fields away investigating the murder you just did?"

I waited until I completely chewed the shrimp in my mouth before saying, "It's called hiding in plain sight. I couldn't leave my car outside without coming back for it, and besides, I'm thinking about going back up there to see if the bitch is still there."

"You are a fuckin' mad man, ock. Just like I said."

***

Outside by Quran's truck ...

"As always, youngin', thanks for coming through. I needed you to ensure that I could make a quick getaway after I fucked slim around. That was the main reason I called you to meet me, but there's another reason too. You told me about your brother trying to get the nigga Baby E, and that's how he got hit, and his man got crushed. You are like the brother that I never had and whoever you love, I love. So, I made some calls. I got a man in the area. Old head named Rodney Shaw. I met him at MGM Grand last night. Nigga loves to gamble at casinos. I breathed on him about the incident, and he knew who all the players were.. One of the dudes who was with the rat nigga Baby E got hit that night but got himself patched up somewhere without going to a hospital. Nigga named Silk ... he got hit. The other nigga's name is Derrick Hill. According to Rodney they are ... two good niggas that fuck with Baby E because he feeding them. To me that makes them bad men. Since one of them shot Jihad, that makes them food in the food chain. I'ma get Rodney to throw all three of them off the backboard for an alley oop. He knows Baby E is business but the other two are personal. Damn, I just thought of something."

"What?"

"That's the second time today I've said that to someone. Hours ago, before I crushed Crud's brother, I told him that killing Crud was business and that killing him was personal. Shit crazy, but anyway, I also told him that I was gonna kill his whole family."

"Are you?" Quran asked.

"Maybe. After we kill Baby E, Derrick Hill, and Silk."

"Well, I'm with whatever you with."

"And I gotta find the bitch. Maybe she'll be dumb enough to go to Crud's brother's funeral. If she does, I'ma roast her ass."

"As you should, ock. As you should."

I walked over to Quran and embraced him. "Be safe, youngin. Love you, slim."

"Same here, big bruh. You already know."

Chapter 17

Bionca Clark
Prince George Hospital Center after midnight.
"Ms. Clark, your mother suffered a grand mal seizure and a heart attack simultaneously. We believe that her preexisting conditions in conjunction with stress, her weight, and the unfortunate news she received this evening triggered her. Once she fainted at the scene of the incident at the funeral home she hit her head pretty hard on the asphalt. That is what brought on the seizure and possibly the cardiac arrest. The frontal lobe of her brain was damaged due to the cerebral infarction. Deep contusions on her brain have left her in a vegetative state even after the surgery to relieve the swelling stop the internal hemorrhage. To be clearer, Ms. Clark, your mother is in really bad shape, and she may not make it through the next twenty four hours. She's sedated and comfortable and is given pain meds intravenously. If I was you, I'd probably prepare the family for more bad news."

The female Asian doctor turned and walked away from me, leaving me alone with her parting words and the sound of my own voice in my head. Death always comes in threes. Death always comes in threes. How did things get this bad, this fast? What sins had we committed to have this enormous cup of suffering poured on our family? I thought about my words to Brion on the night that we found out our brother had been killed, his head severed from his body.

"Did you see the shape that mommy is in?" I asked Brion

"How can I not? I'm standing right here looking, ain't I?" he replied.

"Well, act like you see her then and do something about it. I don't give two fucks about all thwild shit that Crud was into, what he did, or who he pissed off. He was my brother. Our brother. And nobody had the right to take him away from us. Did you hear what I just said about what they did to him?"

"I heard you."

"Somebody killed my brother. Take your ass out in the streets and find out who did it. Then you kill their ass. Kill everybody involved. If you can't do it, then I'm gonna do it. Then I'ma kill your ass."

With heavy tears streaming down my face, I asked myself if I had been wrong to send my youngest brother on a mission to avenge the brutal murder of our older brother. Had I pushed him too hard? Had I sent Brion to his death? Would Brion be dead had I not pressured him to find Crud's killer? Sean Branch had killed my brother, Crud. Had he also killed Brion? I remembered the day that Brion told me that Sean Branch had killed our brother Crud. I remembered the fear that crept over me as I told Brion what I knew about the notorious killer.

"I'm hip to Sean Branch, Brion. Damn near the whole D.C. is hip to him. He's bad news. Dangerous. Vicious. Just came home about a month or so ago, I think. I saw it all over the news. Back in the day, he killed so many people and got away with it, that the streets nicknamed him Teflon Sean. no murder charges were ever brought up on him. No crime could stick to him. The game just got super serious, baby brother. You tried to kill Sean Branch and missed. Didn't you say that he got a look at you?"

"Yeah, he looked right at me and Ren, then he ducked low and got out of there. We put over twenty rounds or better in his car ..."

"Sean Branch is a different kind of killer. He's been rumored to have been killing since he was like eleven or twelve. Maybe younger. He saw your face, so he knows what you look like. Not who you are, but what you look like, and that ain't good. You have to find him, Brion, and find him soon."

I pushed too hard and got too cocky. Knowing that Sean Branch was too seasoned a killer for my little brother, I sent him on a suicide mission anyway. I got Brion killed. Me. The sole responsibility was mine and mine alone. My tears came harder. I had to catch myself and stop myself from being crushed under the weight of my reality. I looked up to face my family. The emergency room lobby was filled with friends and relatives. Their eyes also wet with tears. Slowly, I made my way over to them.

"Bionca, what the fuck is going on?" Aunt Sharon asked.

Everybody stood behind my aunt. Their faces showed pain, despair, and wanting.

"There's some stuff going on that we tried to keep quiet about," I explained. "We... my mother and myself, felt it was best to not involve anyone here. To kinda keep things in our house only. But I guess things have changed. My brother, Byron, allegedly testified against some heavy hitters in the streets last year or a couple years ago, I'm not sure. So, those heavy hitters put a hit on Byron from jail. That's why he was killed in the barbaric way that he was. Brion and myself wanted answers, and we wanted revenge ..."

"Revenge?" my cousin Della questioned.

I nodded. "In my family ... my immediate family ... we live a certain way. We hold each other sacred in ways that most families don't. We are the protectors of one another. So, when Byron was killed, I told Brion to find out who killed our brother …"

"Did he?" another cousin asked. "Did he find out who it was?"

Again, I nodded. "He did. The streets talk about everything. All you have to do is listen. Brion found out who the person was that killed Byron, then he went after that person. He ambushed the dude. Before somebody asks me how he did that, I won't get into details. Brion found a way to get the dude who killed Byron, and he tried to kill the guy. He was unsuccessful. Now, I'm one hundred percent sure that the dude has figured out that it was Brion who tried to kill him. Somehow, he found out about Byron's memorial service. He had to have known that we'd all be there, especially Brion. He came to Stewart's and killed my little brother."

"Who is the dude?" one of my male cousins asked.

"Does the police know all of this?" Aunt Sharon asked.

"Are anyone of us in danger?" This came from my uncle Craig.

"Nobody else is in danger," I told him.

"Not even you and Brechelle? What about Aunt Barbara?"

Tears came to my eyes and started to fall anew. I paused to gather myself and wipe tears from my eyes. "The doctor just told me that my mother is in bad shape. When she fainted in the parking lot, she hit her head and injured her skull. That did some damage to her brain. They had to do surgery to try to stop the internal bleeding. She's holding on, but not on her own. The doctor says that she … that she might not make it through the next twenty four hours."

A gasp and a scream left my aunt's mouth. That triggered everybody in the crowd. Cries, sobs, and wails could be heard throughout the room.

"Bionca … who is the dude that killed both of my cousins?" my cousin asked again.

"Somebody out of your league, Petey. No offense, but it's true."

"You sleeping on me, cuz," Petey replied.

"It's better that I sleep on you, Petey because this dude won't. I don't need no more family members dying behind this. Besides, I'ma take care of it."

"How?" a couple people said in unison.

"The less y'all know the better."

***

The city morgue was located at the rear of D.C. General Hospital. I walked down the corridor and spotted Ren sitting on a bench alone. Her head was hung over, covered by her hands. As I got closer, I could see that her clothes and hands were still covered in Brion's blood. She looked up as I stood over her. Ren's eyes were bloodshot red. I could see the pain and sorrow etched onto her face. I sat down on the bench beside her.

"The doctor said that my mother might not make it."

Ren's tears started anew and ran down her face. Her make up was already smeared all over her face. She looked scary, almost grotesque, like her face was a mask of some kind displayed in a horror movie.

"I'm sorry…" Ren started but dropped her head again and sobbed violently.

My heart was literally broken in half. My hurt was a deep, dark hurt that I had never experienced before. I felt the tears flowing from my own eyes. I let a while go by before speaking again. "I can't believe this shit. Both of my brothers and possibly my mom. My little sister is on the verge of a nervous breakdown, and she's only nineteen years old. If my mother dies …" The words I had just said registered in my head really hard and stopped me mid-sentence. A part of me couldn't fathom life without Barbara Clark in it. My mother had always been there for us. She was the rock, the glue that held the entire Clark side together. My mother was Big Mama, the matriarch that always made things better for everyone around. Then I realized what was really happening. God was taking my mother from the world as a comfort to her. There was no way that she could go on living after losing both of her sons to a violent death. My mind filled with images of Brion. Images from just days ago, to images of him as a kid, a teenager, a grown man. I saw his smile in my mind, and heard his voice. It literally broke my heart to see the light shine in my baby brother's eyes and know that that light had now been extinguished forever. Suddenly, I got more than angry. My soul was tired of crying. My resolve became sturdy. Sean Branch had to die.

"I have never loved anyone like I loved your brother. Blast was everything to me. I can't go on without him. "

"Ren, don't you ever let me hear you say that stupid shit again. We ain't no weak bitches around here. Not you and I. Blast told me all about your deceptive ass. Looking beautiful, acting all shy and shit, but deep down inside you're a killer. Don't look surprised. Brion told me a lot about you and his love for you. So, I know who you really are. You can go on. You will go on just like me. I just lost both of my brothers and may be about to lose my mother. Do you hear me saying shit like that? No. Why? Because I have a warrior's spirit. Just like you. Do you know that I'm the one who told Brion to go out and find out who killed Crud? That wasn't his idea alone. I was upset and hurt. I was pissed off about somebody cutting off Crud's head. I told Brion to kill everybody involved with Crud's death. I ordered him to do it. And as I sit here telling you this, I just remembered something else I said to Brion. I told him that if he couldn't kill the people involved, I'd find them and kill them. Then, I told him, I was gonna kill him."

"Who, Blast? You told Blast you'd kill him?" Ren asked. I nodded. "In my anger, I said that. Yes, I did."

"And you do know that I would've had to kill you, right?"

"I understand. That's what any real bitch would've done. Get it? Any real bitch who truly loved her man. That's you, Ren. A real bitch. A thorough, ride or die bitch that can never again think about anything that sounds like suicide. Real bitches never take their own lives. They get it how they lived and die how they lived. I made a mistake, Ren. A big one. When Brion told me that the person who killed Crud was Sean Branch, I should've game planned differently, better. Why? Because I knew what Sean Branch was and still is. In my arrogance and selfishness about wanting someone to pay for my brother's death, I forgot one of the cardinal rules of war, of the streets."

"Cardinal rules? What are the cardinal rules?"

"To get rich or die trying. To hold your head even in the face of death. To never tell. To always know your enemy. Brion didn't know his enemy. You didn't know either. Despite you rolling with Brion on the move to kill Sean Branch, neither of you knew the animal that you were dealing with. And I blame myself for that. I told Brion that Sean Branch was dangerous, but I never really told him how to move against a man like that. When you and Brion tried to walk up on Sean Branch, he saw y'all. Being a seasoned killer, he read y'all body language. He peeped the move before it could happen. How? Easily. Because he was trained by the streets to spot the move coming. Most dudes would not have been alarmed by seeing a couple. A man and a woman. I get the reason y'all did it that way. To throw him off, but you and Brion miscalculated. I miscalculated for all the reasons I just stated, I blame myself for my brother being on that cold slab of metal in there, his blood all over you."

"Don't blame yourself, Bionca. Blast knew the risk … I knew the risk. When I pulled that gun and killed those two dudes on Orleans Place and wounded the other one, I knew the risk. When I killed Doo Doo …"

"Wait…who…you killed Doo Doo?" I asked incredulously.

Ren nodded her head. "Yeah. I killed Doo Doo on Half Street. Brion didn't tell you that?"

"No. He told me about Doo Doo's death and what he confessed to, but he didn't tell me you killed Doo Doo. I just assumed that HE did it following my orders. Either way, it's cool as long as he's dead for the role he played in Crud's death."

"Like I was saying though, Bionca, Blast and I both knew the risks. You can't blame yourself just because you ordered Blast to avenge Crud. That didn't mean anything. If you knew Brion Clark like I did, he was going to avenge Crud without you telling him to…"

"I told him a lot of shit. What did he repeat?"

"He repeated what you said when you told him, regardless of what was said, it's a rack of niggas out here who ain't living by the code of silence, and they're still alive. Why was Crud so special that niggas wanted him dead because he told? Just because Miguel said it, doesn't make it so. And even if Crud did tell, he was y'alls rat and nobody had the right to kill him. That's what he kept telling me."

"Damn, I almost forgot I said all of that shit. Even though one of the cardinal rules is that you never tell … I feel like a vicious hypocrite, but so be it. The first law of nature is self-preservation, and in Crud's mind that law trumped the cardinal rule. I don't know. All I know is that my two brothers are dead, and my mother is fighting to live … I think. Despite all that has happened, I can't stop now. We …" I motioned to Ren and pointed at her and then me, "can't stop now."

Ren Tyler reached into her purse and pulled something out. "This is a home pregnancy test. I been feeling funny and realized that I might be pregnant. While we were at the memorial, I left Blast to go to the bathroom. I was in the bathroom taking this test when he … I told Brion to go ahead to the car and I'd meet him there. That's how we separated. I took the test and guess what?"

"What?"

"I left the bathroom excited to tell Blast the news about the test. That's when I heard the gunshots. My heart dropped, and somehow, I knew it was him. I knew that he was gone before I even saw him lying there. I felt him leave me. I felt Blast leave this world."

"You said that you were excited and wanted to tell my brother about the test. What was the result?"

Ren showed me the bright pink plus sign still on the applicator. "It's positive. I wanted to tell Blast that he was going to be a father. I was too late, and now he'll never know." Ren broke down crying again.

"Not true, Ren. he'll know. Brion will be looking in on us from the sky."

Ren wiped the tears from her eyes and then stood up. "That's the first lie you've ever told me, Bionca. I hope you never tell another."

I stood up and faced Ren, befuddled. "What lie did I tell you?"

"The one where you just said that Brion would be looking in on us from the sky. I ain't no religious nut, but one thing I know is that the man I loved, your brother, Brion Jermaine Clark, was no angel and that people like him don't go to heaven. People like him and me, we're destined for hell. So, there's no way for Blast to look down on us unless hell is above us. Sorry, but that's real and you were the one that said we're real bitches, right?"

"Right."

"Well, come on, let's go. We got things to do," Ren said with purpose.

"Things like what?" I asked.

"We have to do our research and get to know our enemy. Our common enemy, Sean Branch. Once we know everything about him, we can kill him. We have to kill him. You agree?"

I nodded, grabbed Ren's bloodstained palm, and walked down the corridor out of the morgue.

Chapter 18

Ren Tyler
Gateway Condominiums
Temple Hills, MD

If pain could be measured in pounds, I felt as if mine weighed a ton. The water in the shower was a little too hot, but I stood under it anyway. I needed to steer away the enormous amount of guilt I felt. At any moment, I could have asked Blast to walk away from the investigation into his brother's death. With the right amount of coaxing and cajoling, I believe he would have listened to me, but I hadn't done that. Instead, I'd been turned on by the thug that flowed in his blood. I'd been enamored by the 7.62 bullets that he loaded into his choppa. The way he demanded respect from his peers was an intoxicated breeze that I never could get out the way of. Everything about Blast had allured me. I was drawn into his magnetism, his charisma, his swag, his fly. I leaned back against the wall as I struggled with the emptiness I felt, the sense of loss. My stomach rumbled. It was as if the fetus growing inside me wanted to remind me of its presence. I allowed myself a fleeting moment to rub my still flat belly. My navel was still pierced. Fingering the jewelry that Blast had bought me, I couldn't let the platinum and diamond encrusted letter 'B' go. I was scared that it was all I had left of Blast besides the baby growing inside of me.

"A life given; a life taken …"

Or was it the other way around? Either way, I could hear Brion telling me that. I'd heard it as I sat on that toilet inside of Stewart's funeral home. I was hearing it yet again. I looked down and saw the platinum hoops pierced into both of my nipples. Also a gift from Blast. I fingered the small hoops. Thoughts of those piercings brought on thoughts of the final piercing. The platinum bar that pierced my clit. It was the only piercing that I had gifted myself. Out of all my piercings, that was the one that Blast most enjoyed. Visions of him fingering, licking, and kissing it flooded my thoughts. Then I realized that Blast would never touch it or me again. Tides of extreme grief hit me, and I collapsed under the weight of it. On my knees in the tub while the shower nozzle sprayed me, I let my tears flow, my cries kind of muffled. I couldn't breathe. I couldn't stand. All I could do was let the misery envelope me. I gave in to the darkness.

***

"Ren! REN! Wake up! Ren! Get the fuck up, girl! Ren!"
I felt my face being smacked and opened my eyes. It took a minute to focus, but finally Bionca's face came into view. Then I felt cold and wet. I was being pulled out of the tub as the cold water assaulted my skin and my senses.
"What happened?"
"Did you fuckin' take something?" Bionca yelled.
"No… take what? No," I replied.
"Don't fuckin' lie to me, Ren! Is it drugs? Coke? Dope? Weed? What made you pass out in the shower?"
I struggled out of Bionca's grasp, grabbed a towel from the toilet seat and wrapped it around myself. "I'm cold."
"I guess you are. All this fuckin' time, I'm thinking your ass is just in here taking long as fuck to wash the blood off and clean your ass and your ass in here passed out. I'm glad

I decided to come in and check on you. Did you try to kill yourself? Let me see your wrists."

Snatching away from Bionca, I braced myself on the toilet and stood up erect.

"Get off me, Bionca. I'm good. I didn't try to kill myself. I collapsed in grief, and I must've blacked out. My heart is hurting. "

"Yours too? My heart is broken in ways you can't imagine, but you gotta hold it together, Ren. Real talk."

"I'ma be okay. I just need time. That's all," I said and led the way into the living room. "Turn the heat up some for me. The thermometer is on the wall over there." I pointed at the thermostat before sitting on the couch and tucking my feet beneath me. The towel now covered the upper half of my body.

Bionca walked over to the love seat across from the sofa I sat on and sat down. She pulled out a laptop and powered it up. "Okay. You've had your moment, and I've had mine while you were in there taking a swim…"

"I wasn't taking a swim."

"Whatever. As I was saying, we've both dried our eyes, so hopefully we can see and think clearly. Now, it's time to get to work."

"Get to work, how?" I asked.

"By using our resources… the internet… to find out everything, and I mean everything we can on Mr. Sean Branch, his family and whoever else that he loves. You with me?"

I needed a drink of hard liquor and some weed, but I had to remind myself about the baby. Brion's child. "I'm with you one hundred percent."

Chapter 19

Quran
Southview Apartments
Oxon Hill, MD.

"What the fuck was so important that it couldn't wait until tomorrow, Tosh? You said that it was a matter of life and death, and we couldn't talk on the phone."

Tosheka opened her apartment door wider without saying a word. I took her silence seriously and walked past her into her spot. "I don't have time for no ..."

"I saw you there."

"You saw me where?"

After looking out of the peephole on her door, Tosheka turned and went to the counter near her kitchen. She picked up a glass with a clear liquid in it and drank it. Something about Tosheka was off. She looked afraid. Her jeans lay in a heap by the couch next to her boots. Her coat lay on the couch next to her purse. Dressed in nothing but a blouse, bra, panties, and socks, she repeated what she'd said earlier, "I saw you there."

I was tired and needed a shower. I wasn't in the mood for Tosheka's shenanigans. Turning to leave, I took two steps before hearing, "At the memorial."

I turned back around. "What did you just say?"

"I saw you, Quran. I was at the memorial for Bionca's brother Byron. The streets call him ..."

"Crud. So, what? Why do I need to know that, Tosh?"

"Because if I saw you, and somebody else might have too. I spotted your truck but thought I was trippin' at first. I looked again and saw you behind the wheel ... watching people. I saw through your tint. I recognized that Sean Branch was with you."

"You saw me and realized that Sean Branch was with me?"

Tosheka nodded. "And don't ask me how I know who he is. I was with you on several occasions over the years when you were on jail calls with him. I had your phone one day when somebody sent a text to you mentioning him needing to talk to you. I'm very observant, Que. I watched the news months ago when he was retried on the murder charge he went in for. I saw, like everybody else in the city saw, that he beat the charges and was released. Your head has been so far stuck up in that bitch ..."

"Don't go there, Tosh. Just stay focused. You were talking about Sean."

"I try to be a good girl, Que. You know that. But I'm always in the clubs, and I got good girlfriends and male friends connected to the streets. I've heard all the rumors about Sean Branch killing shit again. Niggas talking about he out here really murdering shit, cutting off people's heads and shit. Since I already knew how you get down out here, it made sense for you to link up with your man. If I had any doubt about who your man was, Jihad told me that Sean was your man, and how close y'all is. He told me that he just met Sean Branch days ago. Sean Branch has one of them faces that once you see it, you never forget it."

My irritation was growing. I was messing with Tosheka off and on for years, and I never had a conversation about what I do for a living. To hear her stand in front of me and tell what she knew or thought she knows about me unnerved me. I silently cursed Jihad for running his mouth to Tosheka when I specifically told him not to. "What's your point, Tosh? You think you saw me ..."

"I drink a lot, Que, and I smoke a lot of weed but don't make me out to be delusional or retarded. I saw you and Sean at the memorial, but I just kept it moving. I never put two and two together until after Bionca's other brother got killed in the parking lot behind Stewart's. Like an epiphany, it came to me. I had heard that Bionca's brother, Crud, had been killed. Then I heard that somebody cut his head off, but I never thought … I didn't talk to Bionca. We've been friends since elementary school. Sometimes super close, sometimes distant. My … our other friends kept me updated on everything, though. Then a couple days ago, out the blue, Bionca called me. We talked a little about her brother and I gave my condolences. Then she came out the blue and asked me about you."

"Me?" I asked, now even more perturbed. "Fuck she know about me?"

"All she knows is what I told her, which wasn't much. I always bragged about you. Not on no street shit. Just how fine you were. The dick being bomb and how you looked exotic with curly hair and grey eyes. I swear to you, Que, that's all I said to her. I told her your name years ago, when I talked about you. I told her how much I loved your name. How different it was and that it was spelled like the Muslim holy book."

"Your ass talk too fuckin' much."

"Que, I was a woman in love … still am. I talked all my friends to death about you. There was no harmful intent. I swear."

"What did your friend ask you? Tell me exactly what she said."

"We were kinda catching up since we hadn't talked in a while. As a matter of fact, she called the same day that I saw you with your new bitch …"

"Zin. Her name is Zin Tosh. Call her Zin when you refer to her."

Tosheka's face depicted a mask of fury. "I'll call her whatever the fuck I want to. Fuck her, and fuck you, too, Que. Standing here defending the next bitch …"

"Get back to the story, Tosh. what else did Bionca say?"

"I was complaining about niggas out here, thinking about you. She just came out and said, that grey eyed nigga driving your ass crazy, huh? What's his name again? I told her Quran. Then she started talking about she needed somebody like you and this and that. But I found it strange because Bionca is on pussy, hard, but she tries to keep it on the low. In all our years, she has never expressed wanting a man. Then she went on to ask me if you have a brother? I told her that one of your brother's was dead and the other was already taken …"

For reasons unknown to me, I laughed out loud. Then it hit me.

"Fuck is so funny, Que?"

"The fact that you told her that my brother was taken. I bet you didn't tell her that you were the one who took him, did you?"

"Fuck you, Que. that shit ain't funny."

"I think it is. Finish."

"Then she comes out and says, I'll take one of his friends. I heard that Quran be with that fine ass old head nigga that just got outta jail, Sean Branch."

"She said that to you, and you didn't tell me that until now?"

Tosheka turned and went back to the counter. She picked up the bottle of Patron and poured a generous amount into her cup. She turned the cup up and drained the glass.

"Like I told you earlier, I never thought anything strange about it until today. I sat in the car and replayed the conversation only because I saw y'all, and I remembered that Bionca asked me to get you to put her on with Sean Branch. I told her that you'd never do that, and she accepted my answer. When I put it together in my head and figured that

Sean must've killed her brother, Crud, I figured that somehow Bionca must've found out that Sean was the killer. Somebody… and it wasn't me… must've told her about you and Sean. You gotta believe me, Que. It wasn't me, but she knows. Now, since her younger brother was just killed, she's either gonna go to the cops or send somebody after Sean or use you to get to Sean. I'm worried about you. That's why I needed to see you tonight. There was no way that I could go to sleep and not warn you. I love you, Que. With all my heart, I do. It would kill me if something ever happened to you."

My cell phone vibrated, and I could see that the caller was Zin. I ignored the call.

"Damn, you love me like that, huh?"

Tosheka walked over to me and grabbed me. I could smell her perfume, the liquor on her breath, and the scent of her shampooed hair. She kissed my face as she tiptoed. I allowed her to pull me into her body. "Love you more than you will ever know." Tosheka buried her face in my chest. Her hand reached down and unbuttoned my pants. Putting her hand inside my boxer briefs, she gripped my dick and rubbed it, stroked it.

I never said a word in protest. I decided to let her do her thing.

***

Do her thing, she did. I sat in the bathroom and visualized all the freaky shit that Tasheka had done. Shit that she'd never done before. I stood up and washed up in the sink. After getting dressed, I walked into the bedroom. Tosheka was lying in bed basking in an after-sex glow. Her ever-present glass of liquor was in her hand.

"I gotta go, but I wanna thank you for everything. The talk, the sex, all of it. I appreciate you, Tosh. and believe it or not, I love you a lot."

"Don't say that to me, Que."

"Why not?"

"Because it hurts like hell to hear you say that and then watch you leave to go home to another bitch. Don't play with my emotions."

"Says the woman who's fucking my brother to get back at me."

"I'm… I told you already. 'm sorry."

"Sorry? How? You're still fucking him."

"Look, we just had mind blowing, beautiful, wonderful sex. Can we please not talk about Jay?"

"You're right. Anyway, I gotta bounce. I'll call you tomorrow, and we'll meet and figure this shit out. Okay?" I walked closer to the bed.

"Okay, baby," Tosheka said, put her glass on the nightstand and got up. She embraced me. "I love you, Quran. I love you with all my heart."

***

Outside in the car, I thought about everything that Tosheka had said. No matter what I felt, I knew what had to be done. I picked up my cell phone and dialed Tosheka's number.

"Hello? Que? Did you forget something?"

"Yes, I did, Tosh. I left a gun in your bathroom."

"A gun? You left a gun in my bathroom?"

"Yeah, my bad. Go and see if you see it in there?" I instructed.

"Okay." After a brief pause, Tosheka said, "I got it. Come and get it."

"Naw. I'm on the other line with Sean, and I need to finish hollering at him. He needs to know about Bionca Clark and what she said to you."

"Please don't let him kill her, Quran. I'm serious. I can …"

"Ain't nobody gon kill nobody. Just bring me the gun."

"A'ight. I'm putting my clothes on now. I'll be out there in a few minutes."

"Bet, and you do know that I love your good pussy, bow legged ass, don't you?"

"Well, you need to start acting like it then. Bye, boy."

The call ended. I put the phone in my pocket and looked around. Tosheka's building was a side building that faced the parking lot and not the street. It was late, and the parking lot was deserted. I pulled my other gun and attached the suppressor. I walked to the bushes next to the entrance to the building and ducked behind them. The building's door opened minutes later and out stepped Tosheka. Dressed in jeans, flip flops, and a coat, she looked around.

"Where the fuck is this nigga at?" I heard her say. Then she walked down the steps to the pavement. As she approached the sidewalk, her head was on a swivel, looking both ways. I crept up behind her and fired the gun twice. Two bullets to the back of her head. Quickly, I searched her pockets for the gun. I found it and pocketed it. A single tear rolled down my cheek. I ran to my truck and hopped inside. I never thought the day would come that I'd have to kill another person I loved, but it had. I pulled away from the street wiping tears from my eyes.

Chapter 12

Zin

There was something definitely going on with Quran, but I couldn't quite put my finger on it. I tossed my cell phone on the bed and looked again at the email from Jon Zucker.

Please find attached attachments. In the attachments are copies of the three motions I filed for your dad. As I told you when we spoke last, I filed three different motions. One under the Rule 33 section citing newly discovered evidence. One under the 4401 section of the actual innocence Act and lastly the successive but new motion under code 23-110. In each motion, I've asked for an immediate evidentiary hearing. Things are moving along now and should move at a rapid pace since it's three motions and not one. I spoke to your father at length, and he's aware of the filings. I also mailed him copies of each motion. Hope you received the amended affidavit from Maryann Settles. Still curious as to why she changed it to omit Susan Rosenthal. Can't figure out the significance of it. Lastly, I've had several calls from Greg Gamble and have not taken any of them. Hope that you can imagine the smile on my face. Take care.

I was reading the second motion when my phone vibrated. I picked it up and saw that it was Quran. I answered the call. "Hey."

"Hey? That's dry as shit. I should've called earlier, huh?"

"Maybe. What's up? I'm kinda busy."

"Naw, you gon' throw me shade, huh? I was at the hospital with Jay, Zin."

"It's almost eleven o clock, brotha! Visiting hours are over at eight."

"I had to take care of some shit, and it couldn't wait."

"And whatever that was meant you couldn't take my calls?"

"I didn't even have the phone with me. It was in the truck. I was on foot. C'mon, with the bullshit, Zin. you sound like you think I been out here fucking or laying up with another chick."

"You might've been. Shit, I don't know."

"You trippin'. Can I come through or what? I miss you," Quran said.

"Naw, I'm kinda vibing with my new condo. Enjoying my solitude. Maybe tomorrow, brotha."

"Brotha? I get it. I'm brotha, now, huh? You on some bullshit, Zin."

"I'm minding my business, sir. Like I been doing all day. You don't get to duck me all day then fuck me when you feel like it. I told you I'm busy. I got a few things to do myself before going to bed. I'll call you tomorrow."

The call ended letting me know that Quran had hung up.

"Fuck you, Quran Bashir," I muttered to myself as I went back to reading the motions Jon filed.

***

The aromatherapy candle burned and smelled wonderful. Taking a hot bath by candlelight was a small pleasure that I tried to enjoy often. Leaning my head back, I thought about my life. I had accomplished my goal of becoming a sought-after criminal defense attorney. I accomplished my goal of battling Greg Gamble and being an adversary with a winning record against him. I had my own law office and a thriving business. Crime was always committed and defending criminals was profitable. I learned that from Nikki Locks and Jen Wentz. Thoughts of Nikki and Jen brought back thoughts of my ex, Jermaine Mendenhall. I thought about how I had hurt Jermaine so bad that he turned to solace in Jen Wentz's fat, funky ass. I remembered the night I caught my former boss and my boyfriend in our bed together. I smiled to myself as I wondered if the two had actually hooked up after I left him. I thought about how hard I'd fallen for Quran and my decision to be with him. I thought about all the times I'd lain with Quran, held him, sexed him, talked to him, and kissed him never knowing that he was my enemy. I thought about my father and my desire to bring him home since I was a little girl. I thought about all the days and nights, I'd cried for him, missed him, visited him, defended him, talked to him, and never had a clue that he was responsible for my mother's death.

"Say their names," a voice in my head said.

"Michael Carter. Quran Bashir. Dontay Samuels," I said aloud with my eyes closed.

"Michael Carter. Quran Bashir. Dontay Samuels."

Dontay Samuels was dead. But killed by who? And why? And why had Greg Gamble set up my father to take the beef for killing Dontay? What was the connection between them? I had always thought that Greg Gamble had made his name on the backs of people like my father and there was nothing personal about it. Now, I knew different.

The questions in my head wouldn't leave. I'd asked myself the same things over and over again. Then something hit me. The second witness, Thomas Turner. Where was he? If I could find him, maybe he could answer some of my questions. I thought about Dontay Samuels's family. Was his mother still alive? If so, would she talk to me about her son? I thought about my Aunt Linda and if she knew anything. Mind totally befogged with questions, desire for revenge and strategy, I got out of the tub. I blew out the candle and went to the hall closet. I had yet to move all my things into the condo on Maine Street in Southwest, but I did have the most important thing; It was the box with my mother's things in it and the letter. Walking naked through the condo, I turned up the heat. Then I went to the closet and pulled out the box. I pulled out my mother's letter and read it again for the one hundredth time. As always, the letter brought me to tears. The memories of my mother and her voice in my head always overwhelmed me. Then a thought hit me. What if I'm pregnant? I'd be carrying the seed of the man who killed my mother. I tried to put that thought out of my head.

"Stick to the script, Zin!" my inner voice reminded me. "Even if you are pregnant. That doesn't change what has to be done. Guard your emotions. Continue to do like you been doing and enjoy yourself until Quran's time comes. Do it for yourself. Do it for your mother!"

Chapter 21

Greg Gamble
United States Attorney's Office

"Have you heard the latest news?" Susan Rosenthal asked as she walked into the office. "Councilman Allen Charles has come out against the new crime bill. He's advocating for the mayor's veto and guaranteeing that the city council won't override her veto."

I looked up from what I was reading. "That's good news. Did you get the electronic copies of the three motions Jonathan Zucker filed on behalf of Michael Carter?"

"I did, but I haven't had the chance to read them yet. I've been preparing for the Jaydon Beauvis murder trial."

"Well, there's an interesting wrinkle in the situation, baffing actually. Jon Zucker submitted an affidavit with all three motions, but it's not the same motion that we had recently. The new affidavit mirrors the old one … except for one thing. Maryann Settles took your name out of the affidavit. Now, it only says that I paid her and coerced her to lie on Michael Carter." I looked at Susan Rosenthal with accusing eyes. "Why do you think she did that? Omitted your name?"

"How the hell would I know? I'm not psychic. Did she really do that?"

"She did," I affirmed and leaned forward. "And I must say that I underestimate you, Susan. I thought you were a guppie and all the time, you're a shark." I clapped my hands together loudly. "Bravo. Bravo. You played me like a fiddle. You met with Maryann Settles and convinced her to leave you out of the fray. Instead of looking out for the both of us, you covered your own ass. CYOA. Smart. Real smart. That was a play that I didn't see coming."

"You're crazy, and delusional," Susan scoffed. "Any bad publicity or inappropriate acts proven or not proven against you, affects me and this whole office. There's no such thing as plausible deniability here. One bad apple spoils the whole bunch, remember? You're being paranoid, Greg. And paranoid doesn't become you."

"Cat's paw. Do you know what a cat's paw is, Susan?"

"A person being used by another as a tool. Of course, I know what a cat's paw is. Why is that relevant right now?"

I laughed despite my vexation. "Because I really don't know who's the cat's paw right now. You or me."

"And I think you've lost your mind. Old age doesn't agree with you."

"Don't be factitious, Susan. I'm only forty five. In any event, whose side you're on doesn't really matter. Because like all great magicians, I have other tricks up my sleeve."

"Do you?"

"Of course. Just stay tuned, Susan. You'll see."

***

The crisp, cold air smacked me in the face when I stepped out of the building. The sun shined bright in the sky but did nothing to warm me. I zipped up my coat and walked to the vending stand near the subway station. Grabbing a bag of pretzels and chewing gum, I made my way to the Municipal Building. Minutes later I was sitting across from a detective friend of mine, Bob Mathis.

"You gave the names of a few guys that we needed to keep eyes on. Well, I've got info on a couple of them. All investigations are in early stages, but we might be able to get a few of these guys," Bob gloated. "Especially Sean Branch."

Opening the bag of pretzels, I popped one in my mouth. "Tell me what you have, Bob. Everything."

"Jihad Bashir is in the hospital as we speak recovering from gunshot wounds. We have some video footage that might place him at the scene of a gunfight where one man died at the scene. Another died at an area hospital …"

"Video footage that might place him at the scene?"

"Yeah, it's a little grainy, but we believe it's him. He got dropped off at the hospital by someone. We're not sure who, but we think it was his brother, Quran Bashir, another one of the names you gave us. But like I said, all the investigations are still early. It's more of the same with Casper Vargas, the MS-13 leader from Petworth. He's been linked to murders in Maryland and Virginia, but nothing here in the District. Now … our guy, Sean Branch is a little different. He's in rarified air. We have a confidential informant named Maurice 'Moe' Best who tells us that Sean Branch is back up to his old tricks. Killing. He's allegedly behind a lot of the murders we've been seeing in the area since his release."

"According to Moe Best, Sean is settling old scores and taking new contracts to kill people. All the people we've found recently with their heads cut off …"

"Get the fuck out of here, Bob! Sean Branch is …"

"Responsible for everyone. Or so we're being told. But again, nothing has been confirmed."

"Set me up a meeting with Mr. Best, please."

***

Carl H. Moultrie Superior Courthouse

"And for some reason, the circuit sought… I'll just read it," Judge Anwar Mehta said from the bench. "The government also admitted evidence showing that Ronald Alford had been convicted on firearm charges in 2001 and

2004. As related to the 2004 charge, the government's theory is that Alford had told his probation officer that he was carrying a gun to protect himself because of several robberies at his place of business. The government then argued that those robberies were linked to Alford's feud with someone who was deceased. From that, the government surmised that the evidence of the 2004 firearms charge would somehow explain his motive for having some people murdered. The next paragraph, the explanation for admitting to the 2001 firearm charge, fares even worse. It is hard to even discern what the government's theory of admissibility is. The government simply wraps the charge up with discussion of a '98, '99 arrest where a kilogram of cocaine was found. Beyond that the government makes no effort to link the firearm charged with Alford being an alleged drug supplier in 2001, much less four years later when he was alleged to have been a part of any gun conspiracy. So, both counsels need to marinate on that, and we can take this up again early next week."

"Your honor, and just so the court is clear," Ian McNealy said, "the firearm in the current case against Angelo Pickens … the prior firearm is 404 (b) and has been admitted only to show knowledge of firearms."

"I know that, Mr. McNealy, and I will say that this may become a balancing issue later on. There are text messages and photos of guns and talk of guns involving Angelo Pickens. So, that does raise questions in my mind about the need for prior convictions, given how old they are even if the purpose is for proving knowledge and intent."

"And I would take the opposite position, your honor. McGill negates any kind of staleness. The circuit court has ruled on that. The government asking that Mr. Pickens past firearm convictions to be admitted at trial shows his knowledge of firearms and familiarity and accessibility to them. And I would also note…"

In between listening to the proceedings in the courtroom and rethinking my strategy, I scrolled through the crime watch DC website. Daily posts about crime and suspects were always good information. And like I'd told Allen Charles, information ... dirt on important people was like gold in Washington. And I was rich with it. Smiling to myself, I thought about the conniving bitch, Susan Rosenthal. Whatever she'd said to Maryann Settles to convince her to retract her statements about her was a boss move. It was machiavellian. The fact that Susan held the second highest rank at Triple Nickel wasn't lost on me. With me damaged, broken, tarnished and out the way, she was next in line to be King, or should I say Queen? I thought about the powerful underworld connections Susan had. Getting ultimate power to influence cases, or lack thereof, would be beneficial to her criminal friends. So, her next play was to remove the king from the board. Gutsy, yet a little premature. I promised myself that I'd teach Susan Rosenthal the lesson of life this time. Because when you live in a glass house, you should never throw stones. Something that my brother Lonnell told me before he was killed came to mind.

"Always be aware of the three crosses. The double cross, the triple cross and the holy cross. "

Something I'd seen online also came to mind suddenly. Be careful of the snake with no hiss. They call you, bae, brother, and friend. Getting up and leaving the courtroom, I made a necessary call.

Donovan Olsen answered on the second ring, "Hello?"

"Hey, it's me again. I got all the info you sent me on Christopher and Maryann Settles. Now, I need you to dig up whatever you can find on Thomas Turner also known as TT. He probably changed his name and left the area, but whatever you can find on him, I need it. Check your account."

"I'm on it," Donovan said and ended the call.

I was out in the hallway about to make a second call when Ian McNealy walked up to me.

"Bossman, I saw you in there. Were you checking up on me or do you need to see me really bad, and it couldn't wait until I was back at the office?"

Pocketing my cell phone, I turned to Ian and said, "That stuff that you said you have on Susan Rosenthal, do you still have it?!"

"Of course, I do. Why?"

"Come on, Ian, let's walk and talk. I have a proposition for you."

Chapter 22

Quran
DC Wharf
Southwest, D.C.

"Gimme two dozen clams and two dozen oysters," Sean told the white man on the boat docked at The Wharf. "I need three dozen steamed shrimp, three pounds of whiting, descaled, and beheaded. I like my fish with no heads."

I laughed at Sean's inside joke. "There's a lot of shit you like with no head."

"Tell me what happened again, and don't leave out anything."

"Tosheka called me and told me that she needed to see me to talk to me about something important. A matter of life and death. Said it couldn't wait. I went to her spot, and she told me that she saw me and you in my truck at the memorial. She said something about hearing that you'd been cutting people's heads off in the streets but never put it together that it was you who killed her friend's brother until after the other brother got smoked. She connected us to that smoking. I don't know if she told that dude's sister or family that either of us was there. She said that her friend, Crud's sister, Bionca called her out the blue and asked about me and you ..."

"Before yesterday?"

I nodded. "Yeah, before yesterday. But that ain't hard to believe because if Crud's brother killed Doo Doo and found out that you killed Crud, that made him use to the phone to attempt to get you. Once that failed, I can see the sister, who has to be in on it, calling around trying to find you. Here's the thing though. Doo Doo must've mentioned both of us. The sister, Bionca, knew Tosheka. According to Tosheka, she'd bragged about me being a grey eyed exotic."

Sean smiled. "Those were her words? Grey eyed exotic?"

I smiled back. "Don't hate, slim, because all the bitches be on my line. These grey eyes done got me so much pussy in my life. And the ones that don't care about the eyes love the hair, bruh. Trust me."

"I already know. My shit is like yours. Finish the story."

"Tosheka had bragged to Bionca about me. Told her my name and all that other shit. Evidently, she remembered it."

"So, how did our association come into play? How does your girl know me?"

"Jihad told her that you and I are friends. That's it. Dumb ass nigga. Tosheka said that she overheard me talking to you on occasion while you were still in. but according to her, she never said anything to Bionca about me and you. All she talked about to her was me."

The white man who worked on the boat reappeared with Sean's order in his hands. He passed Sean four plastic bags. "That'll be a hundred and twenty-five dollars, sir."

Sean passed the man a hundred-dollar bill and three twenty-dollar bills.

"Wait a sec, I'll get your..."

"Keep it," Sean replied and handed me two of the bags. He turned and walked through a labyrinth of people eager to get fresh seafood from The Wharf. Once we were back near our cars, Sean asked, "Shorty said she wanted to warn you and that it was a matter of life and death. Whose? And how did she come to that conclusion?"

I shrugged my shoulders. "I have no clue, but obviously she felt that my life may be in danger."

"The woman was your boo for years until Mike Carter's daughter came on the scene. Mad that you ditched her for another woman, she fucked your brother Jihad. She still loves you, so she called you to warn you that your name is involved in some shit where she witnessed you at the scene and for all her troubles, you killed her?" Smiling, Sean shook his head. "You are a ruthless, heartless animal, youngin'. You been around me too long."

"Although her intentions were good, ock, she was a liability. She saw too much. Knew too much. And under pressure, she might've been forced to try and get me somewhere for somebody. I had to do it. You know the rules."

"I do know the rules. I taught them to you. Well, Ameen, your father, taught me. He taught us both. You did the right thing, young boy Que. I'm proud of you. It's not easy killing somebody you love."

"I killed my own brother, big bruh. Killing her was easy."

"Okay, you're right, but I still wonder if you really killed her because of what she could possibly become in the future, or did you kill her because she fucked Jihad?"

***

United Medical Center
Southern Avenue, S.E

I stood by the bed and tried to read the emotion on my brother's face. I could not. So, finally, I broke the silence in the room. "You just gon' lay there and not say shit, huh?"

"What do you want me to say, Que? Tosheka wasn't my girl. Her heart belonged to you. You felt that she was a threat, so you took her life. That's what you do, right? Anybody who's a threat to you, you get rid of them. I saw this movie before, so I ain't gotta wait until the credits roll to know who starred in it."

"Fuck that's supposed to mean, Jay?"

"No matter what Tosheka said or did, I know that eventually you'd label her enemy ..."

"Label her enemy? What for? Because she gave you the pussy? Is that what you think, Jay? You think I crushed Tosheka because of her being with you?"

"I don't know what to think. Pay me no mind. I'm on medication, remember?"

With my left hand I tapped the left side my chest where my heart was. "Damn, bruh. Is that how you really feel about me? That's what you think about me?"

"Tosheka betrayed you when she started fucking with me …"

"Betrayed me? Betrayed me, how? She wasn't my woman. I told you that I didn't give two fucks about her getting with you, and I meant that. Why would I lie to you about that?"

Jihad lay in the bed and closed his eyes.

"Check this out, slim. You mentioned Sean to Tosheka. She told me that you told her you met Sean days ago, and me and Sean was close. So, basically you did exactly what I told you not to do, pillow talk. Tosheka put everything else together based on what you told her. If you would've kept your fuckin' mouth shut …"

"I should've kept my mouth shut…" Jihad repeated sarcastically. "So, does that make me a threat, too? You gon kill me too?"

Jihad was pissing me off to the highest degree of pissitivity. "Slim, you been acting like a real bitch lately. Fuck is up with you? Do I need to be worried about you, Jay?"

"A bitch, huh?" Jihad laughed. "You wild as shit, big bruh."

"I'm wild! I'm wild! Nigga, you been on some emotional shit every since … ever since I killed Tabu. you actin' like you got over that shit, but you really haven't. Be a man and admit it. Man up, and tell me that you still feel some kind of way about what I did to …"

"I admit it! I fuckin' admit it, nigga. Fuck! I'ma always feel some kinda way about what you did to Tab. I thought I could forget it, but I can't. I thought I could forgive you, but I can't!" Tears formed in Jihad's eyes and fell. I can't get it out of my system."

"Let me ask you a question, slim. The lifestyle you live … I mean, all the whips, clothes, shoes, money you spend … where does all that come from?"

"From the work that I… that we put in."

"From the work that we put in," I repeated, trying to remain calm. "And the work we put in is against who?"

"Rats. Human rats."

"And what was Tab? What was he?"

"A rat," Jihad mumbled.

"Naw, nigga, speak up. What was Tabu?"

"A rat! He was a rat. But…"

"See, that's where you go wrong at, Jay. There ain't no buts! None! Ain't no such thing as a halfway crook. All that he was a rat, but he was my brother shit, I ain't tryna hear that shit. I told your ass months ago, after you buried Tabu, that I wasn't tryna hear nothing else about this shit. You have forgotten the words of our father, Jay. Remember when he said, Boys fight to win or lose. Men fight to live or die. Always strike first in war. As teenagers or men, no matter who it is …"

"Friend, brother, or foe…"

"Crush those who seek to harm you. Never waiver and never show mercy."

"I remember what pop said. I remember everything he said. I don't agree with what you did to Tabu, but I understand that it had to be done. He crossed us, he crossed Dave, he crossed the code. But let me ask you this. Who did Tosheka cross if not you, by fucking me? She wasn't a rat. You say you killed her because she could have become a threat, but what if she wouldn't have? Then you killed her unjustly."

Jihad's words stabbed at my heart strings, and I couldn't bring myself to admit that part of the reason I killed Tosheka was for her betrayal.

"Maybe, maybe not. I can't undo what I've already done. My gut told me to do what I did, and that's how I've managed to stay alive for all these years, Jay. I'm not going to apologize for the things I've done, the decisions I've made. It is what it is. You inherited a killer instinct from pop, but you also inherited too many emotions from our mother. I'm starting to feel like I can't trust you,Jay. You're making rookie mistakes, impromptu decisions. You're harboring ill will, and you're hard headed. I would never do anything to hurt you as long as you don't force me to by breaking the rules. The rules that can't be broken. I'm severing ties with you, Jay. I love you, but I can't fuck with you as my partner no more. I'm out."

I turned around and walked away. I could hear Jihad calling my name as I retreated, but I couldn't stop. I couldn't turn back. I couldn't let him see the tears in my eyes.

Chapter 23

Jihad

"Q - Quran! Que ... comeback!"

The nurse rushed into the room. She was a pretty, young Somalian exchange student studying medicine in America. "Mr. Bashir, are you okay? Are you in pain?"

The pain I felt, medicine couldn't fix. "I'm good, just leave me alone," I replied and turned over to face the wall.

Before I knew it, my eyes were full of tears. I cried without making a sound. I cried and really didn't know why I cried. Who were my tears for? A brother that I felt as if I was losing? The brother that I had already lost? My best friend, Bo, who died because of a bad decision that I had made? Or were my tears really for Tosheka? The woman I had grown to really like? Did my tears have to be for one of them? Or could they be for all of them? I asked myself those questions, but no answers came. The throbbing pain in my gut mirrored the one in my heart. My whole life was unraveling right before my very eyes. Pain and death were like a companion that walked with me everywhere. I thought about what Quran had said to me moments ago ...

"Slim, you been acting like a real bitch lately. Fuck is up with you? Do I need to be worried about you, Jay?"

As I wiped the tears from my eyes and cheeks something else Quran said hit me deep ...

"You inherited a killer instinct from pop, but you also inherited too many emotions from our mother ..."

Had he said that because I admitted that I couldn't get past what he'd done to our brother Khitab? Or was my questioning him about Tosheka the cause for him to declare me untrustworthy and too emotional? Maybe what I'd tried to conceal had been revealed in my voice, in my eyes. I couldn't stop thinking about Bo and Tosheka. I could hear her laughter in my head. Bo's too. The fact that I would never hear either of those laughs again hurt me deeply. That realization settled over me like a dark cloud and hovered. My heart rate quickened, and I felt like I couldn't breathe momentarily. I quickly turned over onto my back and stared at the ceiling, willing myself to relax, to just breathe. Breathe … breathe …

***

The next afternoon
"D.C. police are still investigating several homicides that have taken place in the last seven days. A shootout in a parking lot of a local market left two people dead. In other news, Prince George's County police are asking for the public's help in locating the person responsible for the shooting death of thirty one year old, Tosheka Jennings. Ms. Jenkins was shot in the head outside of the apartment building where she lived in the 2400 block of Iverson Street in Oxon Hill."

Just as I clicked off the TV in the room, the same two detectives that had visited me three times since being admitted at UMC walked in. One was black and one was white. Both men approached my bed.

"Good afternoon, Mr. Bashir," the white detective said. "This is just a follow up visit, and I need to ask you a few more questions."

"What's up?" I replied.

"You said that there was an altercation in the Bliss Nightclub parking lot that led to you being shot, correct?"

"That's what I said."

"And you alleged that you were ambushed and shot a block or so away from Bliss, correct?"

"I think so. Yeah."

"You think so? So, you aren't sure?"

"I don't remember all the details."

"You don't remember the details, huh? Okay. Were you alone or with someone as you left the club?"

"Alone? I was alone."

The white detective turned to his partner. "Math, did you get that? He was alone."

"I got it, Phil," the black detective answered.

The white detective pulled out a radio. "Bill, send them in, please."

The hospital room door opened and in walked three metropolitan police officers. One walked right up to the bed and said, "Jihad Bashir, you are under arrest for murder, accessory to murder and possession of a firearm during a crime of violence. You have the right to remain silent ..."

***

Violent Crimes Division
Pennsylvania and Branch Avenues

Things happened so fast that they made my head spin. I was released from the hospital in a hospital gown and nothing else but footies. Doctors at UMC had prescribed me 5mg Percocet for pain and turned me over to the cops. In a small room at VCD, I sat with my head resting on the table. All I could do was shake my head.

After about an hour alone, the door to the small room opened and in walked a man I'd never seen before. He was black, well dressed, and resembled someone on TV. In the man's hand was a bag. The bag contained food that smelled delicious. My stomach growled despite my stoic disposition. The man sat across from me.

"That hospital food is terrible, so I took the liberty of getting you something better. Ms. Debbie's Soul food and Seafood Cafe has the best greens and macaroni and cheese in the city. Since your last name is Bashir, I took the liberty of having these greens made with smoked turkey, instead of pork. Didn't really know your preferred choice of meat, so I got you fried fish. Whiting of course, so you wouldn't be bothered by bones in the fish."

The man took all the carry out containers out of the bag and placed them in front of me. He sat a plastic fork down and then said, "I forgot your beverage. Hope you like raspberry iced tea and lemonade mixed. I'll be right back. Go ahead and dig in. Enjoy."

Staring at the food, I tried to resist it, but I couldn't. I picked up the plastic fork and dug in. Minutes later, the man returned with the beverage. I picked it up and sipped it until my thirst was quenched.

"Food is good, huh?" the man asked.

I nodded. "Why are you being nice to me?"

"Because I think we can help each other, Jihad. You don't have to say a word unless you want to. I hope that you want to. So, I'll start this talk off. I'll speak and then you can speak if you want to. Okay?"

I nodded again but kept eating.

"I know that the story that you told the detectives is bullshit. They know it, too. That's why you've been arrested. Bole Ndugu is an associate of yours. He hangs in the Sheridan Terrace area with you. We have video footage from the Bliss Nightclub of the two of you exiting the club together. Then you entered a dark colored new model Buick and left."

He continued, "Somehow for some reason, you and Bole end up at the Benco Market at East Capitol and Benning. A shootout ensues. Bole Ndugu is shot and killed. Another man is shot and later dies. You got shot in that parking lot but left it on foot and ended up at UMC. It's only a matter of time before we find the Buick you left parked somewhere near the hospital. Even if we don't get the Buick, we have you on video at the Benco Market firing a gun alongside Bole Ndugu. And the best part is the bullet fragments removed from your body match the bullet fragments removed from Bole Ndugu's corpse. So, we know you were there at Benco Market that night, Jihad, and we know you fired a gun. Whether it was your gun or Bole Ndugu's gun that killed the other victim is still a mystery. Why? Because we don't have your gun to test. But just like the Buick, we'll find it, Jihad. And when we do, if you haven't talked to me and helped me in any way, you'll go to prison for about forty years. Maybe more. Why? Because I'm gonna make sure that you get convicted not just for the second victim's murder. I'm gonna make you pay for Bole Ndugu's murder. I can do that, you know. So, what's it gonna be, Jihad? Do we talk or not?"

"Talk? Who the fuck are you?" I asked.

The man smiled. "Oh, my bad. I thought I introduced myself already. I'm United States Attorney Gregory Gamble."

Chapter 24

Quran
One Week Later ...
Copper Canyon Grill
Woodmore Town Center
Largo, MD.

Exiting the truck, I spotted the black jeep Cherokee that Sean was in and walked over. I opened the passenger side door and slid into the passenger seat. "Assalamu Alaikum."

"Walaikum assalam," Sean said, returning the greeting. "What's up with lil bruh? Have you talked to him?"

"Naw, but I sent Zin to see him. He's charged with one count of first degree murder, one count of second degree murder, accessory after the fact and carrying a firearm during a crime of violence. He's being held without bond at the CTF facility because of his medical status. He got Charles Daum appointed to him by the court ..."

"Charles Daum? Slim is a beast on body cases."

"But some shit at everything else. Barring a conflict of interest, I'ma gets Zin to represent him. She talked to Charles Daum, and he said that their case as it stands is weak as fuck. Grainy video footage from both Bliss and Benco Market. They don't have no car, no gun, no motive, nothing. All they have is the bullet that matched between Jihad and Bo, showing that they were both shot at the Benco. As far as I know, there're no witnesses. The bitch nigga, Greg Gamble is behind that shit. He went to see Jihad at the VCD when he first got transported there from the hospital. According to Zin, Daum said, Gamble tried his usual I am the only one who can help you spiel. Lil bruh ain't go for that shit. Gamble gon' make me roast his ass, ock. Real live. That's a conversation for a later date. Right now, here's what's happening."

Sean Branch said with conviction, "Baby E is in that restaurant. Him, Silk, Derrick Hill, Rodney Shaw and two bitches. One bitch is with Baby E. She's driving that silver Mercedes S550 parked over there." Sean pointed to the car to our left in a row of other cars. "The other bitch is driving that Lexus SUV over there parked between the Kia Sorrento and the BMW truck. Derrick Hill and Silk are riding with her. Rodney came here in his Range Rover parked near the Benz. He's gonna eat and leave. Act like something important came up. We should see him bounce and then later everybody else will come out. You focus on Baby E, and I got Derrick Hill and Silk."

"You know Maryland still got the death penalty, right? This is my beef, not yours. You can still …"

"I can still what, youngin'? Leave?" Sean laughed a demonic laugh. He turned to face me. "I'ma act like you didn't just say that, Que. Again … you focus on getting Baby E, and I got Derrick and Silk."

Nodding, I looked at my G-Shock watch. It was 8:21 pm. The night was cold, and the sky was dark, but the parking lot was well lit. It was as good a night as any for killing. "Three murders or five?"

Sean's eyes were trained on the entrance to Copper Canyon Grill. "What?"

"Are we doing three murders or five?" I repeated.

"Three murders or five? Oh … you're asking if we're killing the bitches."

I nodded as I screwed a sound suppresser onto both of my handguns.

"Depends, youngin'. If the bitches get in the way, they're targets. If they get out the way, they live."

"Cool," I said and zipped up my black Moncler bubble vest to my neck. Underneath the rest, I wore a thick, black Hugo Boss sweatshirt. On my head was a Moncler skully pulled all the way down past my ears. Hugo Boss cotton jogger sweats and black Foamposite boots finished off my outfit. Beside me in the Jeep's driver's seat, Sean was dressed almost identical to me. No other words were passed between me and Sean. The silence in the Jeep was loud. Almost too loud.

"Any luck on finding Crud's sister? Do you think that she was the one with the brother when they ambushed you?"

"No and no. Can't find her or her family, but I will, and I'ma crush them all. The bitch that was with Crud's brother the day they brought me a move, wasn't his sister. It was his woman."

Sean pulled out his cell phone, pulled up something on the screen and passed me the phone. I looked at the picture on the phone. "That's the sister right there. Bionca Clark. They got another sister named Brechelle. She's about my daughter's age, but fuck it, she gotta go, too. I got that picture off Facebook. Swipe to the left."

I did as Sean commanded and swiped the picture to the left. Another picture appeared on the phone.

"That's the brother that I smoked, Brion Clark. The streets called him Blast. Now they call him dead," Sean said and laughed at his own joke. Swipe again. "That's him again with his bitch. That's the bitch that was with him that night on Naylor Road."

"Damn, shorty a killer, huh? She's a bad muthafucka. Pretty as shit," I commented.

"I know, right? It's a goddamn shame that I'ma have to smoke her ass. In the comments on Facebook, people called her Ren. so, I'm on Ren's ass. She was at the memorial with the brother. They rode there together. I saw them both go inside the funeral home, but for some reason, she didn't leave with him. He left alone, and she stayed behind. That in itself saved her life, and she don't even know it. I searched all over social media sites for someone named Ren. A rack of broads came up, but none was her."

"Maybe Ren ain't her name. It's probably short for Dorenda, Lavonda, or Myrenda. Renee, Reniqua and some shit like that. It could be a nickname or something. It's obvious that somebody has been teaching you about social media and the internet. That's a good look, but tell them to make you a Facebook and an Instagram page…"

"What? Are you nuts? How the fuck…"

Laughing, I said, "Not one in your name, bruh. In somebody else's name. An alias, anything. Then you do friend requests for everybody on the sister's page and the sister. That's how you keep up with them. You troll them, old head. Follow them on the 'Gram' and watch all their live posts if they ever go live. Most people can't resist going live. Go to the comments and subtly ask about Ren. Make up something about her being your long lost cousin. Anything. People will get on them social sites and reveal everything. You'd be surprised what you can find out."

"Nothing surprises me nowadays… Hold up! That's Rodney right there leaving…" Sean's words were cut off by the sound of his cell phone vibrating.

He answered the call. "Yeah… I'm here. I see you leaving the spot now. They still eating? A'ight. A'ight. Good looking, big boy. I'ma holla at you tomorrow. Bet. bet." Sean disconnected the call. "He said they are still eating but should be leaving shortly. The nigga Silk is walking with the help of a cane. He's the one that got hit that night at Benco's. So, him and Derrick should be easy to spot. You know what Baby E looks like, right?"

I nodded.

"Good. Let's go, then. We gon' wait for them outside. You by the Mercedes, I'm at the Lex truck. Let's go."

***

As I crouched down beside the car next to Baby E's Mercedes, I thought about one of my favorite movies, *Dead Presidents*. The scene when N'bushe Wright was crouched inside the trash dumpster with the two bangers upheld flooded my mind. I smiled as I let the entire scene play in my head. From where I was, I would rise periodically to see if my victim was coming or not. On about my tenth rise, I spotted a crowd of people leaving the Copper Canyon Grill. Three men. Two women. One man was walking with the aid of a cane.

"For my brother and for Bo," I mouthed to myself as I measured their distance.

The man I recognized to be the notorious rat named Baby E, and one female separated from the rest as they approached the Benz. The woman separated from Baby E as she headed towards the driver's side of the Benz. I moved swiftly around the cars until I came right out on Baby E. He looked at me. Our eyes locked. In his eyes I saw confusion, surprise, fear. In mine, he saw death. I quickly raised the gun and fired. The sound was a little more than a loud cough. Baby E's body dropped. I ran up on him immediately and put two forty bullets in his head. I could hear the woman scream. I pointed my second gun at her and fired inside the car. I could hear the unmistakable sound of suppressed gunshots nearby and knew that Sean was at work. By the time I made it back to the Jeep, Sean was just getting there. We both hopped into the Jeep and Sean pulled off. Mission complete.

***

"One down, two more to go," I said into my cell phone.
"Which one?" Mike Carter asked.
"The baby from Clay Terrace."

"Cool. I'll check for the news clip later. I remember that you said you were having problems getting the other two. One I can help with, the other I can't."

"Bet. Indeed, I need all the assistance I can get on those last two. Sean had to help me get the last one."

"Sean Branch helped you?"

"Yeah, got one of his men to throw the baby off the backboard for an alley oop. There was collateral damage, but that's how life is sometimes. We cooked everything and then bounced. Why do you ask that? About Sean? You already know what's up with me and big bruh."

"Just asked, youngin', damn. I didn't think that the two of you were still working together like that. I figured that he was chilling after all the shit he did when he first got out."

"What the fuck is up with y'all two? Is there bad blood between you?" I asked Mike.

"Not that I'm aware of. Did he say there was bad blood between us?"

"Naw, but it's obvious to me that y'all still haven't spoken. Sean been home almost three months now. I gave him your number like three or four times. He told me that he was gonna holla at you but never did. That in itself tells me that something ain't right between y'all. How the fuck is he gonna be closer to me then you? You introduced us. There's something between y'all that y'all ain't telling me."

"I haven't talked to Sean in almost nineteen years. If there's an issue between us, he had the problem, not me. But anyway, this conversation about Sean is becoming too long. Whatever it is … it is what it is. I ain't about to lose no sleep because Sean Branch ain't tryna talk to me. Fuck him. Like I was saying, I can help you out with one of the two, and that's Kendra. Jojo Morris is yours to find. A good young nigga just left here and went home. Got out on the IRAA joint. His name is Andy, but the streets call him Scambino. I'ma text you his number. Call him. He's already hip to what's what. He wanted to take the hit, but I told him that it was already taken. He's from Sursum Cordas and knows both rats. He's been home about two weeks. He hasn't seen Jojo at all, but he's seen Kendra several times. He says that she's in the hood every day just not always visible. Well, I sent some bread his way, and he's gonna make her visible for you."

"That's what's up," I replied and went on to tell Mike about Jihad.

"Sorry to hear that, youngin', but it ain't that bad. Grainy video footage is beatable all day. Ain't no witnesses, and if any do pop up …"

"You already know."

"Where did you say he is?"

"CTF. Because of his medical situation."

"You trust him?" Mike asked.

"With my life."

"Be careful, youngin'. I remember you said that about Dontay. What lawyer does he have?!"

"Charles Daum, but I'm thinking about getting him somebody better. Somebody like Brian McDaniels," I lied.

"He's good, I hear, but Charles Daum is good at bodies too. Did the courts appoint him or you…"

"Courts appointed him CJA. I'ma figure it out."

"Why don't you get Zin to take his case? She could blow up from it."

"Zin? Who, your daughter, Zin?"

"Naw, nigga, the bottle of wine that she's named after. Of course, I'm talking about my daughter. Give her a call. You got her number?"

"Who, me? Got your daughter's number? Naw. why would I have your daughter's number?"

"No reason. I just thought that y'all might see each other …"

"Where? In the streets? Naw, big homie. I ain't seen Zin since I dropped off the money for Dave's case. Text me her number though."

"Done. I'ma text her number and Andy's number. Let me get off this jack before they count. Find Jojo Morris."

"I will. You take care, big homie. One love."

"A'ight. Same here. Peace."

***

The inside of Zin's condo smelled like potpourri and fried chicken. Zin, dressed in nothing but a t-shirt and panties, stood on a chair and hung a painting of Michelle Obama on the wall.

"What the fuck is up with you, Zin? You been acting funny as shit lately."

"How so, Quran?" Zin replied and climbed down off the chair. "We been fucking, right?"

"Yeah, and that's the problem. Ever since that day on Howard Road ..."

"The day that I was about to get all over your side bitch?"

"Ex, Tosheka was my ex. Normally, she wouldn't have done no confrontational shit like that. I don't know what got into her, but I don't give two fucks about her. Real talk. We been fucking, but things don't feel the same. I hate to sound gay, but we was making love before that day. Now, all we do is fuck. You don't chill at my spot no more ..."

"Quran, I got my own spot now. I like to chill here. Have I ever stopped you from chilling here with me? You be out in the streets doing you, and I be working. I got a business to run; if you haven't noticed. And I'm trying to get my father out of prison. I'm sorry that your fragile male ego is under attack by your emotional side right now."

"Emotional side?" I repeated and laughed. I had to laugh.

"What? What did I say that was so funny?"

"Nothing, it's crazy, though. Last week when I was at the hospital seeing Jay, the day before they took him to jail, I told him that he was being too emotional. And now you gon hit me with the same line. Ain't that a bitch?"

"I never said you were being too emotional. I just think that sometimes you forget that I can't be at your beck and call like them other chicks you be fucking ..."

"I ain't fucking no other bitches, Zin. I told you that a thousand times."

"Just because you said it don't make it so, now, does it?!"

"Wow! Damn... so now, I'ma liar too?"

"I don't know, Quran. You tell me."

My feelings were a little hurt, and Zin was pissing me off.

"Let me ask you this, Quran, and if you can manage it, I'd like to know the truth. I'ma big girl. I got on my big drawers right now. I know who and what you are. You've shown me that without compunction. I understand who you are as a man on every level. There's a lot of shit that I signed up for when I decided to love you, even after witnessing you kill your own brother as if he wase nothing. You told me why you had to do it several times, and I get it. Really, I do. I get the job that you have in the streets. I worry about you all the time, but I still get it. But what I want to know is, what I have to know is ... did you kill that woman?"

"Did I kill what woman?" I asked confused.

"Your ex. Somebody killed her last week outside of her apartment building. What was her name? Oh, ... Tosheka Jennings. Her murder has been on the news all week. It's still unsolved. It's really a coincidence that that woman was killed days after that whole little scene on Howard Road that night. Did you kill her, and if so, why? Tell me the truth, Quran!"

"I didn't kill Tosheka, Zin."

"Did you know she was murdered?"

"Now, that I knew. The streets talk."

"Why didn't you tell me then, Quran?"

"Why didn't I tell you? I didn't know I was supposed to."

Zin walked into her kitchen and opened the refrigerator. She came back with a piece of cake in a plastic carton. Zin took her time eating half of the cake before speaking. "See, that's how I know you're lying. The answer you just gave tells it all. If you had nothing to do with that girl's death, you would have felt obligated to tell me that someone had killed her. Just on the strength of the situation on Howard Road. She was your ex, Quran, and I assumed that you cared for her. Maybe even loved her. And not only did you not shed one tear for her, but you didn't mention all week that the girl was dead. And you knew it. The streets talk, right? That's what you just said. What did she do to you, Quran? Why did she have to die?"

"I didn't kill that woman!"

Zin smiled and laughed to herself. "You know what? I don't even know why I'm ... This conversation is pointless. I knew you wasn't gon' keep it real. It's late, and I got a lot to do tomorrow. Stay if you want, Quran. Sheets and blankets are in the hall closet. The couch is quite comfy. You'll enjoy it. Goodnight, boo."

As I stood there and watched Zin retreat to her bedroom, all I could do was drop my head and shake it.

Chapter 25

Zin

I'll summarize rather than reproduce this copyrighted passage from *If You Cross Me Once 3* by Anthony Fields.

In this opening of Chapter 25, narrated by Zin, she is awakened by Quran performing oral sex on her. Despite initial protests, she gives in to the pleasure and has an intense orgasm.

163

on for several seconds before subsiding. Quran didn't stop what he was doing t until after I'd cum again a second time.

Quran finally got up and climbed on top of me. "Zin, stop fuckin' playing with me. Do you hear me?"

"I hear you, Quran. I hear you."

Then he was inside me. The whole length of him. He felt thick inside me. He filled my walls to capacity. I opened my legs wider to accommodate him. His hips moved rhythmically as if to a song that only he could hear. My fingers dug into the flesh of his back as I held him close, snug, tight. One handheld his powerful back, the other arm wrapped around his neck. Quran's dick hit that spot inside of me that I called the deep spot. It was a place inside me that only he could hit. My loud moans assaulted my ear drums. They sounded like a foreign language. Words escaped my mouth that I couldn't recognize. Damn. Was I speaking in tongues? I shook my head from side to side to clear my thoughts, but it didn't work. Quran had me encapsulated in him, mind, body, and soul.

"Oh. My. Gawd. Quran! Damn! Fuck shit! You in my stomach! Your dick is in my stomach! You too deep, baby! Too deep! Owww!"

***

"Have you decided whether or not you gon represent Jihad?" Quran asked.

"Would you be mad if I say no?" I questioned him.

"Probably so."

"Well, how can I say no? I got you. I'ma go and see him today after I leave the jail. I gotta go see David today."

"What's up with his situation?"

"Nothing new. The government… Greg Gamble ain't revealing his hand. He lied and told David that the victim … Warren Stevenson died. I checked on him. He's recovering from his wounds at the hospital. So, all Gamble can do is charge David with assault. That's three to five years if David goes to trial. If he cops, it will be less. I got to see what Gamble charges David with. I'll keep you posted. I gotta enter an appearance for Jihad the next time he goes to court, which is a week from today. I'll let Charles Daun know that I'll be representing Jihad. Is that all you need from me?"

"Naw, not really. I need one more thing from you."

I could see the salacious look in Quran's eyes. "Uh ... no sir, brotha ..." My protests were denied and ignored. Quran dropped the towel from his waist as he walked towards me. I opened my mouth to protest again, but suddenly it was full of him. I looked up at him and our eyes found each other. Quran put his hand on my head and guided himself deeper into my mouth. I didn't resist one bit.

***

Columbia Hospital for Women
Downtown D.C.

"Hey, Zin, it's always good to see you," Dr. Asma Dairo said when she walked into the room.

I stood up and embraced her. She'd been my gynecologist for almost ten years. "Hey, doc. I'm glad that you could see me on such short notice."

"Anything for you, Ms. Zinfandel Carter. What's the problem today?"

"I need an accurate pregnancy test, Doc. No grocery store home tests will do. I need to be absolutely sure about whether I am pregnant or not."

"I hear you, dear. No problem. I can draw some blood and do a urine sample today. Since it's you, I can have an answer for you today. Is that okay?"

"That's perfect, Doc. Thank you. I'm ready when you are."

"Let me go and get everything I need. I'll be right back. Just sit tight."

"I'm sitting tight. Thanks again, Doc."
"No problem, Zin. No problem at all."

***

D.C. Jail
1901 D St. SE.
David Battle had grown a beard since I'd last seen him, and he looked like he had lost some weight. His orange two-piece uniform fit him snug as if it was tailored. David was chained around his waist that was attached to handcuffs. His ankles were shackled as well. He sat down at the table across from me. "David, how are you doing?"

"I'm good, Ms. Carter. The food on lockdown is small portions, and it tastes bad. But other than that, and the twenty three hour a day lockdown, I'm good. How are you?"

"I'm above ground, David, and everybody can't say that."

"True dat. What's up with Quran and 'nem? They good?"

I told David about Jihad's recent troubles and about Quran ex-girlfriend that was murdered.

"Damn! That's crazy. Somebody wiped Tosheka down like that, and Jay over here fighting a body. I know Que fucked up about that."

"Jihad is not over here. He's at CTF in the medical unit."

"What the fuck going on out there. Somebody killed Lil Bo, too," David said while shaking his head. Shit crazy!"

"I know, right? But Quran is good other than that."

He should be. He's the one who fuckin' killed the woman named Tosheka. And he's probably connected to the Benco Market shootout too.

"The good news for you is that Warren Stevens is getting better every day, and he ain't talking. His lawyer is a guy named Kevin McCants. I talked to him yesterday, and he says that his client is not pressing charges. Said something crazy to him like street justice will take care of it. What he meant by that is anybody's guess because you're both locked up and facing time. He has a murder trial coming up soon. If he's physically able to attend it. Maybe they'll get a postponement. As for you, the gun charge …"

"Gamble said he was dropping it," David interjected.

"Well, he lied, David. Just like he lied about Warren Stevens dying. He was trying to get you to talk, to snitch. I'm glad that you were smart enough to see through the bullshit. "

"It didn't matter what I saw or didn't see. I'd rather die than become a rat and cross my men. It's funny that you said earlier that Gamble did the same thing with Jihad recently. That muthafucka is relentless. He wanted me to give up Jihad, and now he's all over Jihad wanting him to give up niggas. That nigga is wild as shit."

"Agreed, but the fact remains that he holds all the cards at 555. All the prosecutors are under him and will do whatever he says. Most judges are the same way. Empathetic to his charm and charisma. So, we got the gun charge in front of Judge Berger. CPWL carries up to five years, but your priors are not that bad, and judges rarely give out the max on guns. So, even if the judge is on Gamble's side, you're looking at three years max because they'll ask for supervised release and the judge will give you the two years left on the five for that. I'm gonna argue for 12 to 18 months. I'll mention the year and a half you've already been in jail and that you should be given time served. We'll see how that goes in a couple weeks. Gamble and company haven't charged you yet in this Stevenson case, but he will. It's probably going to be an AWIK assault with intent to kill. But there was no gun involved and the situation was a jail stabbing. We can use the video before the stabbing to show a judge that Warren Stevenson was playing with his penis on the tier in front of everybody. I think it will end up a regular assault, punishable by three years max. If we can get to simple assault, that's a year if you cop. So, it's not as bad as it seems. Just hold your head and don't get into any more trouble. Am I clear on that?"

David smiled a wicked smile. "Yeah."

"You told me that before and then you stabbed Warren Stevenson."

"I'm locked down tighter than fish in a sardine can. I can't do shit. I heard what you said, Ms. Carter. And I'ma do what you say. No more getting in trouble. I need to get home to my life in the streets. I got you."

I gathered my things and prepared to leave. "Do you need anything?"

"Naw, I'm good. I got money on the books, and my girl be sending books and shit, so I'm gucci. Give my man Quran my love and respect for me."

"I will, David. You take care and behave."

I signaled the correctional officer in the visiting room bubble that I was done. Minutes later, David was escorted out of the room and through the visiting room. I was at the bubble getting my visiting pass when I heard the commotion. I turned around to see what was happening. The correctional officer who had been escorting David was trying to get another inmate off David.

"You stabbed my man you bitch ass nigga! I'ma kill you!" the man shouted as he warded off the one officer and stabbed David. Seconds later, a wave of correctional officers burst into the room and subdued the man who had attacked David.

"Ma'am," the officer in the bubble shouted after hitting the glass. "We're gonna need you to exit the facility! Now!"

I did as I was ordered. I left the D.C. jail completely shaken and stirred.

***

Central Treatment Facility (CTF)
1901 E Street S.E.

Jihad walked into the legal visiting room. His limp was noticeable now more than ever and he looked a little emaciated. But his grey eyes shined brighter than the sun. "Zin, what's up? You good?"

"Yeah, I'm good, but I don't know if David is," I replied, my mind still on what had just happened at DC jail.

"David? What David is that?"

"David Battle. Y'all friend David. At the DC jail." I went on to tell Jihad what had just happened. "They rushed me out of there so fast that I never even got make sure that he was okay."

"And you heard the dude that attacked him say, you stabbed my man. I'ma kill you!?"

I nodded. "Damn. I ain't never seen no shit like that before. David couldn't even defend himself. He was chained up from waist to ankles. I sure hope that he's okay."

"Damn! Me, too. That's crazy that they let a muthafucka get on slim like that. He was on status. They were supposed to clear the area where he was. Where did the dude come from?"

"The hallway. As soon as the bubble opened the door that led out of the visiting room, the dude rushed in. I assume anyway. My back was turned, but I do know that the dude wasn't in the visiting room anywhere. The whole room was empty except for me and David. He had to have come in from the hallway."

"Well, I'ma need you to keep me posted. Lil Dave is my man. Big bruh gon be fucked up about that. Have you seen him today?"

"This morning. He knows I'm here. I told him that I was coming. He convinced me to take your case."

"Convinced you? Why did you need convincing?" Jihad asked.

Because to be honest with you. I really don't think it's a good idea if you really think about it. Me being on your case is only going to piss Greg Gamble off and put him on your line even more and you don't need that. Any case I touch, he's gonna be on it personally. Believe that. Look what he said to David in the infirmary at the jail. He asked about Quran, you, me, my father, and Sean Branch. He knows that a thin thread connects us all. Do you really wanna rub this in his face? My coming on as your lawyer? Doesn't it play right into his hands and proves his theory that we are all in cahoots together?"

"Yeah, you're right. Never thought about it like that. Everything you just said is all facts, and I can't answer any of your questions with the answer no. I feel you on your concerns and Ima holla at big bruh and tell him that …"

"Which reminds me. You can't talk on any of them jail phones in here. Quran knows that. He told me to tell you that he's sending you something through somebody, so be on the lookout for it. What it is? I don't know, but I'm assuming it's a cell phone. If I'm right, wait until you're on that to tell him that I'm right about not representing you. He'll listen to you. It's better for us all that way. I'm sure of it. So, you can either keep Charles Daum, or you can get someone else, but I don't think it should be me."

"I agree. I'll talk to him, and thanks anyway."

"Don't trip. Other than that, how is your body healing?"

"My body is good. It's healing, but my heart is severely wounded. I can't stop thinking about Bo and Tosheka."

Your brother killed Tosheka and you got Bo killed. "I'm sorry for their losses. Hopefully, you'll learn how to heal. I talked to Charles Daum. Have you?"

***

Standing outside of the CTF, I pulled my cell phone out and made a call.

"Hello, yes, I just left the facility visiting a client about an hour or so ago. He was attacked by another prisoner as he left the visiting room. I need to know if he's okay. Yes, I'll hold."

Chapter 26

Quran

Tomasina was already at the Papa Johns in Fairfax Village when I got there. She stood next to a charcoal grey Infiniti Sedan. She was one of Tosheka's homegirls that I partied with about a dozen times. As I approached, she ended a call that she was on and put her phone away. I got close to her and embraced her. "Tom, how you, baby girl?"

"Considering all the wild shit that's been going on the last couple of weeks, I'm good, Que. And yourself?"

"Fucked up about Tosheka, but you already know that. I'ma body any and everybody who was with that shit. Believe that."

"I already know, Que. Say less. My girl didn't deserve to go out like that."

"What the fuck was Tosheka into lately, Tom?"

Tomasina shrugged her shoulders; the look on her face told the story. "I been working sixteen hour shifts because CTF is short of staff. Have been for about five months. I talked to Tosh all the time, but I hadn't seen her in about two months. Since you curved her, she was always ranting and raving about you and your new woman. For about the last month, she told me that she had somebody new, but never told me his name. I should've pressed her for more info about the dude …"

"You think he did it? Killed Tosh?"

"Who knows. Maybe, maybe not, but right now whoever he was looks suspect."

"Like I said, if you find out anything, hit me asap and tell me. I'ma do the rest."

"Gotcha," Tomasina responded.

"A'ight, look, I need you to do two things for me. Walk back to my truck with me."

Me and Tomasina walked over to the GMC. I opened the passenger side door and gave Tomasina a bag. "In that bag is a carton of Newport's, an ounce of loud vacuum sealed real good, a small cell phone that's made of all plastic components. It's designed to not go off once you go through a metal detector. The charger is small and compact, but it does go off if wanded. There's twenty five hundred in a small bag. That's for you. In an envelope in the bag is twenty bands, all big faces. I need you to give that to Tosheka's mother. Tell her it's from me and that I send my condolences. Have you heard anything about a funeral, yet?"

"Yeah, it's this weekend. At Popes on Marlboro Pike."

"Cool, text me all the info. Get that stuff to my brother, Jihad Bashir. He's in the medical unit. You got that? Jihad Bashir. You need me to put it in your phone?"

"Naw, Que. I got it. It'll be done today."

"Great. I'ma try and get with you every week and drop off more weed and cigarettes. Is that cool?"

Tomasina's face lit up. "Do I get twenty five hundred every time?"

"Without a doubt, you do."

"Well, I'm with it. Just holla, and I'ma get it done."

"Good girl. Hit my phone if something comes up or goes down. Tell bruh to hit me asap. Get that bread to Tosheka's mother and hit me if you hear anything about whoever did that to Tosh."

"Gotcha," Tomasina said, clutching the plastic bag tight. "And thank you for everything. I mean that."

"Naw, baby girl, thank you. Holla back."

***

"What happened?" I asked Zin.

Zin paced the floor in her office. "Some dude stabbed David in the visiting hall as he left out. I had just left him. I was at the bubble when I heard the commotion. I looked back and saw the dude stabbing David while fending off the CO."

"What dude was it? Did you recognize him?"

"Of course not, but I did get a good look at him. He was about David's height, brown skinned and muscular. He had tattoos all over both arms. He had a low haircut, tapered. Looked to be young. In his early twenties maybe. Said something about David stabbing his man and he was gonna kill David."

"What the fuck?!" I asked, exasperated and angry. "Is Lil' Dave a'ight? Or do you know?"

I called the jail after I left Jihad and didn't get much info. They kept spinning me. I ended up just hanging up. I'm about to go back there and demand to know how he's doing, if he survived …"

"He survived. Trust me. Lil' Dave doesn't know how to die easily. Please find out something and then let me know what's good."

"I will. And another thing, your brother and I decided that it might not be a good idea for me to represent him."

"What? Why?"

Zin ran her whole spiel down to me, which was one hundred percent about Greg Gamble. I had to admit that she was right. "Right now, we don't need to poke the one thousand pound bear."

"True dat, I'm with it. It makes sense. So, Jay is gonna keep Charles Daum, then?"

"I think so, but he's still deciding. Let me get going. I gotta check on David then get to court by 2:45 pm. I'll call you as soon as I know something."

"A'ight, baby. I love you."

"Love you, too, Quran."

***

In the truck minutes later …

"Hello, Tom," I said into the phone.

"Yeah, Que. what's up?"

"I need you to do something else for me. I got another stack for you."

"What's that, Que?"

"Can you find out shit that happened at DC jail?"

"Of course. The two jails are connected by a catwalk. Why?"

"I got a man over there that got stabbed today in the visiting hall after a legal visit. I need to know if he's okay and the name of the dude who stabbed him. Can you get that info for me?"

"When did you say this happened?" Tomasina asked.

"A couple hours ago. Three or four hours ago."

"Let me see what I can do. Stay by the phone. I'ma hit you right back."

***

I checked the address on the phone against the one on the tan brick, duplex on Warner Street in Northwest. Bo's family was second generation Nigerian. I had met his parents before years ago. Getting out of the truck, I walked up to the front door of the house and rang the doorbell. I silently prayed that someone was home. The woman who answered the door was not Bo's mother, but their resemblance was unmistakable. She was well dressed and elegant. Regal. Very pretty.

"Yes. May I help you?" the woman asked.

"Yes, ma'am. I'm a friend of Bole's, and I came here to give this gift and my condolences to his mother." I lifted the bag with the twenty-five grand in it.

"I'm Bole's Aunt Lima. his mother's sister. Unfortunately, she's in no shape to accept visitors, even one as beautiful as you. In her stead, I will accept your gift and your condolences for my nephew."

I handed the woman the bag.

"Thank you. What is your name, so that I can tell her who the gift is from?"

"My name is Quran. My brother Jihad was best friends with Bo."

"Quran? Like the book?"

"Yes, ma'am."

"And your brother Jihad? Which means struggle in Arabic?"

"Yes, ma'am."

"Please stop calling me, ma'am. I'm not that old. My name is Halima. I go by Lima for short. Is your family Muslim?"

"Yes, ma... I mean, Lima. They are ... We are."

"Where do you get those eyes from, Quran?"

"My father. Grey eyes and curly hair is a family trait."

"Do you have a cell phone with you, Quran?" Bo's aunt asked.

Nodding, I pulled out my cell phone. "Why do you ask that?" I replied.

"Let me see it."

I passed the woman my cell phone.

After putting something in the phone, she gave it back to me. "All of my contact information is now in your phone, Quran. Please contact me later as soon as you get the chance." Halima Ndugu peered into the bag. "I'll make sure that my sister gets this. Have a nice day, Quran and don't forget to call me."

***

North Capitol Street and K wasn't far from Warner Street, only like ten minutes away. I made it there in five. Andy Daniels lived in the high-rise apartment building called Golden Rule. He was outside on the front when I pulled up. I nodded at Andy, and he walked over to the truck.

"Hop in, bruh," I said after putting the window down.

Once Andy was in the truck, he said, "Pleasure to finally meet you, slim. I heard all good shit about you and your brother."

"Likewise."

"This shit out here done changed like a muthafucka, slim. I'm still tryna get acclimated to all this shit."

"Damn, bruh … speaking of which." I went in the center console and removed a wad of big face hundreds. I passed the money to Andy. "Mike told me that he hit you with some bread already, but I still wanna do my part. That's five bands. Welcome home, bruh."

Andy smiled. "I respect that, slim. No bullshit. Ain't nobody really done shit for a nigga since he been home but one muthafucka. I appreciate that." He pocketed the money. "Now, let's get down to business. You want Kendra Dyson's lil' dyke ass, I can provide her for you. I been heard that she scorched some good men back in the day, but I thought it was just rumors. Until I went to the feds and met Tapole. She cooked Bernard 'Tapole' Johnson and a few other good men. Bitch lied on them dudes and said that they raped her. Them niggas was beefing heavy with some southwest niggas and Kendra got caught fucking with the opp. So, according to the case they raped her and tried to kill her. The rape never happened, but the bitch did almost get whacked. Who tried to off her is anybody's guess. She lied on Tapole and 'nem and said they did it. Bitch hot as shit. Here's how we get to her …"

***

I was back on Howard Road at the spot when my phone vibrated. The caller was Tomasina. "Hey, Tom, what's good?"

"Sorry I took so long getting back to you, Que, but I got the info you need."

"That's what's up. I got that band for you, payable whenever."

"Good, I need that. And just so you know, your brother got that. I put it in his hands personally. About twenty minutes ago."

"Good looking, baby girl. Now, give me the four one one."

"You man that got stabbed earlier today at the jail is okay. He's at George Washington getting patched up, but he's good. The knife the dude had was damn near dull and mostly scratched David. That is his name, right? David Battle?"

"Yeah, that's him. What about the other info I asked for?"

"Gotcha. The dude that stabbed him is Jovan 'Von' Jarrett. He's in jail on a couple robberies. He's from Fort Totten. That's all I could get. He's locked down in South One. When David gets out of the hospital, he'll be moved here to CTF. Probably end up in the same unit with your brother."

"Can you make that happen for another grand?" I asked.

"You better know it. I got a little juice. It's done."

"That's a bet. I appreciate you. Hit me when you wanna meet up and collect your bread."

"I will. I'm doing sixteen hour shifts. Ima hit you tomorrow."

"Bet. Talk to you then. Peace."

I tossed the phone on the couch next to me and was about to roll up some sour diesel when a thought hit me. I grabbed the phone and pressed send on the contact info.

After a few rings, a woman answered the phone. "Hello?"

"Halima, it's Quran. How you? Is this later enough?" I asked her.

"You have perfect timing, Quran. I just got home."

"Is that right?"

"Yeah, that's right. Do you know anything about Bethesda, Maryland, Quran?"

"A little. They got a real nice movie theater that I been to in North Bethesda."

"The iPic theater. I know exactly where it is. I'm not far from there. I'ma text you my address, Quran. I need you to come and see me. Is that possible?"

"When? Now?"

"Now, yes."

"Text me the address."

***

"Hello again, Quran like the holy book."

"Hello again… Lima."

"You hesitated. Why?"

"Because I didn't know whether to say Halima or simply Lima."

"Either is fine, Mr. Quran. Come in, please."

The house on Seawood Lane was huge. It looked expensive. Just like the other houses in the area. The decor was opulent. I openly stared at all the paintings, sculptures, and furniture, Halima led me to the living room.

"This was my husband's house before he left me for a younger woman. We were married almost twenty five years, and I never lived here. Can you believe that? Sit down, please."

"I can't," I replied, then sat on a couch across from her.

"Nobody can. As a matter of fact, I never knew about his house at all until I got it in the divorce settlement. Do you like it?"

"I guess so, yeah. It's a lot different than what I'm used to seeing. Do you live here alone?"

Halima Ndugu nodded her head. "But I'm almost never here. I travel a lot, Quran. But enough about me. What do you do for a living?"

"I'm in the extermination business."

"Extermination? Like Orkin and all those other companies?"

"Exactly. Just like Orkin."

"And what do you exterminate?"

"Rats."

Halima screwed her face up. "Yuck. I guess what you do is important. I hear that Washington D.C. has a lot of rats."

"It does. You heard right."

"What's the name of the company you work for?"

"You wouldn't know it. It's a privately owned company."

"And how did you know my nephew, Quran?"

"Bo and my younger brother were best friends. I considered him a friend too."

"Bole was my favorite nephew, Quran."

"He was a good dude."

"Would you happen to know who killed him?"

"All I can tell you, Halima, is that the people responsible for Bo's death are all already dead. I promise you that."

"There's something in your eyes, Quran. An intelligence, a passion. A darkness like the clouds before a storm. I see truthfulness in your eyes. How old are you, Quran?"

"I'm thirty three years old."

"I'm almost fifty."

"You don't look a day over thirty."

"I can't get over your eyes. The greyness intrigues me, draws me to you."

"You are a beautiful woman. Sexy. Bold."

"And honest, Quran. I'm very honest. I want you so bad right now."

I looked at the woman sitting across from me. Halima Ndugu resembled Iman, the famous model. The robe she wore opened at the chest to reveal the prettiest pair of brown breasts I'd ever seen. The nipples were dark brown and looked like dark chocolate. While my eyes ogled her, Halima stood up and let the robe fall to the floor. She was completely naked. The pubic hairs above her pussy were trimmed and cut low. Earlier her hair had been pinned up on her head, but now it was loose and flowing down her back. Her feet weren't all that, and they looked a little neglected, but I could get around that. I stood up and took my coat off, then my sweatshirt. Her eyes were locked on mine as my jeans dropped. I removed my boots and took the jeans off. My dick was rock hard in my briefs. Lastly, I removed them.

Halima's eyes fell to my raw exposed manhood. "Oh my Gawd!"

Smiling, I walked over to Halima. "Leave the big guy out of this."

***

When I hopped back into the truck a couple hours later, I saw that I had several missed calls. Surprisingly, none were from Zin. Something was up with Zin, but I couldn't figure out exactly what it was. The other calls were from Mike Carter, Sean Branch, Kiki Swinson, Lil Jaha from the Cordas,, and a couple other calls from numbers that I didn't recognize. One call was from Tomasina and two text messages were from Tosheka's mother thanking me for the money. I decided to call the two unknown numbers back first. One turned out to be Jihad.

"Que, what's up, big bruh?"

"I'm good, Jay. still fucked up at your sucka ass."

"I already know, big boy. I apologize for my moment of weakness. I promise you that shit will never happen again."

"It bet not. You good?"

"Hell, yeah. The package you sent was bigger than baseball."

"Do you with it. It's gonna be an every week thing. I'm glad that we connected. Be careful on this jack though. Wiretaps are a muthafucka."

"Say less. I just wanted you to know that everything landed, and I'm good. Oh … and they brought Dave in the block earlier. I didn't get to get up on him, but he got hit over the jail."

"I'm already hipped. Tell him I said to stay tuned."

"Say less."

"And hit him off real good. I'ma hit shorty again this week for him. Did he look fucked up?"

"Not really. He had a rack of bandages on him though. He sounded a'ight when I hollered to him. Tomorrow, hopefully, I'll be able to get up closer to him. Did wifey tell you what we talked about?"

"About her not repping you on the beef?"

"Yeah."

"She told me, and I agree with it. Let me know who you want to go with or if you decide to keep Daum.

"Bet. We need to really chop it up though."

"We will. Just not now. Let me get a different jack. I'll call you from that joint tomorrow evening."

"That's a bet, bruh. Assalamu alaikum."

"Walaikum assalam."

I ended the call with Jihad and called Kiki. She answered the call on the first ring. "You stood me up, Kiki. I'm not too happy about that."

"I'm sorry, Que. when I went to New York, I got stuck there. I'm just getting back to Virginia Beach. I wanna see you though. That's why I called. Can I fly in tomorrow? See you for a few hours?"

"How can I tell you no when your pussy is some of the best I've ever had."

"And here I thought you loved my head and ass."

I laughed and started the truck up. Pulling off, I said, "I love all that shit. Call me in the a.m. and give me the specifics."

"Okay, baby. In the a.m," Kiki replied.

The next person I called was Sean. he answered on the last ring.

"Youngboy Que, what's up, ock?"

"You, big homie."

"I called you three times."

"I was busy."

"I can respect that. Must've been in some pussy."

"You already know. Cougar pussy."

"Your slick ass gon' mess around and catch something out here. Anyway, I need to get with you tomorrow. Is that cool?"

"By all means, old head. Hit me."

"A'ight. One love, youngin'."

"One." I ended the call with Sean and decided to hit Mike and Tomback another time. My next call went to Zin. She answered the phone immediately.

"Hey," Zin said.

"Hey. I haven't heard anything from you since this morning."

"I been busy all day, Quran. Still am. I'm working on a case right now. Typing up some motions. Are you okay?"

"I'd be better if I was with you."

"Uh… no way, Jose. Take your horny ass home, and I'll see you tomorrow."

"It's like that, huh?"

"Sorry, but, yeah, it's like that."

"A'ight, I'll hit you tomorrow. I love you."

"Love you, too. Bye."

I pulled over on the curb and dialed Halima. She answered quickly.

"You must be missing me, Mr. Quran."

"I am. I miss you so much that I wanna come back. Can I?"

"Of course, you can. See you soon."

Chapter 27

Quran

The shower in the bathroom attached to the master bedroom was encased in all glass. The water sprayed all over my aching muscles. I put both hands on the glass wall and let the hot water soothe my body and mind. I was inside the home of a woman that I had just met yesterday. My body was here, but my heart was elsewhere. My mind was elsewhere. I couldn't get Zin out of my head. I fucked women. Fucked. With a capital F. But when I was into Zin, it was love. There were sponges hanging on a hook inside the shower. I used the sponge to soap up my body with body wash. All the while, thinking about my life. Standing under the water, I saw my mother in my head. I saw my father. I saw Khitab. Jihad. Mike Carter. His wife, Patricia, alive and dead. I saw Dontay. I saw Sean. I saw Bo. I saw Tosheka. Dave. Tommy. Landa. Man. The list went on and on. Suddenly, it felt like the shower's walls made of glass were closing in on me and got closer. I was starting to feel trapped in my thoughts. Trapped inside my own head. Maybe it was all the lies I told or the lies I held in. The secrets that held me up. The weight of all the blood I had shed weighed me down. My ability to evade the long arm of the law loomed over me. I felt like a victim of my own success. I felt like a good dude. I felt like a bad guy. I felt strong, yet I felt weak. I loved to hate but hated to love. My life was one of a man plagued by his reality. A man embroiled in hypocrisy. Everything about me was a contradiction. The door to the bathroom opened loudly and broke my reverie. The shower's glass door opened and in stepped Halima. Her eyes found mine as I turned around to face her. Without saying a word, the beautiful woman in front of me dropped to her knees, and put me in her mouth.

***

There were times when I felt like the weight of the world was on my shoulders. Before I could be completely overwhelmed, I did what always relaxed me. I prayed. Inside my condo, I made wudu in the bathroom, then pulled out my small prayer rug. It had been at least a year since I had last prayed. Shoeless, I stepped onto the musala and raised my hands to my ears. "Allahu Akbar."

***

The phone in my center console cup holder vibrated. The caller was Kiki. "Hello?"

"I'm about to book the flight, Que. How does …"

"I'ma have to take a raincheck, baby girl. Something came up. I can't get away today. My bad, but I just found out this morning about the other stuff I need to do."

"Are you sure, Que. I was looking forward to seeing you today," Kiki complained.

"I'm sure. I promise you we'll get together soon. Just give me a few days, and I'ma get at you. We gon' make things happen."

"A'ight, Que. Hit me when you ready to see me. I'll be waiting.

"Bet, you be easy. I'll holla back soon."

I ended the call with Kiki and looked down at my lap. Tomasina's head bobbed up and down as she sucked me. I ran my fingers through her hair and watched her attempt to deepthroat me. She wasn't successful but put forth a helluva effort.

***

"Here," I said to Tomasina as she checked her appearance in the rearview mirror. The bag I passed her contained the stuff for Lil' Dave and the money for her.
Tomasina took the bag. "What's in here, Que?"
"Five bands, the phone for David, some loud, cigarettes and a condom."
"A condom? Fuck is there a condom in there for?"
"Because there's five bands in there. I saved you two. I'm giving you two bands to get that stuff to Dave. that leaves another stack. I'm giving you that to fuck him."
"What? Uh-uh, Que. how the fuck am I gonna do ..."
"Do you want the stack or not?" I asked Tomasina.
"You know I do," she replied.
"Well, make it happen then. My man been in a year and a half and ain't had no pussy, so I need you to look out for him. Can you do it or not?"
Sulking, Tomasina got quiet. Then she said, "Got 'cha."
"Good, and be careful with him. The man just got stabbed."

***

Iverson Mall
Hillcrest Heights, MD.
The cookie spot in the mall always had the best snickerdoodles in the world. I stopped there and paid for five pounds of the sugary treats. Walking off, I popped a piece of cookie into my mouth. Minutes later, I was at my destination, a clothing store called Last Stop.
"How you doing?" a pretty young lady called out as I entered the store.

"Oh my gawd, look at his eyes," another girl said as she walked up. "How can I help you today? We have all the new drip. Rockstar, Cult of Individuality jeans, Hugo Boss, Lacoste, G-Star …"

"Girl, bye, don't you see that he don't wear that shit," the first girl said as she came from behind the counter. "I got him. C'mon, boo, I got you. Damn, you fine. What can I get for you? Some Versace Collection? The new Hugo Red Label? Some Burberry? Balenciaga, Jimmy Choo …"

Smiling, I replied, "Naw, baby girl. I'm here to see Corey. Can you get him for me?"

"Oh… okay. Wait a minute. I'll go and get him," the young girl said and disappeared into the back of the store. Three minutes later, she was back. In her hand was a bag. A large bag. "Here, he asked me to give you this. Quran, right?"

I nodded. "That'll be me," I replied and grabbed the bag. I pulled out a wad of money and gave it to the young girl. "Give that to Corey for me, would you?"

"You bet. Have a nice day, Quran. With your fine ass."

***

Back in the truck, I pulled a large shoe box out of the shopping bag. Lifting the lid, I couldn't help but smile. Inside the box were a mini ARP compact submachine gun and three brand new handguns. All came with new clips and extra ammunition. All I was missing were the sound suppressors. That made me think about my partner, Sean Branch.

***

Planet Fitness
Silver Hill Road

"I need some more of them sound suppressors, ock," I told Sean in between sets of pullups. "I got some new shit. Two forties and two FNNs."

"Ain't no suppressor gon' fit on the FNN. They shooting choppa bullets."

"I'm hip, but I thought…"

"They haven't made 'em yet. As for the forty, I can accommodate that. I got you. I got to get with my man."

"Bet. Bruh, let me ask you something. We talked about it before, but you never really said nothing. What's really good with you and Mike Carter? Why you ain't fucking with him?"

"He said something to you about me?" Sean asked.

"Always. I keep telling him that I gave you the number and all that shit. Keep it one hundred with me. What's good?"

Sean dropped to the floor and did a set of push-ups. Then he got on the dip bar and did a set of dips. I was starting to think he wasn't going to answer me, but finally, he said, "Mike is the one that gave Reese the brick to say that I killed Raymond Watson."

"Man," I said and screwed my face up. "Get the fuck outta here, big homie. Mike ain't do no shit like that."

Sean did another set of pull-ups but didn't speak. I did my set of pull ups.

"If he did that, then that means he did some or facilitated some hot shit. And we both know that Mike ain't with that shit. He's a cold-blooded, stand-up man."

Sean looked me in the eyes and shook his head. "So smart, yet so dumb. There's a lot about Mike Carter that you don't know, youngin'. Believe that."

"Well, hip me, then, bruh. Pull me up. Give me the 411. Ever since we met, you been like a big brother to me. A mentor, a guidance counselor, a teacher. Why that ain't the case now? What's different?"

Sitting on a weight bench across from me, Sean said, "Ain't nothing different. You my man, slim. My little brother, my road dawg, my partner. I love you, but there are a lot of things that you don't know. And it ain't my place … It ain't my job to tell you shit about Mike Carter, about his wife, about your father, about your brother."

"About my brother? Who, Jay? What the fuck are you talking about, big homie."

Sean got quiet.

"Say something, slim. Because you throwing me off."

"I'm not talking about Jihad. I'm talking about Khitab. The one you killed. Did he have grey eyes like you and Jihad?"

Sean's question dumbfounded me, irritated me. "What? He had our mother's eyes. Her pretty brown eyes. But why is that even relevant?"

"It's relevant because it proves my point that you don't know half of what you think you know. Almost all of what you think is true isn't."

Now, I was getting angry. "Like what? Tell me!"

"Not now. Not like this. But understand that you opened this can of worms, youngin'. All because you had to know why I haven't reached out to Mike Carter. Then when I told you my reason, you acted like I'm lunchin' or something. You say that Mike Carter is a stand-up man. How do you know that for sure? You don't. In a lot of ways, you're still that young kid that he groomed. The kid that did whatever he said just because he said it. If that's who you want to continue to be, that's on you. Me, I'm a different man now. Eighteen years in prison got me out of his shadow. Pulled me away from his influence. Opened my eyes to who Mike Carter really is. If I wasn't sure of that when I first got home, I'm sure of it now. When we went at Reese on LongFellow Street, he lied and said that the culprit was Kenny Sparrow who paid him to lie on me. I believed that but it didn't make any sense. Then when we went at Kenny Sperson in his apartment, the things he said to me made me see things more clearly. Remember when he said …

" Think about it. Fuck I get a key of coke from back then? A whole brick that I'ma just give a nigga to lie on another nigga? To get him out the way? That shit don't even make sense. It wouldn't have taken Reese's crack smoking ass to be given no brick to lie, and you know that. Plus, you knew me back then. I wasn't getting that type of money back then. Where the fuck did I get a brick to give away? I don't know why Reese lied to you, but on my mother's grave, he lied. I didn't have shit to do with what happened with you back in the day …"

"Then after I cut off his head we were in the caravan. I told you that what Kenny had said was believable to me and why. Remember that Reese said it was Kenny who did it. But after hearing what Kenny said, I knew that Reese had lied. He lied under the threat of instant death. Remember I told you that Reese had lied to protect someone? Someone he feared more than death?"

"I remember everything you said that day."

"Good, but I remember asking you who in the hell could scare that man that much to protect them even in the face of imminent death. You had no clue and neither did I at the moment. But the more I thought about it, the more it started to come to me. The person that Reese feared, he feared more than me. And the only person that could be is Mike Carter."

"But… why would he fear …"

"Why would he what? Fear Mike more than me? Let me tell you. For the most part, youngin', your father did all the killing for Mike. Everybody knew that but Mike wasn't no slouch. He did a lot of his own killing too. There were whole families that were found dead, and the streets attributed their deaths to Mike Carter. Not Ameen Bashir. Mike Carter. Plus, Mike killed Raymond in front of Reese. Over killed him.

That did something to Reese. Reese had heard about my killing game, but had never witnessed it. In his eyes ... in a lot of people's eyes, Mike Carter was way more vicious than me. So, here's the thing, I always wondered why Mike allowed Reese to live. He allowed Reese to come into a court and testify against me. Why would he do that, Que? Ask yourself that, right now. Why? Mike knew that I didn't kill Raymond. Mike killed him. He knew it and the world knew it. Mike had you on the team. Why didn't he send you at Reese? From what I heard, Reese was never hiding. He was still in the hood. Why didn't Mike kill him? See, where I'm at with this? Can you answer that question for me?"

"Which one?"

"I called home and told everybody that Reese was the rat. That he had implicated me in the murder. Mike knew that. Why didn't he kill Reese or send you to kill him?"

I thought about everything Sean said, and I couldn't for the life of me come up with a good answer. So, I kept quiet.

"See, what I mean? You can't answer that question, either. So, here's what I think ... what I believe. I believe that Mike regretted killing Raymond so publicly, especially out of anger. The heat was on. He knew like I knew that the cops were coming his way sooner or later. I believe that Mike needed a scapegoat. An easy one. Me. Someone who was hated and feared by everyone. If the truth about the incident came to light, but the cops had me, no one would cry over my absence. I lived too uncaring, too ruthless. And since I was in the car with him, Mike knew I'd have no alibi. He knew I'd never rat. Knew I'd never set the record straight and say to anyone, I didn't kill Raymond, Mike did."

"It was broad daylight and people saw who killed Raymond, right?"

"They did, but didn't you hear what I just said. Nobody wanted me around. I was blamed for too many murders. Cousins, brothers, fathers, friends. Nobody would ... nobody did come to my defense and set the record straight.

Nobody. I believe that Mike gave Reese the key of coke to say I committed the murder. Mike was connected to the Carlos Trinidad Cartel back then. He was getting a hundred keys at a time. He's the only person who had coke like that to lose back then. Not Kenny Sparrow. And do you remember when I said that Reese feared somebody else more than me? It was Mike Carter. He'd witnessed Mike kill, not me. Plus, Reese knew that his family was at risk …"

"His family? How?"

"Quran, you are not the only person who kills for Mike Carter. For years, I've been hearing about all the murders committed, all the people dead, all the families. They were all people connected to Mike Carter. People who owed Mike. People who had crossed Mike. I knew it, so Reese knew it too. Reese believed that I'd kill just him. But if he told me about Mike Carter and Mike found out, Mike would call the play to have everybody that he loved killed. You think you know."

I stood up and walked around before coming back to the same spot. "I hear you, but I don't understand why. Why would Mike do that to you? To save himself? Why would he throw you away like that? After all the loyalty you've shown him? He loved you. Always spoke highly of you to me. Boasted about your character, your loyalty and honor. Your dedication to him. Why would he dishonor himself that way? Why would he give the game a black eye like that?"

"The answer to all those questions is the same one. To get me out of the way. I was getting too much press, Que. I was becoming hard to control. I was becoming my own man, and Mike started to fear me. He wanted me out of the way."

"Out of the way? Why?"

"There's a lot of things that you don't know, Que."

"You keep saying that. And then you won't tell me shit. What's up with that?"

"Youngin', there's a time and place for everything and right now this ain't the time or place. I didn't call you here for this. I called you here to tell you that the Baby E hit didn't go as smooth as we thought. I never said anything to you because I didn't think that it mattered, but I never killed the chick that was with Derrick and Silk. My focus was on them and when I started hitting them, the broad got down on the ground and covered her head. I saw no reason to kill her. The other chick …"

"The one I shot?"

"Yeah, she died last night at the hospital. And what I didn't know … because Rodney never told me … is that the two chicks were sisters, and they are a dude named Tony Fortune's daughters. And slim is out for blood. Rodney called me this morning all bent out of shape, talking about he never told us to hit the broads, just Baby E, Silk, and Derrick Hill. He talkin' bout Tony is his man and all this other shit."

I had heard a lot about the notorious gangster from Northeast named Tony Fortune. And since I'd killed his daughter, shit was about to heat up literally. "A'ight, what's the play?"

"Tony and Rodney. Rodney's my man, but he's more loyal to Tony. At least that's what I got from our conversation earlier. So, Tony and Rodney gotta go."

"When?" I asked.

"Tonight. They'll both be at the MGM Grand down at the Harbor. I told you; niggas love to gamble at casinos."

"Done. Anything else I need to know?"

"Yeah. What you said about that social media shit worked. I found out that Ren is Renaissance Tyler. Early twenties and from Ivy city. Her father was a gangsta. A nigga named Von Tyler. Serious nigga back in the day. He was the only one giving your father a run for his money on the killing tip back in the nineties. Ren is his only daughter and rumored to be a chip off the old block. I don't have a line in her, yet though. But I do with Crud's sister, Bionca. She lives at the family house on Southern Avenue, near Chesapeake Street. I'ma get on her ass right after we knock off Rodney and Tony. I'ma make her bring Ren to me, then kill everybody last named Tyler and Clark. Just wanted you to know that." Sean grabbed his towel and shirt off the universal weight machine. "I'ma go and hit the showers. Then I'm going home to relax until tonight. So, be ready."

"I was born ready, old head."

"That's right, youngin'… Talk that talk to me. I love that shit," Sean said and turned to leave.

"Aye, ock?" I called out.

"What's up, youngin'?"

"One day soon, we gon' have to finish that conversation we was having earlier. I'ma respect what you said about time and place and all that, but we gon' have to find the place and make time because you leaving me in the blind ain't cool. I wouldn't do it to you. How the fuck you gon know some shit about my family that I don't and not tell me? What type of shit is that? But, again, I'ma respect the time and place thing. I'ma let it go, for now. But we gon' have to talk soon. And I mean real soon."

"That's what's up, youngin'. Later," Sean replied and disappeared.

***

"I love you. But there are a lot of things that you don't know. And it ain't my place, it ain't my job to tell you shit about Mike Carter. About his wife. About your father. About your brother."

"About my brother? Who, Jay? What the fuck are you talkin' about, big homie? Say something, slim. Because you throwing me off."

"I'm not talking about Jihad. I'm talking about Khitab. The one you killed. Did he have grey eyes like you and Jihad?"

Driving through the streets, I was in a daze. I couldn't get what Sean had said off my mind. What did Khitab have to do with anything? Especially the color of his eyes. Where the fuck did that come from? Then to add insult to injury, Sean refused to explain what he'd meant by his words. Talking about, it's not the time or the place to tell me everything. Then why even bring it up? All I did was ask him about his issue with Mike Carter and why he hadn't called him. I still couldn't see what Sean said had to do with Mike Carter. My cell phone vibrated loudly, pulling me out of the fog that I was in.

The caller was Andy Daniels. I answered the call. "What's up, bruh?"

"You, homie. You busy? I got somebody I want you to meet. Can you come through the Corda's right quick. I'm in the Tyler house building in North Capitol."

"I'm on my way, bruh. On my way."

***

Andy met me in the lobby. "I told everybody that you are my cousin from out P.G. and that you looking for a good weed connect. The woman that you looking for is in the apartment but you can't kill her in there. I'ma make the connection, and y'all work out a plan to do business. Then you get her somewhere and push her shit back."

"That's a bet, bruh. Lead the way."

Andy led the way to an apartment on the third floor. Inside apartment 320, there were people everywhere. There were drugs and alcohol all over and clouds of weed smoke filled the air. In the corner of the living room, three women leaned against the wall. All three were bad as hell, but my focus was on just one of them. The one in the middle. She was short, about five two and pretty as shit. Her hips struggled to fit in the jeans she wore, and the shirt seemed about to burst from her large breasts. The woman's outfit was accented by a pair of stylish Gucci high heeled boots. Her lips were painted red and luscious. Her eyes were locked in on me.

"This is my cousin, Quintay. We call him, Que," Andy introduced.

"Hey, cuz," one woman said and smiled.

"Damn, he fine. Looking all good. Pretty ass eyes," another said.

I smiled. "All three of y'all is top flight, but what's your name?" I asked the woman in the middle.

"Kendra," the woman replied, "but you can call me, KD."

"KD, huh? My cousin says that you have the best weed in DC. Is that true?!"

"All facts."

"You got any samples for me to try out?"

"Sure. KD tapped the girl to her left. "Give him an eighth."

The woman next to KD produced a small bag filled with lime green weed with red hairs all over it. She passed the bag to me. I popped the bag and sniffed it.

"Smells good, but I need to see how good it tastes," I announced.

"Let me roll up something for you then," the other woman with KD said and grabbed the weed out of my hand.

Andy stood beside me, eying the woman silently. I looked around the room and spotted a familiar face. The man was sitting on a couch across the room smoking, drinking, and talking to a woman seated next to him.

"Aye, cuz." I leaned in close to Andy. "Who's that dude sitting on the couch over there next to the exotic looking chick?"

Andy looked in the direction that I pointed in. "That's my wild ass homie, Jojo."

"Jojo? Joseph Morris?"

Andy nodded. "Yeah, that's him. He on the list too?"

I nodded. "Told on a good Baltimore man named Gutta. Line him up."

"Say no more."

Chapter 28

Greg Gamble
U.S. Attorney office for the District of Columbia
555 4th St. N.W.
6:18 pm

"Set the coffee down on the table, Ari, then read the Rayful Edmond motion back to me. Wanna see how it sounds."

Ari Weinstein put a steaming pot of coffee down on the table across from my desk. "Do you really support Edmonds getting a time reduction after all he's done to ruin communities in DC?"

"You don't believe in second chances, Ari?" I asked.

"Of course, I do. I hand them out every day, just like you do. But to give Rayful Edmonds a commutation of sentence and not Tony Lewis, that makes no sense to me."

"Why not? Tony Lewis never assisted our office in any way, but Rayful Edmonds has. Lewis made his choice to hold out to the code of silence. That was his decision. Now, he's living and dying with that decision."

"I get that, Greg. God knows I do, but Lewis wasn't even a major player in the Edmonds organization. And all of the other co-defendants are home. All except Tony Lewis. Why is that?"

"Simple. Because everybody else had better lawyers. Now, can we get back to the motion to reduce?"

Defeated, Ari Weinstein took the chair in front of my desk, turned the laptop to face him and began to read. "The government hereby submits, as directed by the court, the following proposed finding of fact with respect to the government's pending motion for reduction of sentence pursuit to Federal Criminal procedure 35 (b) 2: Background in the District of Columbia, after trial, on December 5, 1989, the defendant was convicted of the following: Engaging in a continuing criminal enterprise, in violation of 21 USC 848 as to count one, conspiracy to distribute and possess with intent to distribute more than 5 kilograms of cocaine and more than 50 grams of cocaine base, in violation of 21 USC 846 as to count two; Unlawfully employing a person under 18 years of age, in violation of 21 USC 845 (b) as to count five; Interstate travel in aid of racketeering, in violation of 18 USC 19552 (a) as to count eleven and unlawful use of a communications facility, in violation of 21 USC 843 (b). On September 17, 1996, the defendant pleaded guilty in conspiracy to possess with intent to distribute more than five kilograms of cocaine, in violation of 21 USC 841 and 846 (a). This matter was based on the defendant being involved in narcotics trafficking while imprisoned at United States Penitentiary Lewisburg. In connection with his plea, the defendant assigned the benefit of his cooperation to his mother. On July 24, 1997, the defendant was sentenced to thirty years and based on his cooperation, the defendant's mother's sentence was reduced. Hey, is Rayful Edmonds' mother still alive?! If so, what happened to her?"

I shrugged my shoulders, befuddled. "Don't have a clue, Ari. She was released from prison in 1998, I believe and probably relocated to WitPro somewhere. Don't know if she's still alive or not."

Ari Weinstein turned back to the computer. "Testimonial cooperation. First in 2002, the defendant testified in the United States versus Kevin Gray. The defendant knew many of the defendants in that prosecution and had conducted drug transactions with them before his arrest in 1989. The Gray racketeering drug enterprise covered criminal activity spanning more than a decade and was perhaps the most violent drug trafficking group ever prosecuted in the District. The defendant testified for four days. After a lengthy trial, the Gray defendants were convicted of racketeering and related offenses. Additionally, the defendant testified for the government in the state of Maryland and secured convictions of known members of the Carlos Trinidad organization. Now, I never heard that before, Greg," Ari said, stymied. "Is that true? Did you just add that?"

"Ari, if I had my choice, and I might well do, I'd choose you to sit in my seat after I'm gone. Why? Because no one can match our intelligence, will to win, wit and perceptive nature. You can spot a crock of shit from a mile away. Of course, I just added that. No one is going to fact check me. And if they do, it was simply a typographical error. You know like I know that no one, no district of any state has ever successfully prosecuted any confirmed members of the Trinidad organization. And no one probably ever will."

"No one ever will? What makes you so sure of that?" Ari asked.

"Because Carlos Trinidad controls people. He always has an ace in the hole. And as long as you have a Susan Rosenthal in this office …"

Susan Rosenthal? What does Susan have to do with the most elusive, most notorious crime boss that this city has ever seen?"

"Susan is fucking Carlos Trinidad, Ari. From my mouth to God's ears, it's true. So, just in case you ever get to sit in my chair, you'll know exactly who you have on your staff. And I know you're probably a little incredulous. Probably thinking that I'm making this up. Well, I'm not. I confronted Susan about it, and she didn't deny it."

"But… but, she's married. Her husband Grant is a well-known …"

"Whatever Grant Rosenthal is known for, it's not satisfying his wife. Susan has been in cahoots sexually with Trinidad for over a decade. Do you remember the woman who controlled DC drug trade back in the late nineties, early two thousands?"

"Who, Angel? Of course, I remember Kareemah El-Amin. I was on the team that tried to prosecute her for all those murders after her sister was killed."

"Do you remember how that case ended? What happened?"

Ari gave the look of being deep in thought. "Wait… Angel walked because the DNA samples that implicated her in the tourist home murders disappeared. And the sole witness against her, Fatima Muhammad, was killed while in witness protection. So, we had to dismiss all charges."

"Susan Rosenthal destroyed the DNA samples. She informed an inside associate of Trinidadabout where Fatima Muhammad was being held. Do you remember that it was rumored that Angel was getting her drugs from Trinidad?"

Ari nodded.

"Turns out it was true, and Susan did everything she could to derail that case amongst others."

"So… so, why are you telling me this now, Greg? What does it have to do with Rayful Edmonds?"

"Rayful Edmonds? Nothing at all. But there's a reason that I'm telling you this now. There are a lot of things at play that you know nothing about. Can't know about. But I need you to do something for me. If anything should ever happen to me …"

"Greg, you're starting to scare me. What do you mean by …"

"Ari, listen, I need you to put on your steel reserve hat right now. And let me get out what I'm saying. I'm not specifically implying death. I'm saying if something happens to me, meaning disbarment or removal from office. Or if I'm jailed, I want you to contact a man."

I quickly grabbed a pen and wrote down contact info onto a piece of paper. I slid the paper to Ari.

"Contact Martin Mayhew and tell him to get you into my house. This piece of paper and the fact that you know him and contacted him will gain you entry. There's a safe in my bedroom that's built into the wall. Martin has the combination. The safe is behind a painting on the wall above my bed. Move the bed, remove the painting, and you'll see the safe. You knowing where it is will get Martin to open it. Take out all the contents out of the safe and store it somewhere safe where only you have access to it. There are mostly files there, Ari, but what's in those files will be enough to get you my seat in this office. The proof about Susan Rosenthal is in those files. Damning evidence about a lot of people is in those files, Ari. Even you."

"Me?"

"Yes, you, Ari. I knew all about your connection to the Jewish terrorist group Al-Shalom in Israel. I know how hard you try to cover your tracks and disseminate misinformation about its leaders. I know about the drug pipeline that you oversee to generate funds for the Al-Shalom organization. The proof of what I'm saying is also in those files. And before you get any bright ideas, Ari, there are other copies. Other people in place to expose whatever I want exposed. So, while I know that you're perceptive and cunning, you never saw this coming, did you? Why? Because I am the big kahuna for a reason, Ari. No one here is smarter than me. You might have more perception, and more wit, but no one's will to win is greater than mine."

I got up from my seat and walked around the desk until I was directly in front of Ari Weinstein. I know that you're the devil, Ari, but I'd rather deal with the devil I know than the one I don't. Your secret is safe with me, Ari. Susan Rosenthal is the one that we both have to watch. She's a ruthless bitch. She's going to try to ruin me. She thinks I don't know that, but I do. So, you become the equalizer. She wants my chair, my office, my title, but I'd rather you have it."

"But, why? Why me?"

"I just told you the answer to that. I know who you are. A bird in hand is always worth two in the bush. Besides, when you take over, Ari, and you will take over when I'm gone, you'll owe me. And the knowledge I have will keep me in the loop. You'll answer to me. Me and only me. How does that sound to you, Ari?

"Always heard that you were manipulative and unscrupulous, but I never believed the things I heard. Now, I see that words such as those describe you perfectly."

"Coming from you, that's a compliment, and I'll take that as a verbal agreement that we understand each other." I walked back behind my desk and sat down. "Now, finish reading me that motion, would you, please."

Ari Weinstein had no choice but to acquiesce. He turned back to his laptop and began to read.

"The defendant provided background and associational information that has been used in doing trafficking investigations and numerous wiretaps. Based in part, on the defendant's assistance in this regard, over one hundred drug dealers were arrested, prosecuted, and convicted."

Chapter 29

Sean Branch

In the game I played, paranoia was always a friend. Vigilance was also a constant companion. I played my rearview mirrors the whole ride on Interstate 66 in route to McLean. There was one car that caught my attention. A burgundy Acura truck. The MDX SUV. The windows were tinted, and the occupants were barely visible. The car stayed at least three car lengths behind us. At the Tyson's corner exit, I checked to see if the Acura turned off with us, but it didn't. The four door Porshe Panamera was brand new, courtesy of Alex at the car dealership. My daughter, Shontay, lounged in the back seat, her attention on her cell phone. My girlfriend, Bolivia 'Liv' Santos, was to my right in the passenger seat. Her eyes were closed as she listened to music on her phone through earbuds. I pulled up to the hotel where the restaurant Eddie Vs sat on the top floor. A valet appeared to park the car.

Minutes later, our trio was seated at tables inside the upscale eatery. "Dad, this is far as hell just to get some food. We could've hit Adams Morgan," Shontay said as she studied the menu.

"Adams Morgan? Adams Morgan is in the hood. 18th Street to Columbia Road and all the streets in between are nigga's hoods. I'm one of the most hated dudes in the DMV. We come out here to eat in peace. To be safe," I replied.

"Niggas that's mad at me ain't coming out here to do nothing. These crackas out in VA ain't playing with niggas."

"You think?" Liv added as she looked at her menu. "When was the last time you really paid attention to the news, baby. Niggas is killing like shit in Virginia too."

"I know that, but that's mostly in Southern Virginia. Richmond, Portsmouth, Newport News, Norfolk ... the whole tidewater area. These niggas in Northern Virginia ain't on shit. Menassas, Dumfries, Woodbridge, Fairfax, Arlington ... ain't nobody out here killing shit but them wild ass MS-13 niggas. And they killing with machetes and meat cleavers and shit. I ain't talking about them. Niggas in DC don't come out here doing no killing. Virginia got the death penalty and niggas scared of shit of that. Just ask Wayne Perry."

Liv and Shontay both laughed. "Dad, you wrong as shit for that."

"What? It's the truth. They threatened slim with the death penalty, and he took a cop for natural life. Who does that?"

"Uh... I think I'ma get the sticky Salmon with sushi rice and steamed, vegetables, "Liv said. "We gon' leave that man out of this. Wayne Perry ain't here to defend himself. What are you getting, Shontay?"

"I'ma get the Kobe burger with onion jam... whatever that is... and onion rings on the side layered with three kinds of cheese and bacon bits. "

"Bacon who? Bacon what?"

"Dad, please... stop what you doing. Bacon bits is tiny sprinkles. It ain't like I'm ordering chitlins."

"Chitlins, pork chops, hog maws or bacon bits. It's all the same. If they bring it to the table, I'm leaving."

Shontay was the exact image of me, only a woman. The face she made reminded me of the ones I made when I was angry. "You be doing too much, Dad. It ain't nothing but little ole bacon bits, but since you being dramatic, I won't get them. Gosh! You act like you didn't eat port back in the day."

"Never said I didn't. I used to love that shit, and bacon was my favorite …"

"See, what I mean?"

"Let me finish. That was before I found out how wild that dirty ass pig is."

"And you want us to believe that Islam had nothing to do with it?" Liv added, picked up the menus, and passed them to the waiter.

Everybody ordered their food. After the waiter was gone, I said, "Of course, Islam had something to do with that. That's how I learned about the pig. That'll shit'll kill you."

"Dad, please stop it!" Shontay said and laughed. "Pork ain't never killed nobody. My grandparents on mommy side are in their seventies, late seventies, and they been eating pork all their lives. They still eat it rooter to the tooter and love it."

I sipped water from my glass. "Yeah but look at 'em. Both of your grandparents big as shit, on medicine, and both of their feet stink."

Everybody laughed at that.

"Bae, you crazy as shit."

"My grandparents' feet don't stink!"

"You shittin' me!"

My cell phone vibrated loudly. The caller was Quran.

"What's up, youngin?!"

"I need you, bruh," Quran said.

I looked at Liv and Shontay. "Let me holla at Quran. I'll be right back."

I walked through the restaurant and paused in the lobby. "You a'ight, slim?"

"Yeah, I'm good. I ain't in no jam or nothing. I'm in a spot on North Capitol Street lining up one target and the one I been looking for for weeks is here, too. I can try and get one of 'em, but I want both of 'em. I need you to come through."

"Do both targets know who you are?"

"Naw. Neither one of 'em is hipped to me. They have no clue how close the Grim Reaper is to them."

"Grim Reaper? There ain't but one Grim Reaper, youngin', and that's me. You gotta find something else to ..."

"Old head!" Quran snapped with impatience. "You on joke time, I'm not. The nigga, Jojo Morris is right here in this spot. I been looking for his ass for about a month. I gotta get him, but I can't get both of 'em."

"Kill both of 'em in the spot, then. Fuck it."

"Can't. It's too many people in here. I'd have to body like fifteen muthafuckas. I need you to come and get at Jojo while I trick the bitch KD and knock her off."

"You already know that you wouldn't have to ask me twice, slim, but I'm all the way out Mclean, near Tyson's. It's family night out. I told you that earlier. I got baby girl and wifey with me. We at a spot waiting on food. I can't ditch 'em and plus, I drove. You gon' have to figure something out or just get one. We'll get the other one later after we get Rodney and Tony."

Quran exhaled loudly. "Damn! A'ight, old head. Let me figure out what I wanna do. I'm in the bathroom and can't stay in here long. I'ma do something and bounce. I'll hit you later, and we'll get together then."

"Aight, youngin. Be safe."

"You, too. Assalamu alaikum."

"Walaikum assalam."

Chapter 30

David Battle
Central Treatment facility
1901 E St. S.E.

Warren Stevenson wanted to handle our beef in the street, but Javon Jarret thought it was a good idea to ambush me as I was leaving the visiting hall. I eyed my wounds in the mirror above the sink and got mad all over again. The killer inside me roared like a lion in the wild. The beast inside me wanted blood and so did I, but vengeance would have to wait. Warren Stevenson, the creep I'd stabbed in the unit, was still in critical condition at an area hospital. And the dude that stabbed me, Javon Jarret, was at the jail on lockdown at SouthOne.

"If that guy would have had a better homemade weapon, you'd be dead," the doctor told me before releasing me to correctional staff.

"God must've been with you, Battle," the female lieutenant said as they wheelchaired me from the jail to CTF's medical unit.

While I never said a word in response to what Lieutenant Talley said, in my head I thought, *God better be with them niggas if I ever catch either one of them again.*

The gauze bandage on my shoulder wound was saturated with blood, so I removed it first to clean it. The naproxen I was given for pain did little to dull the aches in my body, but I ignored the pain. Accepted it. Reveled in it. The dude named Javon had actually stabbed me three consecutive times in the same spot on my shoulder. The wound was a nasty one. Using soap and water, I cleaned the wound, then doused it with peroxide and lastly an alcohol pad. I smoothed A & D antibiotic ointment onto the wound and replaced the gauze with fresh bandages. Then methodically, I did the same to my other wounds. The gash on my neck was like a deep scratch. It was near the jugular, and the reason why everybody kept telling me how lucky I was. The wounds on my arms, chest and stomach were bad, but not that bad. The stomach wound was the only one that required stitches. I rubbed my palm over the stitches.

"I'ma burn them niggas asses up if I catch them," I said aloud after grimacing for a long time to stifle a moan.

I was just about to put the uniform top back on when the intercom in my cell came to life.

"Battle?" a female voice said.

"Yeah, what's up?" I replied.

"Can you walk?"

"Yeah, I ain't crippled. Why?"

"Come over here to the CO office. I'm about to pop your door."

"A'ight. Here I come."

Since DC jail didn't have a medical unit, if anybody at the jail got hurt in any way, they had to be brought here to CTF. The unit was smaller than any unit I'd ever been in. There were only like thirty two cells. Sixteen on the bottom tier and sixteen on the top tier. All cells in the unit were single man cells. The buzzer sounded on the door, and the lock opened. I pushed the door open and walked gingerly to the CO station. There was one female CO inside the office and one standing near the door. When I approached the door, the one inside the office looked me up and down. I looked around the empty unit. She was looking at me.

"Go with her, Battle."

My suspicion aroused. "Go with her, where?"

The CO at the door was bad. "Just come on," she said and led the way down a corridor that ended at a room.

The CO used a key to open the door. The room was an examination room. There were medical devices everywhere and an examination table just like the ones at the hospital. The CO motioned me inside the room and shut the door. She reached into her pants after unbuckling her belt. While I stood there totally confused and turned on, I watched her remove something in plastic from her pants.

"Here," the female CO said and passed me a cell phone.

She removed a small charger from the bag and passed me that. "That's from Quran. His new cell number is already programmed in the phone and mine is the 240 number. When you call me, don't ever say nothing about this place, or say my name …"

"I don't even know your name," I muttered, perplexed.

The CO smiled. "Well, you will in a minute."

She pulled her pants down to her ankles, revealing a sexy pair of lace panties. The CO's hands went back into her panties as she squatted a little. A small package appeared in her hand as she removed it from her panties. She passed the package to me and didn't even attempt to wipe it off. My dick was suddenly hard as granite. The female CO eyed the bulge in my pants. She smiled again, then pulled her panties down to where her pants were.

"My name is Tomasina, and I'ma good friend of Quran's. Everything I just gave you, he sent it. There's only one thing left to give you."

"And what's that?" I asked.

"This pussy. I had one rubber and used it to put the weed and shit in, so either you can go raw or not at all. You decide."

The female CO named Tomasina had a pretty pussy. The pubic hairs were trimmed and cut low. I made my decision in seconds. I sat the stuff in my hands down on a chair near me and walked across the room.

The CO smiled and turned around. She bent over the examination table. "Yeah, that's what I thought. Come and get this pussy."

Chapter 31

Zin

"There has to be an evidentiary hearing in this matter, Zin, you know that."

"I do know that, Jon."

"And I'm assuming that the judge will contact us in the next few days to give us the date. Your dad will be moved to Warsaw …"

"Warsaw? Why Northern Deck?"

"DC jail got something going on where they're not accepting federal prisoners on writ. So, Mike will most likely end up at Warsaw?"

"Have you tried to locate the second witness?"

"Thomas Turner? No, not yet."

"Okay, then, Jon. Just keep me posted about the evidentiary hearing date."

"I will, Zin. Bye, bye."

Disconnecting the call, I sat my phone down in the cup holder of the center console in my Infiniti. I drove down South Capitol Street vowing to myself that I'd buy myself a new car soon. I crossed the bridge and turned onto Howard Road. I looked to my right at the Anacostia Subway Station and remembered when it wasn't even there. The extension of the Metro's green line didn't open until 1991 when I was six years old. The light at the intersection ahead caught me. I pulled into the far-left lane and signaled to turn left on MLK Jr. Avenue. Five minutes later, I was at my destination. I parked my car on Banger Street behind a red Chrysler 399. I looked across the street at the house with the burgundy door and black wooden shutters. The red, brick, two story colonial was just as it appeared on the Google Earth app. The app made finding Delores Samuels easy. The address on the mailbox read 1413 Banger St., and the house was surrounded by a black, cast-iron gate. I wondered what secrets and what answers lay beyond the gate. I wasn't even sure about what had brought me to seek out the mother of the man who had killed my mother. At least, he was accused of doing it. I sat in my car staring at the house, not knowing if Delores Samuels was even home or not. I thought about all the questions in my mind. The questions I had asked my father but got no answers. The lights inside the house were on.

"It's now or never," I said to myself and got out of the car.

The wind snuck up on me and chilled me to the bone. I tightened the belt around my wool peacoat trench. I walked across Banger Street, confidence building with each step. Opening the screen door, I knocked on the burgundy door. Minutes later, the door opened, and a woman stood on the other side of it. Familiarity passed through me as I stared at the woman. The multicolored hijab she wore over her hair was pretty and a stark contrast to her dark skin. She openly stared at me. Recognition shined in her eyes. It was strange.

"Uh… I'm sorry to bother you, but I'm looking for Delores Samuels. My name is …"

"Zin. Zinfandel Carter. Zinfandel Marie Carter."

"Yes… but… how… how do you know my whole name? Nobody knows my middle …"

"It's good to see you again, Zin. It's been twenty years, but I can still see your mother in you."

"But… how?"

"Come in, Zin," the woman said and turned to enter the house.

I followed her inside. The house smelled of brewed coffee and baked goods. In the living room, Delores Samuels moved a few things off the sofa. She turned back to me.

"Please, Zin, have a seat."

"How do you know my mother?" I said, still standing.

"I saw you on TV once. At the news conference for that man who loves to kill people. Sean Branch. After he won his freedom in that retrial, I saw your face and couldn't contain myself, couldn't hold back my tears. You looked just like Patricia. It was as if she'd come back from the grave. I looked you up online. Awed at your accomplishments. All the while, saying to myself, her mother would be so proud. I always made dua to Allah that one day, I'd see you again, talk to you. And today, my prayers were answered. I will tell you whatever you want to know, Zin. but please, sit down. Give me a minute to compose myself."

I did as she requested and sat down on the sofa. "If you know who I am, and know who my mother is, then you also know who my father is…"

"Your father is Michael Carter. I know who your father is," Delores Samuels said.

"And you still…"

"Still what, Zin? Want to talk to you? You thought I wouldn't because of what your father is in prison for. What he was charged with?"

I nodded. "I thought that you might not want to talk to me."

"Since you thought that, but still came here, you must not know the truth."

"The truth being what, Ms. Samuels?"

"Please, Zin, call me Deloris? You always called me Auntie Delores."

"I did?"

Delores Samuels nodded. "As a child you did, yes, but before I get into that, let me answer your question. You asked me what the truth was. The truth is that your father, Mike Carter, didn't kill my son. I know that and everybody in Sheridan Terrace knew that. Your father did a lot of things in those days, but killing Dontay isn't one of them."

"Are you sure about that?" I asked.

"Positive. I know exactly who killed my son, Zin, and so does everybody else who was outside that night."

Suddenly, I was totally confused. "Wait a minute… wait a minute. You know that my father didn't kill your son and according to you, a lot of other people know that, too. Yet nobody came forward in 1996 at his trial to tell the truth?

"I remember that look. The one that's in your eyes right now. The accusing, judgmental look. The look of anger, yet confusion. It was the look that was in your mother's eyes at times. I understood her then, and I understand you now. There's something that you have to understand, Zin. Ameen Bashir was one of the most feared men in the entire District of Columbia back then. He was brutal in his savagery. He was heartless, ruthless, and beasty. Even though he was killed years before Dontay was, we all knew that his son was more dangerous than his father. So, nobody came forward to implicate him."

I closed my eyes and wanted to close my ears. I knew exactly what Delores Samuels was about to say.

"Nobody wanted to come forward and tell the truth. The truth being that Dontay was killed by Quran Bashir. His best friend."

To be continued…

Note From Author

I use names in my stories that are familiar names. Oftentimes, it's just to remember the person. Some I do to shout them out. Most of the characters depicted in this story are actual people. If I've named them as someone who has dishonored the code of silence, then in real life they actually have. I don't apologize for exposing human rats. It's my intention to let readers from my city know who they are dealing with. The Byron 'Crud' Clarks, Artinis, Whistle' Winston's, Kendra Dysons, Joseph Morrises, Baby E's (wish I knew his government joint), Maurice 'Moe' Bests and countless others who've eaten the government cheese.

I have to say again, in this book, that Sean Branch is a real person, but none of the events that I've written about are real. Everything I have attributed to Sean is completely made up and false. None of it is real! Quran and his brothers are not real people. Greg Gamble and all the prosecutors are made up. Renaissance Tyler, Bionca and Tosheka (well the name Tosheka Jennings is actually a real name) but the characters are not real. There's no Ren Tyler running around DC killing people. Mike Carter and Zin are made up. Aunt Linda too, but Mike's celly in USP Canaan is not made up. Henry 'Lil Man' James is a real person, and a friend of mine who I've known since juvenile jail. And lastly, although he appears in quite a few of my books, there is absolutely no Latino drug lord named Carlos Trinidad running my city. Make no mistake about that. I mentioned Rodney Shaw in the book. He's a real person who's a good man. Had to shout him out. I also mentioned his partner, Anthony 'Tony' Fortune. Tony Fortune has been dead since 1991, but I wanted to remember him. Rest in power, homie. With that said, I believe I covered the whole disclaimer thing. This book is a work of fiction. It says so at the beginning. No part of this story is real.

DC Stand up,
Buckeyfields

TURN THE PAGE FOR A SNEAK PEAK AT
IF YOU CROSS ME ONCE 4
LET THE TRUTH BE TOLD

Chapter 1

Quran
Tyler House
1200 North Capitol St.

I put my phone up and stepped out of the bathroom. Andy Daniels was where I'd left him in the apartment living room. Walking straight up to him, I grabbed the blunt out of his hand and lit it. "Let me get that, cuz. You on papers ain't you?"

Ignoring me, Andy continued to flirt with one of the women with Kendra, his eyes darting from her to Jojo Morris. Mine did the same. Inhaling the pungent aroma coming from the weed, I coughed and almost choked. The weed was potent as shit. The three women on the wall laughed at me.

"What the fuck?"

"Told you," one of the women said.

Kendra Dyson just smiled.

Bitch, you ain't gon' be smiling when I get through with your ass. I hit the weed again and passed it to the woman to Kendra's left, my eyes never leaving Kendra's.

"You like the weed, pretty boy?" Kendra asked.

"I love it, pretty girl," I told her.

"Well, you might not like the price."

"And that is?"

"Three thousand a pound. No exceptions."

"Three bands is some skinny shit."

"Good, that's what I like to hear."

Kendra grabbed the blunt from her girl and puffed it. She hit the weed and never coughed, never choked. Her eyes never left mine. Kendra tried to pass the weed back to me, but I shook my head.

I pulled Andy to the side. "Slim, how well do you know this building?"

"Grew up running around in it. Why? What's up?" Andy replied.

"How many exits?"

"Three. The front door, a back door and side joint that's always locked unless there's an emergency, like a fire or something."

"So, Jojo has to leave the building by either the front or the back, right?"

Andy nodded.

"KD is gonna have to wait. The priority for me now is Jojo. You fuck with him?"

"He the homie. We ain't never been buddies, but we ain't never bumped heads neither. I been in, and he been cooking niggas on the witness stand, so…"

"A'ight, I get it, but I need you to disarm him…"

"You want me to take his gun?"

"Naw, slim. Not like that. I want you to go and holla at him. Shoot him something like you tryna get some money since you just came home. Ask him if he can put you on with a lick or something. I'ma go ahead and bounce. I'ma need you to somehow get him to leave. Find out where he's parked at. Then you text me one word, front or back. I'll do the rest. I got a bankroll for you if you pull it off."

"Now, homie if you pull it off, he's a free one."

"Bet. Let me go and get KD's info."

I slid back up on Kendra Dyson. "I'm tryna get with you for some of that. I need at least five of them joints. Can I get ten of 'em for 25 racks?"

Kendra smiled. "Didn't I tell you no exceptions?"

"Not even for the pretty boy?"

"I'll think about it. When you gon' be ready?"

"I'm ready now, but we'll meet up tomorrow. Is that cool?"

"You come recommended by Andy, so, yeah, that's cool. Have 27.5 on deck and you got ten of them."

I passed Kendra my cell phone. "Put your number in there."

Kendra Dyson did as I instructed.

"What time tomorrow?"

"Early. I'll hit you."

'Aight, pretty girl. Thank you."

"Naw. Thank you."

Chapter 2

Zin

The revelation that Quran was the person that killed Dontay Samuels hit me like the green line train during rush hour. They were friends. Close friends. According to Delores Samuels, they were best friends. Why would Quran kill Dontay? Was it for my father? I thought about my mother's letter locked away inside my purse. She had put Quran and Dontay together. Said they rode with my father everywhere and killed for him.

"Quran killed Dontay?"

Delores nodded. "Everybody witnessed it. He walked up to Dontay on the front porch, pulled out a gun, and shot him."

"But if they were friends…"

"Best friends."

"If they were best friend why would Quran kill Dontay?"

"Now, that's what we don't know. No one knows why."

"From the very beginning, my father always said that he was innocent. He maintained that for years, but I always thought he was lying to protect my feelings. I thought he didn't want me to look at him differently, like a crazy killer."

"There's a lot of things that you don't know, Zin. I can see the confusion on your face, in your eyes. I have a lot to tell you. A lot of truths. You asked me how I knew your mother earlier. How I knew your middle name was Marie. I can tell you everything you need to know… if you want to hear the truth."

"I want to hear you out, hear the truth as you put it."

"Well, this may take a while, Zin. Would you like something to eat or drink?"

***

"Your grandmother's name was Pearl Ann Mitchell. She was five foot two but her inexorable spirit made her appear a giant. She embodied confidence and power. Her fiery personality made living in Jackson, Mississippi in the forties, fifties, and sixties a serious problem. So, she boarded a Greyhound bus in 1965 and headed North. With her were three children, Paul Jr., Preston Earl, and Pamela Rose. Paul was 7, Preston was 6, and Pam was 4. It was on that bus that your grandmother met my mother, Deborah Louise Allen, a twenty year old escaping a bad marriage to a man in Tupelo, Mississippi. All my mother had to her name was sixty five dollars, one suitcase, and one daughter. Me. I was born in Tupelo in 1960. I was five years old when that bus arrived in the Nation's Capital.

Why Pearl and Deborah chose Washington, DC to migrate to, I never knew. Never asked. Being two young women… your grandmother was only twenty three years old then… from Mississippi, they bonded together and scraped out a life for themselves in the city. Then in 1968, everything changed. Martin Luther King Jr was assassinated in Memphis and that same night, your mother was born. Ms. Pearl named her youngest daughter Patricia, after one of her distant relatives. I was eight years old by then and never did meet or even knew who Patricia's father was. Nobody ever mentioned him. Ms. Pearl and my mother lived in the same building on Sayles Place in 2022. They helped each other out in every way possible. The city was consumed with riots that year after MLK's death, and a lot of the white citizens of DC ran for the hills. The mass exodus of white folk fleeing to the suburbs left DC with a majority black citizenship after that, and DC was later nicknamed Chocolate City. I loved baby Patricia and spent a lot of time taking care of her while Ms. Pearl worked. So much so that I couldn't stand to be away from her for long periods of time. I used to pretend that Patricia was my child. In the latter part of 1968, tragedy stuck. Your Uncle Paul Jr. ran into the street on Stanton Road trying to cross and was struck by a car and killed. Ms. Pearl remained stoic and graceful, but we all knew that the death of her oldest child had ripped away something inside of her that was needed. Your grandmother went back to work at Savoy Elementary in the cafeteria and did all she could to maintain her composure. My mother worked in the cafeteria too and was always there for Ms. Pearl in every way. Then tragedy struck a second time. In 1973, I was thirteen and your Aunt Pam was twelve. Preston was fourteen and your mom, Patricia, was five. Me and Pam were only a year apart in age, but two people could never have been more different. Pam took after Ms. Pearl in the looks department. She was a beautiful girl. A hair over 5'2, long black hair, big brown eyes, she had the body of a woman grown. She was a smart one in school, but that girl was a fast one. 'Hot in the drawers' was what my mother called her. Pam linked up with an older guy from Barry Farms named Tony Edelin and snuck around like nobody knew her business. One day in the summer, Pam was hugging a boy from Howard Gardens on Bowen Road. Tony Edelin saw Pam with the boy. He walked up to them and shot them both, killing them. The death of your Aunt Pam crippled Ms. Pearl. She was inconsolable. It was a sad, sad time. Tony Edelin went to jail for both murders, but nobody was satisfied with that outcome. Especially your Uncle Preston, who'd been very close to his sister.

    One year later in 1974, Preston, who was fifteen at the time, went to the Edelin family home on Eaton Road in Barry

Farms and shot five members of the family as they cooked out in their front yard. Tony Edelin's brothers Wayne, Ray Ray, and Tommy, all died. A sister and the mother survived. Preston was declared clinically insane by a judge and never did a day in jail.

He was sent to Saint Elizabeth's mental hospital. Two years later in 1976, Preston killed a doctor and a nurse, then he hung himself. Preston's death did to Ms. Pearl what the other two didn't. It broke her. Completely. She left her job and became reclusive and sick. My mother cut her hours at work to part time just to care for her. Then in 1978, two things happened. I had sex for the first time and got pregnant, and your grandmother passed away. My mother said that Pearl Ann Michell had died of a broken heart and nothing more. My mother, who was 33 at the time, became the sole legal guardian for Patricia. Your mother moved in with us on Sheridan Road. She was ten years old. I was seventeen about to turn eighteen, and that's when I met Donnie Samuels.

In the sixties, a lot of men in DC became a part of the 'Black Muslims' movement. I think it was mostly to get away from white people's culture and their religion. Christianity. In 1975, Elijah Muhammed died, and the Nation of Islam became something else. Sunni Muslims. Donnie was a Sunni Muslim. He wasn't my child's father, but he took responsibility. So, I had my son and named him Dontay Samuels, giving him Daniel last name. Dontay was born in 1979. Donnie and I married a year later. I converted to Islam that same year. I moved in with Donnie, leaving Patricia as the only person in the house with my mother. Living as a Muslim woman and wife was new to me, but I adapted. I catered to my husband and son. Donnie had all Muslim friends that came to our house. All except one. Kevin Carter. Kevin was Donnie's only non-Muslim friend, but they were close. Kevin had two brothers and one sister …"

"My Aunt Linda, my Uncle Kirk, and my father."

Delores got up from the kitchen table where we sat. She walked over to the counter and retrieved a pie. "When you were a kid, you loved strawberry cheesecake. Is that still the same?"

I nodded.

"Good," Delores put the pie down on the table. Then she went to the cabinet and pulled out two small plates.

She got silverware and returned to the table. After slicing two pieces of cheesecake and putting a slice on each plate, Delores set back down.

"Donnie's mentor in all things was a man named Amir Bashir. Amir was one of the most enchanting men you could ever meet. And damn was he handsome. Almond complexion, dark curly hair and light grey eyes. He had one son. A man named Ameen Bashir. In 1979, Ameen was seventeen years old, I think, and the spitting image of his father. All the girls in our neighborhood fawned over him as if he was a celebrity. In 1980, I turned twenty and life was good. My husband had turned to the streets selling drugs. Dontay was one, and your mother was twelve years old. I was working at the time and rarely saw Patricia. My mother had met the man she'd eventually marry and was working a lot. So, that left your mother to basically fend for herself. And just like her Aunt Pam before her, Patricia was twelve but built like a grown woman. She had the family's pretty, hazel eyes, long hair, caramel complexion, and diminutive height. The girl was beautiful too. Really attractive. How Ameen Bashir got to Patricia …"

"Ameen Bashir? Back then? Before my father?"

"Yes. Ameen came before Michael. He was every bit of eighteen years old and the most sought-after dude in the hood, but he wanted Patricia. We were still very close, although I couldn't see her often. But we made time to get together. She was my younger sister. Patricia told me that Ameen had taken her virginity and did things sexually that she had never known were possible. And over time, she confessed that she loved him more than the air she needed to live. Patricia looked like a woman but wasn't one on any level. When she found out that Ameen belonged to Katherine Bell who was pregnant with a son, she went crazy. It made Ameen back away, but not all the way. Katherine converted to Islam, became Khadija, married Ameen and gave birth to a son…"

"Quran."

"Exactly. Patricia was devastated by Ameen's marriage but learned to play her position if she wanted to be in his life at all. She did. Michael Carter… Your father was three years younger than his friend, Ameen Bashir, and was about to turn sixteen when he met Patricia at a store on the Avenue. If I was working then, I was spending a lot of time at the masjid. I wanted to raise Dontay in the Islamic religion to help him become a good man and Muslim. So, I kept Dontay there with me. Another person who was always at the masjid with me was Khadijah Bashir, Ameen's wife. Her son, Quran was ever present as well. It was there in the masjid that Quran and Dontay met and formed their bond as children. I want to say that Patricia was 14, maybe 15 when she came to me and professed her love for Mike Carter. Yet she still continued to love and sleep with Ameen. Unbeknownst to your father, of course. At some point, Patricia moved into an apartment with Mike Carter. Then in 1984, she became pregnant with you. One day, Patricia came to my house and broke down crying. She was hysterical, inconsolable. I thought that someone else had died. It was that day that I learned of the pregnancy and the fact that Patricia feared that the baby was Ameen's. She had managed to hide her relationship with Ameen for years, and the thought of Mike finding out and her baby being Ameen's scared her to her core. I did and said everything I could to comfort Patricia, but in actuality her concerns were real. If Michael Carter had found out about Patricia and Ameen, he would have killed them both. And make no mistake about it, Ameen Bashir, and Michael Carter were two of the most feared men in Southeast at that time. Ameen Bashir had gained a reputation for being sadistic and barbaric. I watched him kill two men right there by the walk bridge. Once both men had fallen, he stood over them and pumped more bullets into their corpses. He was a skilled killer, a butcher, a menace. And while Mike Carter was more patient with people, more diplomatic and focused on money, he was rumored to be just as vicious as Ameen. Your mother's fear was that the baby would be born with light grey eyes, thereby revealing her deceit and Ameen's betrayal of Mike. Something happened one day to make her almost tell Mike about her and Ameen. Patricia told me one day that she had went to Mike's apartment only to find Khadijah Bashir leaving it. She said that it happened a few times before, and Ameen was never present. Patricia said that she dismissed Khadijah's visits as business or her handling something for Ameen. Then Khadijah got pregnant with the third child, and Patricia always wondered. But she kept quiet about Khadijah and about her and Ameen… How's the pie?"

"The cheesecake is delicious. Made it yourself?"

Delores nodded. "I did actually. Suddenly, I feel like ice cream with my cheesecake. How about you?"

"I'd love some."

Lock Down Publications and Ca$h Presents Assisted Publishing Packages

BASIC PACKAGE $499 Editing Cover Design Formatting	UPGRADED PACKAGE $800 Typing Editing Cover Design Formatting
ADVANCE PACKAGE $1,200 Typing Editing Cover Design Formatting Copyright registration Proofreading Upload book to Amazon	LDP SUPREME PACKAGE $1,500 Typing Editing Cover Design Formatting Copyright registration Proofreading Set up Amazon account Upload book to Amazon Advertise on LDP, Amazon and Facebook Page

***Other services available upon request. Additional charges may apply

Lock Down Publications
P.O. Box 944
Stockbridge, GA 30281-9998
Phone: 470 303-9761

Submission Guideline

Submit the first three chapters of your completed manuscript to ldpsubmissions@gmail.com. In the subject line add **Your Book's Title**. The manuscript must be in a Word Doc file and sent as an attachment. Document should be in Times New Roman, double spaced, and in size 12 font. Also, provide your synopsis and full contact information. If sending multiple submissions, they must each be in a separate email.

Have a story but no way to send it electronically? You can still submit to LDP/Ca$h Presents. Send in the first three chapters, written or typed, of your completed manuscript to:

LDP: Submissions Dept
P.O. Box 944
Stockbridge, GA 30281-9998

DO NOT send original manuscript. Must be a duplicate.
Provide your synopsis and a cover letter containing your full contact information.

Thanks for considering LDP and Ca$h Presents.

NEW RELEASES

BLOODLINE OF A SAVAGE **BY PRINCE A. TAUHID**

THE MURDER QUEENS 4 **BY MICHAEL GALLON**

THE BUTTERFLY MAFIA **BY FUMIYA PAYNE**

KING KILLA 2 **BY VINCENT "VITTO" HOLLOWAY**

BABY, I'M WINTERTIME COLD 3 **BY MEESHA**

THESE VICIOUS STREETS **BY PRINCE A. TAUHID**

TIL DEATH 2 **BY ARYANNA**

CITY OF SMOKE 2 **BY MOLOTTI**

STEPPERS **BY KING RIO**

THE LANE **BY KEN-KEN SPENCE**

MONEY GAME 2 **BY SMOOVE DOLLA**

THE BLACK DIAMOND CARTEL **BY SAYNOMORE**

CRIME BOSS 2 **BY PLAYA RAY**

THUG OF SPADES **BY COREY ROBINSON**

LOVE IN THE TRENCHES 2 **BY COREY ROBINSON**

TIL DEATH 3 **BY ARYANNA**

THE BIRTH OF A GANGSTER 4 **BY DELMONT PLAYER**

PRODUCT OF THE STREETS **BY DEMOND "MONEY" ANDERSON**

Coming Soon from Lock Down Publications/Ca$h Presents

BLOOD OF A BOSS VI
SHADOWS OF THE GAME II
TRAP BASTARD II
By **Askari**

LOYAL TO THE GAME IV
By **T.J. & Jelissa**

TRUE SAVAGE VIII
MIDNIGHT CARTEL IV
DOPE BOY MAGIC IV
CITY OF KINGZ III
NIGHTMARE ON SILENT AVE II
THE PLUG OF LIL MEXICO II
CLASSIC CITY II
By **Chris Green**

BLAST FOR ME III
A SAVAGE DOPEBOY III
CUTTHROAT MAFIA III
DUFFLE BAG CARTEL VII
HEARTLESS GOON VI
By **Ghost**

A HUSTLER'S DECEIT III
KILL ZONE II
BAE BELONGS TO ME III
TIL DEATH II
By **Aryanna**

KING OF THE TRAP III
By **T.J. Edwards**

GORILLAZ IN THE BAY V
3X KRAZY III
STRAIGHT BEAST MODE III
By **De'Kari**

KINGPIN KILLAZ IV
STREET KINGS III
PAID IN BLOOD III
CARTEL KILLAZ IV
DOPE GODS III
By **Hood Rich**

SINS OF A HUSTLA II
By **ASAD**

YAYO V
BRED IN THE GAME 2
By **S. Allen**

THE STREETS WILL TALK II
By **Yolanda Moore**

SON OF A DOPE FIEND III
HEAVEN GOT A GHETTO III
SKI MASK MONEY III
By **Renta**

LOYALTY AIN'T PROMISED III
By **Keith Williams**

I'M NOTHING WITHOUT HIS LOVE II
SINS OF A THUG II
TO THE THUG I LOVED BEFORE II
IN A HUSTLER I TRUST II
By **Monet Dragun**

QUIET MONEY IV
EXTENDED CLIP III
THUG LIFE IV
By **Trai'Quan**

THE STREETS MADE ME IV
By **Larry D. Wright**

IF YOU CROSS ME ONCE III
ANGEL V
By **Anthony Fields**

THE STREETS WILL NEVER CLOSE IV
By **K'ajji**

HARD AND RUTHLESS III
KILLA KOUNTY IV
By **Khufu**

MONEY GAME III
By **Smoove Dolla**

MURDA WAS THE CASE III
Elijah R. Freeman

AN UNFORESEEN LOVE IV
BABY, I'M WINTERTIME COLD III
By **Meesha**

QUEEN OF THE ZOO III
By **Black Migo**

CONFESSIONS OF A JACKBOY III
By **Nicholas Lock**

JACK BOYS VS DOPE BOYS IV
A GANGSTA'S QUR'AN V
COKE GIRLZ II
COKE BOYS II
LIFE OF A SAVAGE V
CHI'RAQ GANGSTAS V
SOSA GANG III
BRONX SAVAGES II
BODYMORE KINGPINS II
By **Romell Tukes**

KING KILLA II
By **Vincent "Vitto" Holloway**

BETRAYAL OF A THUG III
By **Fre$h**

THE MURDER QUEENS III
By **Michael Gallon**

THE BIRTH OF A GANGSTER III
By **Delmont Player**

TREAL LOVE II
By **Le'Monica Jackson**

FOR THE LOVE OF BLOOD III
By **Jamel Mitchell**

RAN OFF ON DA PLUG II
By **Paper Boi Rari**

HOOD CONSIGLIERE III
By **Keese**

PRETTY GIRLS DO NASTY THINGS II
By **Nicole Goosby**

PROTÉGÉ OF A LEGEND III
LOVE IN THE TRENCHES II
By **Corey Robinson**

IT'S JUST ME AND YOU II
By **Ah'Million**

FOREVER GANGSTA III
By **Adrian Dulan**

GORILLAZ IN THE TRENCHES II
By **SayNoMore**

THE COCAINE PRINCESS VIII
By **King Rio**

CRIME BOSS II
By **Playa Ray**

LOYALTY IS EVERYTHING III
By **Molotti**

HERE TODAY GONE TOMORROW II
By **Fly Rock**

REAL G'S MOVE IN SILENCE II
By **Von Diesel**

GRIMEY WAYS IV
By **Ray Vinci**

Available Now

RESTRAINING ORDER I & II
By **CA$H & Coffee**

LOVE KNOWS NO BOUNDARIES I II & III
By **Coffee**

RAISED AS A GOON I, II, III & IV
BRED BY THE SLUMS I, II, III
BLAST FOR ME I & II
ROTTEN TO THE CORE I II III
A BRONX TALE I, II, III
DUFFLE BAG CARTEL I II III IV V VI
HEARTLESS GOON I II III IV V
A SAVAGE DOPEBOY I II
DRUG LORDS I II III
CUTTHROAT MAFIA I II
KING OF THE TRENCHES
By **Ghost**

LAY IT DOWN I & II
LAST OF A DYING BREED I II
BLOOD STAINS OF A SHOTTA I & II III
By **Jamaica**

LOYAL TO THE GAME I II III
LIFE OF SIN I, II III
By **TJ & Jelissa**

IF LOVING HIM IS WRONG…I & II
LOVE ME EVEN WHEN IT HURTS I II III
By **Jelissa**

BLOODY COMMAS I & II
SKI MASK CARTEL I, II & III
KING OF NEW YORK I II, III IV V
RISE TO POWER I II III
COKE KINGS I II III IV V
BORN HEARTLESS I II III IV
KING OF THE TRAP I II
By **T.J. Edwards**

WHEN THE STREETS CLAP BACK I & II III
THE HEART OF A SAVAGE I II III IV
MONEY MAFIA I II
LOYAL TO THE SOIL I II III
By **Jibril Williams**

A DISTINGUISHED THUG STOLE MY HEART I II & III
LOVE SHOULDN'T HURT I II III IV
RENEGADE BOYS I II III IV
PAID IN KARMA I II III
SAVAGE STORMS I II III
AN UNFORESEEN LOVE I II III
BABY, I'M WINTERTIME COLD I II
By **Meesha**

A GANGSTER'S CODE I &, II III
A GANGSTER'S SYN I II III
THE SAVAGE LIFE I II III
CHAINED TO THE STREETS I II III
BLOOD ON THE MONEY I II III
A GANGSTA'S PAIN I II III
By **J-Blunt**

PUSH IT TO THE LIMIT
By **Bre' Hayes**

BLOOD OF A BOSS I, II, III, IV, V
SHADOWS OF THE GAME
TRAP BASTARD
By **Askari**

THE STREETS BLEED MURDER I, II & III
THE HEART OF A GANGSTA I II & III
By **Jerry Jackson**

CUM FOR ME I II III IV V VI VII VIII
An **LDP Erotica Collaboration**

BRIDE OF A HUSTLA I II & II
THE FETTI GIRLS I, II & III
CORRUPTED BY A GANGSTA I, II III, IV
BLINDED BY HIS LOVE
THE PRICE YOU PAY FOR LOVE I, II ,III
DOPE GIRL MAGIC I II III
By **Destiny Skai**

WHEN A GOOD GIRL GOES BAD
By **Adrienne**

A GANGSTER'S REVENGE I II III & IV
THE BOSS MAN'S DAUGHTERS I II III IV V
A SAVAGE LOVE I & II
BAE BELONGS TO ME I II
A HUSTLER'S DECEIT I, II, III
WHAT BAD BITCHES DO I, II, III
SOUL OF A MONSTER I II III
KILL ZONE
A DOPE BOY'S QUEEN I II III
TIL DEATH
By **Aryanna**

THE COST OF LOYALTY I II III
By Kweli

A KINGPIN'S AMBITION
A KINGPIN'S AMBITION **II**
I MURDER FOR THE DOUGH
By **Ambitious**

TRUE SAVAGE I II III IV V VI VII
DOPE BOY MAGIC I, II, III
MIDNIGHT CARTEL I II III
CITY OF KINGZ I II
NIGHTMARE ON SILENT AVE
THE PLUG OF LIL MEXICO II
CLASSIC CITY
By **Chris Green**

A DOPEBOY'S PRAYER
By **Eddie "Wolf" Lee**

THE KING CARTEL I, II & III
By **Frank Gresham**

THESE NIGGAS AIN'T LOYAL I, II & III
By **Nikki Tee**

GANGSTA SHYT I II &III
By **CATO**

THE ULTIMATE BETRAYAL
By **Phoenix**

BOSS'N UP I, II & III
By **Royal Nicole**

I LOVE YOU TO DEATH
By **Destiny J**

I RIDE FOR MY HITTA
I STILL RIDE FOR MY HITTA
By **Misty Holt**

LOVE & CHASIN' PAPER
By **Qay Crockett**

TO DIE IN VAIN
SINS OF A HUSTLA
By **ASAD**

BROOKLYN HUSTLAZ
By **Boogsy Morina**

BROOKLYN ON LOCK I & II
By **Sonovia**

GANGSTA CITY
By **Teddy Duke**

A DRUG KING AND HIS DIAMOND I & II III
A DOPEMAN'S RICHES
HER MAN, MINE'S TOO I, II
CASH MONEY HO'S
THE WIFEY I USED TO BE I II
PRETTY GIRLS DO NASTY THINGS
By **Nicole Goosby**

LIPSTICK KILLAH I, II, III
CRIME OF PASSION I II & III
FRIEND OR FOE I II III
By **Mimi**

TRAPHOUSE KING I II & III
KINGPIN KILLAZ I II III
STREET KINGS I II
PAID IN BLOOD I II
CARTEL KILLAZ I II III
DOPE GODS I II
By **Hood Rich**

STEADY MOBBN' I, II, III
THE STREETS STAINED MY SOUL I II III
By **Marcellus Allen**

WHO SHOT YA I, II, III
SON OF A DOPE FIEND I II
HEAVEN GOT A GHETTO I II
SKI MASK MONEY I II
By **Renta**

GORILLAZ IN THE BAY I II III IV
TEARS OF A GANGSTA I II
3X KRAZY I II
STRAIGHT BEAST MODE I II
By **DE'KARI**

TRIGGADALE I II III
MURDA WAS THE CASE I II
By **Elijah R. Freeman**

THE STREETS ARE CALLING
By **Duquie Wilson**

SLAUGHTER GANG I II III
RUTHLESS HEART I II III
By **Willie Slaughter**

IF YOU CROSS ME ONCE 3 | ANTHONY FIELDS

GOD BLESS THE TRAPPERS I, II, III
THESE SCANDALOUS STREETS I, II, III
FEAR MY GANGSTA I, II, III IV, V
THESE STREETS DON'T LOVE NOBODY I, II
BURY ME A G I, II, III, IV, V
A GANGSTA'S EMPIRE I, II, III, IV
THE DOPEMAN'S BODYGAURD I II
THE REALEST KILLAZ I II III
THE LAST OF THE OGS I II III
By **Tranay Adams**

MARRIED TO A BOSS I II III
By **Destiny Skai & Chris Green**

KINGZ OF THE GAME I II III IV V VI VII
CRIME BOSS
By **Playa Ray**

FUK SHYT
By **Blakk Diamond**

DON'T F#CK WITH MY HEART I II
By **Linnea**

ADDICTED TO THE DRAMA I II III
IN THE ARM OF HIS BOSS II
By **Jamila**

YAYO I II III IV
A SHOOTER'S AMBITION I II
BRED IN THE GAME
By **S. Allen**

LOYALTY AIN'T PROMISED I II
By **Keith Williams**

IF YOU CROSS ME ONCE 3 | ANTHONY FIELDS

TRAP GOD I II III
RICH $AVAGE I II III
MONEY IN THE GRAVE I II III
By **Martell Troublesome Bolden**

FOREVER GANGSTA I II
GLOCKS ON SATIN SHEETS I II
By **Adrian Dulan**

TOE TAGZ I II III IV
LEVELS TO THIS SHYT I II
IT'S JUST ME AND YOU
By **Ah'Million**

KINGPIN DREAMS I II III
RAN OFF ON DA PLUG
By **Paper Boi Rari**

CONFESSIONS OF A GANGSTA I II III IV
CONFESSIONS OF A JACKBOY I II
By **Nicholas Lock**

I'M NOTHING WITHOUT HIS LOVE
SINS OF A THUG
TO THE THUG I LOVED BEFORE
A GANGSTA SAVED XMAS
IN A HUSTLER I TRUST
By **Monet Dragun**

QUIET MONEY I II III
THUG LIFE I II III
EXTENDED CLIP I II
A GANGSTA'S PARADISE
By **Trai'Quan**

IF YOU CROSS ME ONCE 3 | ANTHONY FIELDS

CAUGHT UP IN THE LIFE I II III
THE STREETS NEVER LET GO I II III
By **Robert Baptiste**

NEW TO THE GAME I II III
MONEY, MURDER & MEMORIES I II III
By **Malik D. Rice**

CREAM I II III
THE STREETS WILL TALK
By **Yolanda Moore**

LIFE OF A SAVAGE I II III IV
A GANGSTA'S QUR'AN I II III IV
MURDA SEASON I II III
GANGLAND CARTEL I II III
CHI'RAQ GANGSTAS I II III IV
KILLERS ON ELM STREET I II III
JACK BOYZ N DA BRONX I II III
A DOPEBOY'S DREAM I II III
JACK BOYS VS DOPE BOYS I II III
COKE GIRLZ
COKE BOYS
SOSA GANG I II
BRONX SAVAGES
BODYMORE KINGPINS
By **Romell Tukes**

THE STREETS MADE ME I II III
By **Larry D. Wright**

CONCRETE KILLA I II III
VICIOUS LOYALTY I II III
By **Kingpen**

THE ULTIMATE SACRIFICE I, II, III, IV, V, VI
KHADIFI
IF YOU CROSS ME ONCE I II
ANGEL I II III IV
IN THE BLINK OF AN EYE
By **Anthony Fields**

THE LIFE OF A HOOD STAR
By **Ca$h & Rashia Wilson**

THE STREETS WILL NEVER CLOSE I II III
By **K'ajji**

NIGHTMARES OF A HUSTLA I II III
By **King Dream**

HARD AND RUTHLESS I II
MOB TOWN 251
THE BILLIONAIRE BENTLEYS I II III
REAL G'S MOVE IN SILENCE
By **Von Diesel**

GHOST MOB
By **Stilloan Robinson**

MOB TIES I II III IV V VI
SOUL OF A HUSTLER, HEART OF A KILLER I II
GORILLAZ IN THE TRENCHES
By **SayNoMore**

BODYMORE MURDERLAND I II III
THE BIRTH OF A GANGSTER I II
By **Delmont Player**

FOR THE LOVE OF A BOSS
By **C. D. Blue**

KILLA KOUNTY I II III IV
By Khufu

MOBBED UP I II III IV
THE BRICK MAN I II III IV V
THE COCAINE PRINCESS I II III IV V VI VII
By **King Rio**

MONEY GAME I II
By **Smoove Dolla**

A GANGSTA'S KARMA I II III
By **FLAME**

KING OF THE TRENCHES I II III
By **GHOST & TRANAY ADAMS**

QUEEN OF THE ZOO I II
By **Black Migo**

GRIMEY WAYS I II III
By **Ray Vinci**

XMAS WITH AN ATL SHOOTER
By **Ca$h & Destiny Skai**

KING KILLA
By **Vincent "Vitto" Holloway**

BETRAYAL OF A THUG I II
By **Fre$h**

IF YOU CROSS ME ONCE 3 | ANTHONY FIELDS

THE MURDER QUEENS I II
By **Michael Gallon**

TREAL LOVE
By **Le'Monica Jackson**

FOR THE LOVE OF BLOOD I II
By **Jamel Mitchell**

HOOD CONSIGLIERE I II
By **Keese**

PROTÉGÉ OF A LEGEND I II
LOVE IN THE TRENCHES
By **Corey Robinson**

BORN IN THE GRAVE I II III
By **Self Made Tay**

MOAN IN MY MOUTH
By **XTASY**

TORN BETWEEN A GANGSTER AND A GENTLEMAN
By **J-BLUNT & Miss Kim**

LOYALTY IS EVERYTHING I II
By **Molotti**

HERE TODAY GONE TOMORROW
By **Fly Rock**

PILLOW PRINCESS
By **S. Hawkins**

IF YOU CROSS ME ONCE 3 | ANTHONY FIELDS

SANCTIFIED AND HORNY
by **XTASY**

THE PLUG OF LIL MEXICO 2
by **CHRIS GREEN**

THE BLACK DIAMOND CARTEL
by **SAYNOMORE**

THE BIRTH OF A GANGSTER 3
by **DELMONT PLAYER**

BOOKS BY LDP'S CEO, CA$H

TRUST IN NO MAN
TRUST IN NO MAN 2
TRUST IN NO MAN 3
BONDED BY BLOOD
SHORTY GOT A THUG
THUGS CRY
THUGS CRY 2
THUGS CRY 3
TRUST NO BITCH
TRUST NO BITCH 2
TRUST NO BITCH 3
TIL MY CASKET DROPS
RESTRAINING ORDER
RESTRAINING ORDER 2
IN LOVE WITH A CONVICT
LIFE OF A HOOD STAR
XMAS WITH AN ATL SHOOTER